ELIOT SCOTT

THE WALLACE GIRL

The Feud Series

The Wallace Girl
The Feud Series Book 1
Text copyright © 2019

Ginger Scott, Anne Eliot
Writing as Eliot Scott
Butterfly Books, LLC
ISBN: 978-1-937815-16-5

We dedicate this to the old-school romance readers who miss the days of sneaking Mom's dog-eared paperbacks and reading them by flashlight.

1.

ALEX SINCLAIR, PRESENT DAY.

I don't know why I'm surprised to find JoJo Wallace standing near some crap rental car as I pull my Mercedes into the Memorial Hall parking lot to attend my father's funeral.

The girl had promised to see my father buried six feet under. Promised me while naked with her lips still swollen from my kisses and her thighs covered in my sweat.

Jojo's never been the type to break a promise. But she's a Wallace, so it's expected, I suppose. They're steadfast, honorable, kind, trustworthy, considerate and loyal to a fault.

Personality traits that irritate the shit out of my family.

We Sinclairs specialize in promise-breaking, lies, murder, fucking up people's lives through severe emotional torture and, above all, destroying the Wallace girls from each generation by using all of the above against them.

Over the years, as the youngest male member of this family, I've made a shit ton of promises to this particular Wallace girl, and because I was so good at breaking them, I've made my daddy very proud.

The last promise—the promise not to hurt her—I made to JoJo Wallace before we made love. And it was broken while my cock still pulsed inside of her sweet body. Dad beamed when I told him. Yeah...my deeds required every detail shared. My father and my older brother, Grady, hung on my every word when I told them, as if they'd done the deed themselves.

Because she'd been a virgin, I forced myself to go slowly that night. I told myself it was to make sure that JoJo at least had some sort of pleasure out of her first time—before I destroyed her.

When I'm honest with myself about it all—when I look back and remember the unthinkable things I've done on behalf of my father to hurt her—I know that somewhere I'm also guilty. I'm probably the guiltiest of all. That night, the worst night of my life, I got a lot of what I didn't want, but I also got exactly what I *did*.

Defining what happened between me and Jojo depends on how you look at it; which side you're on.

Which family you were born into.

That first time, she'd come so long and so hard we knocked our favorite fishing rods halfway across the room, and her moans had nearly shaken down the walls of my parents' boathouse. After, I was panting for breath like I'd run a marathon. But Jojo simply sighed, sounding sleepy and satisfied, as she wrapped her arms so tight around me I couldn't pull out—didn't want to pull out. And she whispered how much she loved me all mixed up with the kisses she was pressing onto my skin.

I can still feel where each of her words hit against my neck between her kisses. Those spots are my curse to bear.

FIVE YEARS AGO

"You're the best boyfriend in the world."

Her soft hair was tickling my chin, and her gentle fingers reached up to twine into my hair.

"Have I told you yet how...I think I'm the luckiest girl in the world? How I can't wait to do that again. And we're so much closer now, and I can see our future..."

Jojo had a dreamy way about her sometimes. She was nervous and excited with her rambling—one of the things I loved about her. I was still full on pulsing lightning bolts into her wet, slick tightness. I was *also* wishing to do it again, relishing how my cock ached beautifully from my release. My eyes saw only flashing stars, and I'd never felt more alive, while at the same time, my entire being was so consumed with regrets that I wanted to die.

As if she'd sensed my conflicts, which was always her way with me, her hands stilled and landed on my cheeks. She kept them there, waiting for me to focus on her heat-flushed-face before slaying me with the sweetest kiss on my lips and the even sweeter question. *"Did I do it right, Alex? God...I love you somehow even more now. I'm so happy we waited until today. It was amazing. Was it amazing? For you?"*

I planned for her elation, anticipated her sweetness and sentimentality, and I even expected her to love me more, because—*love?* That's JoJo Wallace's essence. It's what she is, and what she does, and how she hands it out to the world like she owns a pocketful of self-replenishing hundred dollar bills.

I dug into that rotten part of my soul for strength, imagining my father's face waiting for me to "get it done"—conjuring my brother Grady's laugh, and picturing their rough, cruel hands on JoJo's soft skin, "doing the job for me." That's what they threatened to do if I didn't come through—that's what helped me stay strong.

I locked on the stony facial expressions I'd perfected while staring myself down in the bathroom mirror weeks and days before, and turned my voice into the well-practiced ice tones copied from my father, and I looked down at her and shook my head.

Her smile faltered. *"No? It wasn't good?"*

I shifted my hips, making sure my weight was heavy and uncomfortable against her in a way I'd never done before. JoJo's frame is slight compared to my six-foot-three one, and until then I'd been holding myself up with my forearms.

"We're done now, JoJo." I gritted out the words, choosing to look at a point on her forehead to avoid her clear, beautiful and loving gaze. I couldn't let her see the torture I was feeling. She needed to believe. "I got what I wanted. Now that you've finally put out, there's nothing left for me to do. You and I are—and were —*nothing.*"

A ruthless laugh slipped out, just as I'd practiced. It made me sick to be this man, but that wasn't enough to fight off the inevitable evolution. Monsters are born to be monsters.

"We're less than nothing, actually, and we always have been." I added that last bit for me more than her. I had to lie to myself.

"What?" She blinked, trying to breathe under me, while I pressed down more weight against her, willing her not to argue, and damn me to hell, memorizing the feel of her skin...her scent, the way her lips bruised from my kisses.

"We're not *together* anymore. I guess you could call this break-up sex." I readied myself to look in her eyes, and I accepted my destiny.

While those deep pools of hers widened with surprise and shock, I spewed out so many of my truths mixed with lies. It was critical she dialed in, and even more critical that she believed me.

"Our friendship, the one that started just before freshman year, was set up by my father. Our relationship was simply a game."

"'Mhmm. *No. You're—what are you doing? No.*" She was shaking her head. This was hurting her. She was fighting it already. It killed me, but I pressed on.

"Yes!" I shouted and she recoiled a little because I never, ever shouted at her.

I left off telling her that I didn't know about the plan until years after we met. Not until I was so much in love with JoJo—not until things had gone too far. That fact... it was irrelevant now. My love for this girl was how my father manipulated me. It was how he leveraged me to do so much.

"The lake, the fishing, the poles...how we met..." I pressed on. "And all of high school. Every suck-ass school dance. All of it was a twisted set up, JoJo. We're over. This was—*is*—the end of the game. So I hope."

"Game?"

Long ago, she and I agreed that this feud between our families wasn't real, only I was pretending. I knew better. I came to know better. This feud quickly became the realest thing in my life.

"My father's game. You and I...the players." I grinned a smile I hoped was as wicked as one of my father's. "Nightly entertainment for my entire family—better than any series you can find on TV. This is just the end of it. I guess my father's bored with it now that your mother is dead. As long as you leave town as promised, and as long as you don't come back, it's the end. You know my father's mantra: Pain for Pain. That's what he was doing—fucking with your mother, waiting for me to fuck you."

I shrugged like it was not a big deal, and again I left off what was not important for her to know. It was easy for me to say all of that convincingly because my father's game was very real. It terrified me—made me obedient. It had real rules and dangerous plays. Rules I once tried to escape—plays that I tried to alter. I had many failed attempts at *rebellion,* so my father called my behavior back then when I balked at all of this.

I was punished for it—threatened. They had taught me a lesson, one that brought me in line with the Sinclair ways. It had cost JoJo too much. To keep her safe I'd never broken them again.

The one lie I'd spewed to her in all of this was as cruel and as practiced as my words and my expressions, because I had to make her believe it. "I do not love you, JoJo. Never have. This whole thing was a four-year joke."

Somehow, through it all, I held on. I kept it up when she surprised me by wrapping her arms tighter around me. When she repeated how much she loved me and said that she didn't care about my family or my father or his games. And when I didn't answer after JoJo smiled up at me and continued with confidence: "We can change everything. It will be 'Love for love' not 'Pain for pain' instead, okay? Please, Alex...please. We can do this."

I smiled at her sweet face, leaned down and kissed her soft smile, stole those too idealistic words off of her lips.

I kissed her because she was right.

I also kissed her because she was wrong—because love for love was not enough to keep her safe from my father or my brother. She thought this was familiar, that this was just more of the stern father-to-son relationship she'd seen. She had no idea how deep it all was.

Then, because her smile up at me was part love, part laughter and part lust, and her amazing body was bare, because she was so damn beautiful to me—and because she still smelled half like lavender and now half like me —I kissed her again as my cock swelled inside of her.

I was selfish.

I kissed and kissed and kissed her until she'd gone limp with desire, and I had her moaning under me again, and I pumped myself into her willing softness.

I licked, bit, and pressed kisses all over her already kiss-bruised skin. I ran my hands thrice over where they should *never* have been in the first place, and this second time?Shit...it was the last thing I deserved.

Worse, if my father found out, it would please him, the last thing I want when I've vowed to never please him on purpose.

I brought her higher and higher—relishing her cries and how her heated skin rolled against mine. I made love to her until I had her fingers digging into my back while she rocked up into me hard and fast and hungered. I lost my mind when she'd called out my name, over and over again. Instead of lingering inside of her and lying against her hot-skin how I did the first time, though, I rolled off of her with a groan.

Even though it killed me, I said, "You make me sick. One time and you're as talented as your whore of a mom. Get dressed and get out."

I could see her tremble. I couldn't go back on any of what I'd said. I changed her forever.

I changed me.

Us.

So I told her again.

"We're done. Don't contact me again. Don't even try; you'll be sorry if you do. Let me be clear. My father will kill your aunt—if not both of you. No more family for you. Got me?"

She'd nodded, tears staining her skin. She was in shock, but she'd asked still: *"Why? Why? Why?"*

I couldn't be sure if she was agreeing to just erase this part of our lives and move on to the next, or agreeing because she understood. So I repeated it all again. Her cheeks drooped and her bottom lip quivered, but there was no cry. She'd moved beyond that to a deeper sadness.

She was in despair.

One last word croaked from her lips.

"Why?"

As if I could answer that honestly—at all—ever. Because the answer to that was *"if I didn't, my father and my brother would have killed you."*

"Happy fucking birthday, JoJo," I said instead, a cruel smile locked on, that barking laugh coming out again. "Emphasis on the *fucking*."

2.

JOJO WALLACE, PRESENT DAY.

I don't know why I stopped at the Sinclair boathouse to grab the fishing rods before the funeral. Looking at them bent in the trunk of my rental car like they still have some spring left for casting while the fishing line is impossibly tangled is only making me feel pathetic. The lure Alex gave me as a gift, one that I used to actually wear as though it were as valuable as any diamond necklace, is tied in there too. Its broken chain, and the fact that Alex had to be the one who wound it into the middle of the mess and obviously never looked back, actually hurts.

It makes me feel even more pathetic.

As if that's possible.

It's been years since Alex Sinclair and I were those kids—the ones who didn't care about appearances, about our parents, about his father's company.

The company that runs this town and everyone in it. The man who ran all of us.

I hate that company. I hated that man, and I'm happy Mr. Sinclair is dead.

It—*he*—took innocent people and shredded them to dust. That oil company of his swallowed great men whole, including my own parents—my house. Though no one could ever prove any of it, or pin anything to the venerable Sinclair name, everyone knows Michael Sinclair created demons, gutted out hearts and left everything cold.

It left me cold for the last six years.

Or maybe...*maybe* it just left me alone. Alex is alone now too, finally. And that fact is why I've come back.

Well, maybe he's not entirely alone. He has Grady, but they've never been brothers or friends. He also has his mother, May. Such a bright month for such an awful human being. She never liked me, but it wasn't personal. I think she's not capable of liking anyone. She's the best actor of the bunch. She...all of them...fooled me for so long.

That was when I wore pigtails and cut-off shorts. Those were the days when she let me fall asleep in the Sinclair's basement during a marathon of Star Wars movies with Alex. It took a while for her to accept me as his friend, but she had. I was welcome in their home. That was before I understood they'd thought of me and my mother—the Wallaces—as a *threat*.

Dangerous. Disgusting. Prey on which to feed.

"*Nice dress,* Josephine," May calls out from behind me like my thoughts have conjured her out of a mist.

I jump, but don't turn yet, pausing to pull off the Post-It note I'd left on the dent in the driver's door before I pulled away from the rental lot just to make sure the attendant saw it and wouldn't hit me with a random fee when I came back.

"I hope you know you're not invited." Her crackled, nicotine-laced voice sounds the same, like death's fingers reaching around my neck to choke me. I'm sure she hates that I'm here. That she can't control me anymore. That I'm still alive while the rest of my family is dead all thanks to them. But the Sinclair hatred is why I came. I'm here to face it.

To defeat it.

That...and I'm here to save Alex. My Alex...not theirs...not anymore.

"May, the paper said the service was open to everyone."

"You're not *anyone* to us. Remember?"

I turn to face her clutching my sweater to my stomach to hide the snag in the black chiffon fabric draping down the front of my dress. This was my mother's dress, and it's the only black dress I own. I know it's tattered and old, but it's one of the few things I've got left of her and it is still beautiful. I won't be ashamed of it, but I won't let May point out its flaws.

I deliberately close off my expressions.

"I remember everything." If I were feeling anything

but her hatred, I'd add, "I'm sorry for your loss." But I'm not a liar, and even though she's as dark as they come, I would assume she's not sorry for her loss one bit.

"I hope you're not planning to stay long." Her eyes graze my whole body—up and down like she's evaluating me, then she swallows and her gold-brown eyes, eyes that match Alex's, flick away to track the line of people filing out of the parking lot before she returns them to me. "You're staying with your Aunt in that tourist-trap antique store in Old Town?"

I don't answer. I'm sure she knows where I'm staying.

"Well..." She sniffs, stepping away from me, lips parted, breath held as if she has more to say. There's a note that lingers there between us, something hidden, tense. And for a moment when she looks back at me... the voice in my head whispers *"she knows"* while my stomach clenches in irrational fear.

If she does know—what will I do?

It would be so like her to shake me down like this, to draw it out of me, to pretend she doesn't know. She breathes deeply, nodding at me like she can read my mind, and she closes her lips in this tightly protective, sinister and curious smile before turning away and following the long empty pathway to the church, where the rest of the demons in suits pretending they're upset that Michael Sinclair is dead have gathered.

I watch her walk away, and for a moment, I consider getting back into the tiny Kia, driving back to the airport, and charging whatever it costs to get back to Ohio to the credit cards I can't afford to pay anyway just so I can undo this decision I made when my Aunt Shelly called me four days ago. All of my fears from the past— the voices of these Sinclairs, this town, and the fears about the feud I've come here to end—come crashing in.

Is it dangerous here for me? Is any of this safe? Is it worth it to be here...is it really?

"They can't hurt me anymore." I say the words out loud while my core, my heart and my soul screams...*but they can, they can...and if they find out, they will try!*

As shivers prick the back of my neck and my stomach rolls as I remember fully what these inhumane people are capable of, I resolve to go with plan B: To retreat to the car and escape.

But then Alex pulls into the lone parking spot next to mine—and I can't move.

I'm frozen, suddenly afraid that somehow he'll *know* I was just looking at the lure and the stolen rods, even though they're tucked inside the trunk.

He sits in his car, engine turned off. His hands grip the wheel for almost a minute before he rummages in the back then gets out. His profile is obscured by the height of his car, so I watch the shadows and reflections in the nearly blacked-out windows while he opens the back door, pulls out a black suit jacket, and slips it on.

I'm terrified to actually see him.

I want to see him.

I want to run.

I haven't seen him since my eighteenth birthday. Since he made love to me. My words. My experience.

Since he *finally fucked me*—his words, his lies.

Then, he called me a whore and told me to leave town and not come back.

I haven't seen him since I obeyed that order.

All I can make out are angles of his form, but even just seeing those stabs at the center of my being with a hot, sharp knife. He's exactly as I imagined, the real-life man that I'd stolen glimpses of online and in tabloids. He's the prodigal son, the *real* bad boy and playboy that the media says he is. Except I know he's not. I know it, with that very aching center I feel burning with hurt right now.

His feet shuffle on the other side of the SUV, and I wring my hands in front of my body, kneading the collar of my sweater, nearly tearing a few of the threads. I hold my breath, just so I can hear him, and listen to the flicking sound of the lighter, the glow of fire now shining through the tinted layers of windows I'm looking through. I smell the smoke before I see him, and he passes without as much as a glance at me.

He knows I'm here.

I feel him feel me.

I could always feel him—see him—find him, and vice versa.

But seeing him now, like this—his tall body cloaked in the same black suits his father wore, his light brown hair curled at the ends, long enough to tempt my memories but short enough to tell me this isn't the same hair I once pushed my fingers through while I felt my heart beat faster because I knew he was going to kiss me—it makes that cold feeling that accompanies being alone only grow chillier.

It makes me so unsure...

"So you're smoking now?" I blurt out when he's several paces away. I don't say, "I'm sorry to hear about your father." I don't say I've missed him. I don't ask how he is, or tell him I hope it's okay that I came. I don't say any of those things because those things won't reach him.

His feet stutter to a stop, the loose gravel beneath them sliding around, mimicking the sound of a drumroll for the leveling he is about to deliver. He pulls his cigarette up to his lips, looking to the side, to the full lot of expensive SUVs and sports cars, all driven here by people pretending to care, pretending they aren't already plotting to destroy Alex Sinclair, the heir to the Sinclair fortune, next.

He looks...furious.

Annoyed.

Handsome.

I hate that my belly is already swirling with longing, that my lips are involuntarily tingling with some sort of hope.

He surveys the cars around us and takes a long drag, holding the smoke hostage in his mouth, almost as if he's mocking me, then he steps closer to puff out a long trail, filling up the air between us before saying, "You came back for more? Still so stupid, huh?"

His voice is all gravelly heat, and nearly too much for me. The words he's uttered cut me, but not too deep. I've come to terms with who I am—and my dyslexia—and I'm not stupid. He's being mean to me on purpose. Salt in old wounds.

"Make my life easy and drive away, here and now, would you, Jojo? I deserve that luxury, because as you probably know, I didn't have that the first time we all got you to leave this place. I was forced to deal with you, and you kind of fucking owe me for saving your life, so...just *go*, would you, before one of us finally kills you."

I manage to shake my head, a massive wall of sarcasm buckled on my face. I'm proud of myself, because I've even rolled my eyes as though his words are a joke.

His face stays frozen. The warm golden brown eyes I remember so well are hooded behind this squint he's maintaining through his next mega puff of smoke.

I expected this.

It hurts all the same.

He pulls in another drag off the cigarette, and I move my stare to where it rests, smoking in his big hand.

"You *know* my mom died of lung cancer," is all I respond, letting him know the cigarette hurts way more than everything else.

His eyes travel to the horizon like they always did, but instead of flickering bright to my challenge, they remain away from me. Dead and cold, shutting me out. This is his defense, and I can break it. I must.

"Since we all get that your family has a history of being a little *slow*, I'm going to say it clearly in some of those *shorter* words you can understand. Get the fuck out of here, Jojo. No one wants you anywhere near here. I can guarantee my father didn't ever feel an ounce of guilt. Not about you, or your mom. Nor did he have you added to the will, if *that's* why you came."

His words do their intended job. They insult, they cut, pummel, and they wound me deeper than a fist to my gut. But I'm not a kid anymore. I know what he's doing. I'm better than he is at this game now. After all, the Sinclairs taught me how to play, and I did learn all of my best poker faces straight from Alex.

"I'll go." I nod. "After we bury your dad, after I do some...*fishing*. See...I'm here..." I shrug, keeping my eyes on the cigarette dangling from his hand, because being this close to his beautiful face has rattled me. "I'm here," I repeat—locking eyes with him then.

As if he knows what I'm trying to do, I feel him pull back. Before he can escape I drop my voice and finish quickly and clearly, "for a little adventure." I smile openly at him then, instantly regretting it because I wonder if I've revealed too much of how I'm longing for this to work. I just uttered words meant to scratch at our past, memories I wish to flood his chest and revive the man I know still breathes inside of this beast.

I watch as his whole body tenses and his brown eyes

tangle into mine—this time they're hard and wild. I've cracked him. I can tell. It takes every effort I have to open my eyes wider. I try to let him see all the way to my heart, working to let him see me. See that I'm keeping my promise—pleading, asking, loving and searching for the boy who used to love me back.

He tears his eyes off of mine to take one more huge drag of the cigarette, and he puffs out enough smoke to choke us both. I wonder if I've seen him wince slightly before he flicks the butt to the ground between us, crushing it with the weight of his black, leather shoe before walking away without another word.

I cling to the idea that he winced because I can't fathom the idea that there might not be a heart still beating in there somewhere. Will it be enough for me to reset its rhythm?

But, oh God. My chest twists and I feel my knees threaten to buckle. Those blank eyes. His obvious anger that I've come. I'm not going to lie. I'm terrified. Have I come too late?

I won't run again. I repeat my promise to myself over and over in my head, working to regain the edge and calm my nerves. He scared me once. I can't be scared for this to work.

He follows the same path his mother took into the Memorial Hall, and I wait, heart thrumming in my throat with hope as he turns the corner. He never once looked back at me to see whether or not I heeded his warning or stayed put.

Counting extra seconds in my head, I will my legs and limbs to finally move, and I walk back, open my trunk and stare at the fishing rods. The lure he gave me. My necklace. And I think about how he just acted...and us at the lake, his voice full of love for me always saying: *Our lake. Our lake. Our lake.*

3.

JOJO, SPRING BREAK, SOPHOMORE
YEAR OF HIGH SCHOOL.

It's a hot spring break night, and because of the unseasonably warm weather, we've been doing this lingering, making out thing at the lake every evening.

Our lake, that's what Alex always calls it even though it's actually only *his* lake.

He's been saying that ever since he officially asked me out just before freshman year started. It's perfect here; a total of sixteen miles around the beautiful shoreline. No one's sure how deep it really is. Alex's father sent divers in once, but after 300 feet, they had to stop measuring. The divers said it may be as deep as Lake Tahoe is down in California. One thing for certain is it's the deepest in this region, which makes it the only privately owned freshwater lake of its kind in the Pacific Northwest. And it does, truly, belong to Alex. A gift from his father...if you can imagine a gift as big as that. I

ELIOT SCOTT

still can't hardly wrap my mind around giving something so big to someone. Though if I could, I would…to Alex. I would give him everything.

Alex's fingers trail over my bare arm absentmindedly, sending shivers of hope down my spine. I can tell he's all languid and relaxed like I am. How much I love the lake, *our lake*. I love me and him here together, doing all of this kissing and—touching—under this endless sky.

I'm late getting home tonight, and he hasn't argued about it yet. This is not like Alex, so he's giving me even more hope that he also wants to go to the next step with me.

Please. Let tonight be the night. We've waited nearly two years. Two years. And I love him. He knows that I do…

He turns to rain kisses down on my face before pulling me up next to his body so I can snuggle in closer to him again.

"You warm enough?" He nestles me next to him, my back against his chest.

I nod my answer and he sighs, and I sigh, but still we both remain quiet and contemplative. He doesn't try to make out with me more, even though I can feel his desire for me, now pressing against my backside.

The lake is the place Alex and I always hang out. The place we feel safe—where Alex feels free from his family. It's where our friendship started, and it's where Alex asked me to be his girlfriend. Where I think it would be perfect to finally do…everything.

I squeeze his hand, and he squeezes back. I've been pretty clear with him that I'm ready. I think he knows that, but I always wonder if he also holds back because of all of the negative stories that are out there about the Wallaces and the Sinclairs.

People say it's taboo that Alex and I are dating. Dangerous. All of Tacoma has this superstition that a Wallace and a Sinclair are fated to never work out. Fated, at the very least, to destroy one another.

Those are the whispers. Worse, people in town know who we are, and that we're dating which has caused all kinds of scandal. We've even been approached by strangers who ask us about it. Ask if we're *afraid*. As if he's a vampire dating a human like the books and movies and how strange this must be for us.

They always want to know if *I'm* afraid. *Of what?* We always answer just like that. I think they just like the drama.

I've met Alex's family many times now, and yeah, they're strange, even a little...unfriendly sometimes, but it's all been fine. They're just people, after all. I do hate his older brother, Grady. I think he's an ass. Even Alex thinks Grady's an ass. Alex and I are great character judges so I think we're right about him. Sometimes people are just born to be slimy, snake-eyed jerks. Grady wears it proudly.

Ass.

As for the rest of them, May, Alex's mom—and his father, Mr. Sinclair? They're normal enough. Except for the part where they're super rich. They were worried I was too poor to date Alex—*dirt poor* is what May called me to my face when she first met me. She wasn't being insulting, just literal. That was her label for me, and it was something I told her I'm never going to be ashamed about. And I told her that to her face. Alex says that earned me some respect in her eyes.

At first I wasn't welcome near them or their house, but they seem to be warming up to me now. I've been over to his house all summer without a problem. I eat dinner with them sometimes, too, but I try to avoid it because I don't know what all the extra forks and tiny spoons are for, and they both watch me as if I'm a zoo animal.

They allow me to watch movies with Alex in the basement anytime I want—even when they're home now, which is a big change. I used to have to sneak in. I think it's because Alex and I are about to hit the two year mark on our relationship. Like my own parents, the Sinclairs have relaxed about us dating. They all probably realize we're actually in love for real. This isn't pretend or some fling.

I've directly asked Alex about the Wallace and Sinclair rumors that fly around town. *The feud* is what my father once called it when I asked him about it, too. But Alex always swears he's never heard anyone mention anything called an official *feud.* Not in his family. He also didn't know any of the stories I've heard from my side of the family. He was actually shocked when I told him about the stories.

Where my parents have been pretty open about the past, Alex apparently grew up without one whisper of it on his parents' lips.

Not one. Never.

But that could be because his father and mother rarely interact with him. Not how my parents do with me.

Although it's incredible to me and my family that the Sinclairs never brought it up, I do believe Alex. That's mostly because Alex is a terrible liar. I can see right through him when he's trying to hold something in, my father has that ability, too. My father thinks the Sinclairs' silence about the past was maybe their way to bury the feud and move on with life. Why bring it up, if it's over and done? It would be like adding fuel to a fire that's long burned out.

Problem is, the Tacoma History Museum has an entire display about the Wallaces and the Sinclairs. *They* talk about it—the feud—and keep it alive. Every generation around here was raised on the story about how our great-great grandfathers were the first settlers in this region. The Wallaces were (and we still are) farmers. The Sinclairs were (and still are) owners of the ports and the entire shoreline in the area, from Tacoma all the way up to Canada.

In the past, the Wallaces owned as much land as the Sinclair family empire owned, and both families used to be really big. Where the Sinclairs had the shorelines and the shipping industry locked down, we Wallaces had the farmlands and the lakes—probably even this lake, too, once…long, long ago, I'll bet.

We also had the streams, and more importantly, all of the water rights, which was a very big deal my father once said. All of this was more than a hundred years ago. It's common knowledge the Wallaces sold everything off to the Sinclairs, little by little. During the Great Depression and after, the Wallace lines died out or moved away. Life here was hard, and opportunities made it impossible not to move. The family lines dried up, though, as men were lost to war and women married into other families. As far as I know, me, my mom and my dad are the last ones—not counting distant cousins back in Ireland.

When oil and gas came into play for the growing US economy, the Sinclairs made even more money because there's tons of oil in the tide flats off the coast of Tacoma as well as up to the North. The Sinclairs own it all, and they're still making money off of those ports and pieces of land today.

We weren't so lucky. Everything was sold off to the Sinclairs except my parents' small farm where we live now. I figure what we're living on must be junk land—or we'd have sold it off long ago, too. Either way, it just barely supports us; it's enough to hold the most comfortable farm house in the world and it has a giant garden that feeds us all year long. We survive thanks to some huge wheat granaries left over from the 1950s where we charge a fee to store wheat for other farms in the area when there's overflow.

"It's all we need," my father always says, and I agree with him. Money like the Sinclairs have is extra—and it has never brought smiles to their faces, at least none that they've shown me.

All of the land is what's documented. Deeds and trusts with small payments recorded…sometimes. But when Alex and I went into the museum to ask about the feud a month ago, the curator told us that there was no real proof, no news articles ever written about it. It's nothing but legend pointing to the Sinclairs and Wallaces actually having murdered each other over grudges and deals gone sour.

The woman also implied that the families were fighting not over land—but over *love!*

That last part—the love stuff—comes from a story I *know* is true. I was the one who surprised Alex when I told him about my grandfather being in competition with Alex's grandfather. There was an old fashioned fist fight—kind of like a duel or something, over which one of them would marry my grandmother.

He couldn't believe the story, told me he would have heard of it from his side. But I, and later my father, confirmed it to be true with photos and my grandmother's diary where she'd written about everything. I also confirmed it because, well, my mom was born, and then I was born—wasn't I? So there.

I also was the first to tell Alex that my own mother and Alex's father—back when they went to the same high school Alex and I are attending now—used to be *friends!* Friends like us, although maybe not as close as Alex and I are right now. But still, friends.

Again, Alex didn't believe me.

It took some time to prove that, but finally Alex and I found an old yearbook in the school library archives that showed a photo of my mom and Mr. Sinclair laughing together as they were crowned Homecoming King and Queen. I tried to pester my father with questions about this, but he said it was my mom's private business...a story that was not his to tell, even though my father also attended that high school, but wasn't in any of the photos besides the class one. That was because he said he couldn't be in any activities. He had to work on the farm after school.

When I asked my mom about it once, about her friendship or whatever went down with Mr. Sinclair back in high school, she laughed it off as teenage silliness. She said that Mr. Sinclair had a big case of "pouting-sour-grapes" when she started dating, and then later married, my father.

She clammed up even more than my father did when I had more questions about it. She told me it just made her uncomfortable, then she begged me to not tell Alex. She called it silly and trite again and again, and finally she told me it was embarrassing for her and probably also embarrassing to Mr. Sinclair, which is why I was to never—ever—bring it up in front of him most of all.

I kept that promise mostly, but I had whispered about it to Alex. I told him that I think it had to be true that Alex's father maybe wanted to marry my mother or something like that. That's when Alex started to really believe. My mom is *that* beautiful, and kind. She's loved by everyone in town, everyone who meets her, really. Back then, she'd worn her brown hair down all long and wavy, how I do.

Even now, in her late forties, my father and I would die for her. She had a scary battle with lung cancer that she won last year after they took out half of one of her lungs. Though I'm not too religious, I still thank God every day that he didn't take her away from me, and I never once complain how my chores have doubled because Mom can't do anything strenuous like run, or carry laundry. I won't even let her do the dishes, though she swears she's fine. I will never get over her being sick, nor will I ever let her risk being sick again.

"Are you ready to go home yet?" Alex wraps his arms tighter around me, jarring me out of my thoughts. "We might be in trouble...it's getting beyond late, you know?" He presses a kiss against the top of my head.

"No. Not ready." I point upwards. "Look. The sky is so black it's nearly nothing, and the stars look like millions of grains of salt spilt against granite. I never want to end this night."

"Beautiful." He answers, but when I glance back at

him he's not looking at the sky. He's looking at me and rubbing his cheek against my hair. "You're so beautiful. Smell so good…skin feels so soft." His fingers dance along my midriff, toying with the bottom of my shirt. My body is spooned against his, my head resting on one bicep while the other holds me close.

Every tickle inches closer, moves my shirt up, and then up some more so my waist is exposed. Those fingers travel along the curves of my skin but he hesitates every time he heads up too high.

Every. Frustrating. Time.

Impulsively, I take his hand and guide it up and under my shirt, all the way to cover my breasts, and he freezes as he pulls in a huge startled breath.

"Fuck." He responds in a short, fast pant. "What are you doing?"

I shift and press his hands tighter. "Please," I whisper, loving how his palm feels cupping my aching breasts.

"Jojo…hold up…I—" his voice is pained, straining for control.

I can feel he's harder now as his body involuntarily jerks against me. He stays pressed and throbbing into my backside, so tightly that I can feel the shape and the heat.

The thought of that—heat—the thought of how sexy and sweet and patient he is with me, how it will be when his skin is next to my skin, how that might feel *inside my body*, has sent my belly into a fluttery spin. I've thought of this so much that I think I've melted with how badly I want him right now. I can only hope he's feeling the same.

"Alex..." His name comes out in a vibration.

He groans and starts kissing my neck, rolling with me until his lips find my collarbone. We're sixteen. That's how old everyone is for their first time. This is how I imagined it all.

My body presses and turns to inch for more, but his arms are locking me still. "Alex…"

"Mmmmm," he hums, burying kisses against the side of neck and into my hair. I feel him press and pulse against my hip this time. I press back—hard.

It's so hot. He's…so…very…hot.

"You're killing me. You know that?" he whispers.

"I trust you. You know that, right? I…want you. I want to…I want you to…"

My heart is pounding so hard my vision is shaking, so I close my eyes.

"Damn…JoJo. I know," he answers, his voice all want and restraint, his body grinding into me, the force of it increasing with his own pounding, shaking desire.

"I know that you won't hurt me, and I want to keep going, you know I do." To prove it, I press against his erection again, and his whole body goes rigid. This time he stops kissing my neck and groans like I've hurt him.

I stop in a sigh and move my palms up fast to cover my face, hiding my burning skin in embarrassment. "You…don't?" I say, mortified. "Oh, God! You don't want to. That's why you never? Is that why?"

"Are you kidding? I want to as much as you, I'm just more—patient. Less…desperate?" Alex pulls my hands away from my face, chuckles as I pull a face in response to his words, and finally, he shifts me, so we're face to face. He's now looking down at me as I lay half beneath him flat on the ground—hoping—hoping, and yes, desperate. I raise my head to kiss him again, hard.

He pulls back and his tongue passes over his lips as though he's trying to still taste me, as his eyes dart from mine back to my mouth. He leans down and kisses me softly again, sucking my bottom lip gently before shifting me further under him, then lowering his body along mine and tilting his chin up to stare into my face.

I say nothing and force myself to breathe slowly until eventually I don't breathe at all. No sudden movements. Nothing about me will signal him to STOP. Except for this one small motion.

Impatient, my fingers deftly unclasp the hook in the center between the two cups, and I feel the tension release.

He gasps, surprised at my move, and his gaze envelops me; the wanting I can read off of his face consumes me.

I moan a little and repeat, "*Alex.*" My eyes and hands say everything else as I touch the sides of my breasts. My nipples have hardened into high peaks in the cold night air, and I know from the way he's biting his lower lip and looking at me that he thinks I'm beautiful—and that maybe he wants to put his mouth just where I want him to put it, too.

"Please...?"

"Can't...not yet, damn." His eyes are molten boring into mine. "Do you know what you do to me? How you look right now, that fucking impish smile on your face? Your eyes—with the stars reflecting in them as you look at me—asking what you're asking me to do? *Fuck...*" he grits out, running the side of one hand along the curve of my breast. "JoJo...please, I just can't. I promised and I won't—not here not now, not all the way," he whispers back.

The look he's giving me is filled up with apology and with what I know is love for me, but it's also loaded with something I just can't read. Something that, I can tell, is still holding him back from me.

But what? Why?

Whatever it is, like him, it's sexy—it's mysterious, but it's also frustrating as hell. The look he's giving me now is not coming from the face of the boy who has always been so sweet with me. It's this expression that makes him appear like he's suddenly turned into a man. I like how he's growing older, how he and I have grown older together since we met, and I wonder if finally I'm seeing the man he's going to become. Maybe he can see me, wanting so badly to be a woman, but maybe he simply thinks I'm not ready?

His right hand slides up the center of my chest, testing the weight of my breasts, and pauses where the fishing lure he gave me after we'd made things *official* hangs on a thin chain I bought at the town's Five & Dime. I'd made the necklace after he'd told me he loved me back, right after I'd awkwardly told him—months ago. I love how we say it to each other easily all the time now. I feel his fingers close over it gently, then he rests it back against my beating heart before moving on to the lacy bra. With both hands, shaking fingers and a little shifting on my part, he manages to re-clasp the bra over my breasts.

"You deserve more than a blanket on the hard ground. I also don't have any condoms...so..." He sighs, eyes burning into my face.

I nod, pretending to understand, because I do, but knowing I'm still wide-eyed and wishing and so...wet, like I've never been before.

I'm watching the path his fingers are making over the edges of my now re-clasped bra, and I'm still about to lose my mind. I'm also trying to hide my disappoint-ment as he adds roughly, "I swear to God, Jojo, I don't know what I love more—the way you feel...the way you look at me...the way you moan when I touch you..."

His words make me lose it and my whole body tenses up again as his fingers slide over the delicate material that is now covering those hard peaks of my breasts. I shiver some because I can't help it, and because the hungry look on his face is so sexy, and because... even to me...I know that I look attractive in this moon-light. "Or..." he continues, "Maybe I love the way you love me back, so simply. The way you let me call the shots."

"For now, I do." I frown because he's pulled his hands away from me. "On this *one* topic, yes. But soon, I swear Alex, I'll be the boss of you for making me wait like this," I blurt out, touching my breasts again, and gently circling the lace-covered, rock-hard nipples with my index fingers, watching his eyes go wide as I add, "I wanted you to kiss these. And damn you for not doing it." I pout, while I still my fingertips at the peaks.

"Did you?" His voice comes out low and slightly pained again. "I'm not a mind reader...and I'm sorry to have disappointed you."

His eyes are now transfixed on the movements of my fingers, and he startles me when his mouth comes down fast, pushing my hands aside as his lips clamp over my left nipple along with the fabric of my bra.

It's surprising, and scratchy—and it feels so crazy good I gasp out, "Oh..."

I squirm under him and watching his mouth on me makes the hot spot between my legs get hotter, all while the pull of his mouth is so intense on my nipples that I'm moaning and pushing myself—my breasts—everything that is me, up and towards him while his body and his erection presses back into me, hard. He does it over and over again, and it feels amazing. My arms twine around his back, and I hold him there, loving the weight of his body against me. I'm wishing he'd never stop.

As he groans and I moan back, all that was rational

thought in my mind turns to me bucking upwards and him pressing back. I become sweat and heat and two million more wishes that he would just go all the way with me. Somewhere between kisses, his fingers have unbuttoned my shorts and I've helped him pull off his swimsuit. He's reached down my bikini bottoms, and I'm touching the length of his hardness. He rubs and rubs his fingers gently into me, and presses and flicks them against the wetness, and the stars spin above us as I lose track of how I'm touching him because he's made me come hard and shudder against his hand. While I lie there, panting and smiling, he jerks himself off, and he's huge and he's beautiful and he's staring at me. I can't take my eyes off of what he's doing. I watch hungrily as he finishes, sending white hot moisture into the dark grass next to me, and when he's done with that, he collapses flat on his back, our sticky arms barely touching where we lie exhausted and blissful.

"Fuck. Jojo. That was..." He glances at me, one arched brow high. "Should I apologize?"

"Never. Not for anything as amazing as that," I breathe out and smile over at him.

When we come back down to earth, I'm blushing and out of sorts, and maybe he's right—maybe I wasn't as ready as I thought I was, because that—holy cow—that was more than enough between us for one night.

More than he and I have ever done.

And...already, I can't wait to try this all again, but I don't tell him that.

"I love you." It's cliche, I know it, but it's all I can think to say right now that sounds right. He owns me at this moment. He owns me completely.

His voice is rough and full of emotion as he helps me back into my shirt. "I love you, too, Jojo. So much. *So damn much.*"

PRESENT DAY

I realize I'm nearly the last one left in the funeral parking area. I've been staring at the fishing rods and remembering so long my eyes feel weighted. The memories—or the damn sound of Alex's voice reminding me of our past, and that he used to love me— it's all made me feel like I'm going to cry.

But since I'm not going to do that, not before this funeral at least, I pull hard on the fishing line until the lure I used to wear around my neck as though it was more valuable than gold, pops off of where it's been tied.

It was tied and forgotten for almost six long years.

I know Alex must have found it the night after we had finally made love, because that is the last night I saw him up close. That is the night he broke my heart, or tried to. And it's where I left the necklace on the floor of his family's boathouse. It was laid out on the canvas sails, just where I had been abandoned by him.

But I know—I know deep down—nothing that went wrong that night was his choice.

The chain is rusted through, so I work it off then flip the lure upside down and force it in place, using the little fish hook so it dangles into the fabric of my dress like a brooch.

This lure...it's lucky. And it means something to both me and Alex. It means friendship, love, promises and home. It means, to me, at least, that I still love him, and I hope when Alex is finished being angry or mad and worried about me—because he was always that—he will realize that me wearing it today is a symbol that the past is over and he still loves me, too.

I know he'll see it. Alex never misses details.

I run my fingers along the cold metal of the lure, thinking on the boy I left behind here and the devastatingly gorgeous man he's grown into, knowing that if I press my fingers too hard the minuscule hook will dig into my flesh and draw more blood. This will remind me to be careful as well as remind me why I can't leave here without Alex.

I know I'm his only hope, *our* only hope. So I can't fail.

Alex doesn't belong to them. He's always been different, and he's always been mine, and I've been very patient for the last six years.

Wherever or however it is the Sinclairs have buried the Alex I used to know, I've come to set him free. Based on what I just saw in his eyes, in his reaction to me, Alex Sinclair is very close to death. If I fail, his funeral will become the fourth funeral I attend because of these

Sinclairs: my mother's, my father's—now Mr. Sinclair's. But not Alex's.

If that happens—if they, or the feud, or whatever darkness that rules this place gets Alex too—it will also kill me.

4.

ALEX, PRESENT DAY.

I get my shit together—get my memories shoved back some, and analyze how she's leaning against that car like she needs it to hold her up, like the sight of me might have already inadvertently hurt her all over again.

She straightens her slight shoulders then runs her hands nervously through the thick, mahogany hair at both sides of her ears like she used to do when she was trying to gather her courage. From her stance, I see she's undecided about approaching me directly, but I can also tell she's not going to move until I get out of this car.

"Fuck," I mutter, gripping the steering wheel tighter. "Of course she hasn't changed. Stubborn...stubborn girl."

I hate how, like a starving man, my eyes have already gone over every inch of the exposed, luminous skin that makes up her long, bare legs. I've trailed over the curve of her cheek. Noted faint shadows under her eyes.

I can't look away from curve of her delicate collar-
bones, and I hate that I've let my eyes linger just where
they meet at that soft indent at the base of her neck.
Hate even more how I long to place my lips there, how
my fingers itch to feel those wild wisps of her untam-
able hair curling its softness around them.

The wheel is all that's giving me balance as my heartbeats punch into my temples, doubling the crippling
headache I've had for days. I swear I'm about to black out.
Wouldn't the town gossips love that. Even dead, my
father's lingering dark ghost would force The Tacoma
News to print the headline he'd want to read over the real
truth. Something like: *Loving son, Alex Sinclair, found uncon-
scious in car overwrought with grief before his father's funeral.*

I'd always daydreamed about how JoJo would look if
she came back here. It—she—should look and feel like
anger, vengeance, hatred. But, shit...the girl who's
silently staring at my car and waiting patiently for me to
find enough balls to exit has me feeling unprepared to
build walls against her like I need to build.

It's all got something to do with the way she's biting
her lip. I know exactly how that lip tastes.

I've never forgotten. Never will.

"*Fuck,*" I say again and shake my head to clear it,
looking desperately for some sort of weapon to use
against how JoJo Wallace affects me.

I've brought the suit jacket Grady, my older brother,
had asked me to bring for the funeral. As I'm stepping

out, I hold it in front of me like it's some sort of shield, and reach into his pocket to find one of his cigarette packs and a lighter.

Even though I don't smoke, I tap out a cigarette and pause to light it, almost giving myself away in a fit of coughing before stepping around to where JoJo and I will have to cross paths.

Long before I reach her she blurts, "So...you're *smoking* now?"

Like she's hit me with a slingshot, my feet slip on the gravel and I stop dead in my tracks. I was right to be afraid of her. The sound of her clear voice chastising me just how she used to has undone me as much as her words have humbled me. Of course she's concerned, upset...*worried*. About me. This is Jojo, after all. She's the only person in the world who ever worried over me about anything. About everything.

Should she still smell like lavender and look up at me with stained-glass-window eyes that hint that she still loves me despite everything, I will pull out the gun I've stashed in my glove box and put it exactly where someone placed it on my father's head, right between my eyes, and pull the trigger right now.

That kind of fast death is preferable over letting myself die a second time, year after year, over JoJo Wallace when she can never be mine.

Keeping my eyes off of her, I pull the cigarette to my lips again, sucking on it hard, willing the smoke and the heat to burn the scratchiness and tightness at the back of my throat away.

I pretend to stare at the *just-washed-for-the-funeral* cars all around us and force my expression to angry-annoyance. When I'm about to choke on the excess amount of smoke I've pulled in, I puff it all out slowly so I can only smell the stale and sour scent of tobacco instead of the memories of her, then I step closer and risk looking at her face, hoping the smoke between us will also blur out some of her beauty.

It doesn't.

"You came back for more? Still so stupid, huh?" I spit out words that mean to maim, and I make sure I say her name like it's poison on my lips, hoping to scare her off. "Make my life easy and drive away, here and now, would you, Jojo? I deserve that luxury, because as you probably know, I didn't have that the first time we all got you to leave this place. I was forced to deal with you, and you kind of fucking owe me for saving your life, so...just *go*, would you, before one of us finally kills you."

Instead of rising to my bait she's rolled her eyes at me and after a long pause, she glares at my cigarette and answers simply: "You *know* my mom died of lung cancer."

I return the cigarette to my lips, dragging in more smoke to cover a smile of admiration as a telltale crease of worry forms above the bridge of her nose. Despite what we did to her, this mini-lecture and that scrunched face means we didn't break her.

I get that she is older, more beautiful...maybe more composed—a lot more composed—but still...this is *her*. This is still Jojo Wallace.

Even though I want to pull her into my arms, and laugh with relief over that realization, I play this carefully and layer on a lecture of my own.

A warning.

"Since we all get that your family has a history of being a little *slow*, I'm going to say it clearly in some of those *shorter* words you can understand. Get the fuck out of here, Jojo. No one wants you anywhere near here. I can guarantee my father didn't ever feel guilty. Not about you or your mom. Nor did he have you added to the will. If that's why you came."

She holds her ground, surprising me yet again.

"That's not why I came." Her eyes latch onto mine. Clear. Bright. Unwavering.

The way she's looking into me has me sucking in a breath. She has *me* threatening to quake—to pull a one-eighty and drive the hell out of here, just how I'd wanted her to do.

What the fuck?

The Jojo of the past would have fired at least twenty wounded expressions at me by now—maybe even pleaded or cried, all things that kill me to see. But the only reaction she lets slip through now is a slight tilting at the edges of her eyes—and, damn her, she licks her lips, which is sexy as hell. That, plus her voice, because it was completely devoid of the anger I'd expected, has coated me with the kind of goosebumps I'd long forgotten.

"After we bury your dad, after I do some...*fishing*. See...I'm here..."

She shrugs, and my eyes are drawn to how vulnerable her slight frame looks in her mother's old, faded black dress.

I take in the stubborn set of her shoulders, the solid lift of her chin, before I risk letting my eyes trail up the soft curves of her face again. The only change I can note in this adult version of JoJo is that her freckles have faded. The soft scent of lavender snakes around me as though to taunt me. "I'm here," she repeats, her eyes rise up and glue onto mine. This time what she's said has come out stronger and makes me reel back some. Because *damn her*, I *know* exactly what she's going to say next. Exactly.

"...for a little adventure."

She blinks, and then smiles, those fucking smiling, kissable lips of hers causing all of the blood to rage into my pants.

The first words she'd ever said to me. That fucking smile.

Check. And mate. Fuck. I think I just winced. I know I just winced.

Those are the words that started our friendship.

The smile she's pinning on me is the one that instantly stole my heart.

She's bringing up the beginning and the end.

The Wallaces and the Sinclairs.

Everything, here and now.

Everything that will never be.

Like an addict heading back to the pipe, I do what I swore I wouldn't. I look deep into her wide, open eyes. I probe the blue-green depths, and I try to hide my apologies, my devastation and, more importantly, *myself* from her unyielding gaze, because the monster I was when my family made me break her heart six years ago can't compare to the monster I am now. Not. Even. Close.

Like she's a mind reader, and is still unafraid of that monster—as she always was—she simply blinks calmly and smiles up wider. She's got this hopeful look on her face that's made me want her twice as much as I ever did, all while it makes a cold sweat break out along my spine. If she stays I will succeed in destroying her, or worse, she'll end up dead like my father is now, like her parents are—and that is the last thing I ever wanted. It's why I did everything that was asked of me—to save her. To keep her alive.

Panic thrums through me. Suddenly I'm eighteen again, pressing against the walls of a boathouse listening to this girl cry, while covering up my own tears.

"*Why? Why? Why....*" She'd asked me, unbelieving, hurt and broken.

"*Happy fucking birthday, JoJo Wallace,*" I'd said to her that day after treating her like an animal. "*Emphasis on the fucking...*"

She cannot stay here. She cannot stay here. I will not let all that I've been through to protect her be for nothing. I will keep her safe.

I shove my swirling thoughts back into the present and pull in yet another huge drag of the hateful cigarette. Then I manage to puff more smoke than a forest fire over her, all without coughing or letting the mask she's just fucking tried to crowbar off of me drop from my face.

Acting like she's not worth one more moment of my time and pretending that my now rock-hard cock hasn't nearly debilitated me, I grind the butt under my shoe and turn away without another glance. It's all I can do to hide the second wave of goosebumps that are coursing down my spine, because this time, I'm afraid.

Jojo hasn't come back here for blood or the paybacks she deserves to give us all.

I should have known when I saw the faded black dress. Jojo's here for something else. Something more.

This girl has come back for me, for my soul.

Only it's not there anymore. *I'm* not there anymore. My family killed both long ago. I'm like them—I am them, and I can't change that.

But even so…I can't push away the memories of who I was back before it all went wrong. Before I even knew about the feud.

Nor can I stop the flood of memories about the day I first met JoJo Wallace from happening as they pour into my mind.

5.

ALEX, SUMMER BEFORE FRESHMAN YEAR.

I think I hear splashing when I reach the lower path that leads up to my lake, but it could just be my imagination.

My lake.

I love saying that. *My lake.*

As I get closer, there's even more splashing. My chest tightens, because it can only mean that someone is in *my lake*, scaring the fish I'd come here to coax out of the water with my rod, some dry flies and sheer patience.

My fish.

I smile at that thought, trudging along, trying to imagine what my father would say if he were as disappointed as I feel right now, because frightened fish never go for flies. I try on his voice and say, *"Fucking hell."*

Father always cusses with such perfect authority.

I sound like a toad.

Pausing to catch my breath, I try again, this time with less force so my changing voice won't crack, "Is it too much to ask for a little privacy after walking six miles? *A little hell-fucking-damn-privacy?*" I crack up at that last one. Cussing and trying to act like my dad is a first for me, as is this epic solo hike to the lake.

"My lake," I whisper again, admiring the curling ferns filling in every inch of space between the cedar trees. I'd never been allowed to *just hike* in the woods alone before today. My parents are such helicopter types that I actually thought personal freedom like this would never happen for me.

All the way up until my fourteenth birthday a few days ago, my father had insisted on hiking *with me* wherever and whenever I'd wanted to go. Sometimes twice a week, and always around our property lines. I thought he and I had been everywhere on the Sinclair property, but because our estate is so huge, and because I'm always stuck studying or doing whatever sports my dad thinks I need to be doing besides fishing (which is the only sport I *want* to do), this route and even the existence of a lake on our property had been unknown to me.

The first time father brought us here, he'd acted all strange, studying our reactions to the secret he'd revealed to us like we were rats in a scientific test.

I, of course, was ecstatic. There is no better lake than this lake.

Grady, my sixteen-year-old, know-it-all brother,

simply complained and whined that his feet hurt and that he couldn't care less.

Father, like he was on some sort of mission, had us hike to the lake three times in a row—day after day— and he had been acting so strange Grady and I started getting really nervous about his intentions. Our father had never really shown this kind of concentrated interest in us—in our reactions to things, for sure. Father also knows Grady hates hiking and that Grady hates me.

At least I think Father knows that Grady hates me, because he's never done much to stop my brother's endless tormenting. He always says, "brothers will be brothers; you two need to sort it out," no matter what Grady does to me. And that kid has pushed me off my bike, thrown rocks at my head, and once, when we were little, he shoved me down the stairs so hard I broke my arm.

This summer, I grew to be just as big as Grady is now. Six feet tall; skinny, though, but I'm still growing. Although I don't outweigh him yet, my retaliation punches as well as the fighting skills I've learned from watching YouTube videos have started to find their marks. It's to the point where Grady's backed off some. "Brothers will be brothers. I was sorting some stuff out," was my comment to Grady and to my father the day the big, whining baby went crying to our father about how I blackened one of his eyes.

Father, I think—though he didn't say anything in

front of Grady—was secretly proud of me. He was also pissed off at Grady for showing his weakness; we're not allowed to do that. Grady looks bigger and stronger than I am, but my brother has always cried louder and longer about everything. I never do that. I just take it and clam up, simmering with anger while I start hatching plans for revenge.

Father also hates when Grady and I are together now that we are older, because he says *I* bring out the worst in my brother. Father hasn't realized yet that it's not at all about me.

Grady is just...the worst. Period. He's a horrible person.

He and I had decided the hikes to the lake were our father's final attempt to force us to *bond*. But no matter how much he orders us—how much he commands us, pesters us, bullies us—our disdain for each other seems to be something permanent, genetic and growing bigger every year.

Grady says it's because he's sure I was switched at birth, of course. Our mother assures me that isn't true, and the part where Mom and I have the same golden brown eyes proves it.

My father sees mine and Grady's bad relationship as his one and only failure. But I see it as a survival tactic. Grady and I were terrified that Father was going to make us do this same hike on a *fourth* day, so we pretended to get along for once. We talked to each other and laughed at every one of Father's crass jokes.

We also said stuff we never say, like, "Father, this has been an amazing week—all of us together." Grady even said that he wished we'd do stuff like this all the time, "together."

It worked.

That last day, I'd snuck along my fold-up fishing rod, and I begged and begged to stay at the lake and fish, or hike back alone. But my suggested ideas were not in Father's plans.

Father had also brought some things along in his pack that day, too. Guns.

He'd planned to stop on the way back to the house so we could all shoot the crap out of distant tree branches or take aim and waste any poor bird the noise of the guns had flushed out.

As much as Father hates fishing, he loves watching Grady and I shoot guns. Father wants Grady and I to shoot better than military snipers. We've been shooting at the range since way back when we were little kids, so we're both amazing shots, whether we like it or not.

Father always says he wants us to be able to take care of *things* when we grow up. We were raised on lecture after lecture about how *"we Sinclairs handle things on our own, outside the law if need be, because we own the law in Tacoma."* Whatever that means, because how can someone own the law?

At this age, I only nod and go along with whatever Father says, because when I was younger, I'd ask questions about all of the stuff he would say. The wrong questions got me hit, so I stopped asking. I learned —*wised up.*

I have no clue what Father means by these *"things that might need to be managed with guns,"* so I've made up my own answers. And I was really into zombie books and movies for a number of years, so I've decided that knowing how to handle a gun could have its benefits, and I suppose Father, in his own weird way, just wants us to be able to stay safe.

TURNS out all of the hiking, the lake, the information about the lake and the surrounding lands Father was drilling into me and Grady was all about *me.*

About me being a Sinclair. A real one. And my four-teenth birthday.

That thought warms my heart because I've been thinking about it—and my birthday—all the way up here.

See, instead of the usual cash for my birthday gift, which is what I've gotten every year since I can remember, Dad had handed me a thick, weighted manila envelope, already addressed to the *County and Clerk Recorder of Tacoma, Washington.*

It contained a map, along with a legal-looking paper with the words TRANSFER OF DEED across the top. The middle of the document had all of these extra-tiny-font legal sentences I couldn't begin to understand, but the bottom had two columns. One had my father's name and our address with his signature already on it. The other had four blank lines that read: *Type or Print Full Names of New Property or Shared Property Holders.*

My father asked me to sign the line next to my typed name, which I did very carefully. He told me the lake we'd been hiking to was now mine, really and truly *mine.* He'd explained that these papers meant he had also given me all of the lands we'd hiked through for the past three weekends—lands so vast that I couldn't believe it when he'd shown me.

He'd talked about how one day I could build a house up there if I wanted, and he said that we would refurbish some of the old buildings he would soon give us in the downtown—and that together, as our profits from Father's new oil investments grew out on the mud flats, we three Sinclair men would own all of Tacoma. Everyone and everything in it.

Grady had laughed as I smiled and hugged Father, I was so humbled by this amazing gift. Overwhelmed. Happy that I didn't have anything to say besides, "Thank you."

Always competitive, Grady bragged that Father had gifted him better land on his fourteenth birthday. His gift was made up of the city waterfront—lands that held the family business, not crap-land and a soggy lake in the middle of nowhere that held a few sea lions that no one cared about and wetlands that would be impossible to develop into anything good.

I'd just kept on smiling at my Father, not caring about anything Grady was saying. For the first time ever, Father had just smiled back at me. He never does that. It was like my silence made him proud of something. He'd even defended me against Grady. He'd said the lands he'd given me suited my future and my *duties to the family perfectly*, just how Grady's suited his, and then he shut my brother right up.

I figure now that I'm growing up, I should stop wishing for a different family, a different father like how I used to do. Because of this gift, I mean to try to understand Father a little bit better, just how obviously Father is trying to do the same by me. Because why else would he have given me this perfect lake?

As I round the final switchback, I hear the splashing start up again.

I pause to listen and realize it's not the rhythmic sound of a fly fisherman tromping around and then pausing to cast, nor is it a *swimming* sound like I'd thought I would hear if someone were trespassing there to swim.

This splashing is wild—erratic even. Which means it's possible the person messing up my water and freaking out my fish isn't a person at all.

It's got to be a bear.

The thought of a bear being this close makes my heart pound and my throat go dry with anxiety because we don't just have black bears around here, we have grizzlies.

The salmon are also running right now. This lake connects to wetlands on the far side, and it's fed by a big river that pours out into it on one side then travels out to the sound and connects to three other tributaries that also head into the ocean. It's a perfect place for salmon to breed and lay eggs as well as for all kinds of animals to hang around.

I prepare myself to face something big. *Maybe it's not a bear, maybe just a moose—still an animal that can kill someone, but usually they're more dangerous in the spring...*

Just in case, I set my fishing rods, hang up my backpack full of lunch, water bottles, and a pile of books (ones I regretted bringing at about the four-mile mark) high up on a broken branch while I listen again.

The splashing sound repeats, followed by a noticeable pause. It's definitely something running in the shallows.

Splashes sound again, sporadic, loud enough to startle birds nesting in the trees above.

The sound moves a bit away from me, and I grow frustrated because there is no way to tell without looking. Hoping it will be focused on the lake, and not consider me any sort of food source—and because I can't resist watching a bear catch fish—I inch around to drop down behind some scrub bushes.

My eyes follow the line of the lakeshore. I track wide water arcs that seem to be going off to the right and the left as something bends and ducks fast toward the surface of the water.

I'm completely disoriented when my gaze trips, then locks on these flashes of dark brown hair, flashes of blue denim shorts and gangly limbs all wrapped up in what sounds like peals of happy laughter.

"Got you. *Yes!*"

The dripping wet creature has just hand-plucked a squirming salmon out of the shallows. Without a blink she tosses it up onto the beach next to three others as though she does this all the time.

It's—she's—a girl!

A girl who looks to be about my same age, too. She can't be from around here because our town has only one school that includes elementary through high school, and I've never seen her before.

I would—*anyone would*—remember this girl. That's because even in cut-off shorts, pigtails, and thoroughly covered in mud, she's the most beautiful girl I've ever seen.

When she spots me staring, she's startled—I can sense it, but her calm and open expression is exactly the opposite of the awkward, galloping horses that have invaded my heart.

"Oh. Hi!" She turns and takes two steps in my direction, and I notice she's barefoot.

Because I'm on this huge Lord of the Rings reading-binge, I get this crazy sensation that she and I are from opposite worlds. In fact, her willowy limbs, and wild, dirty brown hair tinged with red, as well as her wise, blue-eyed gaze make her a dead match for the Elfin people of Rivendell. Seriously, it's like she fell out of the exact pages I'd read last night.

Surely only elves can run barefoot over sharp stones to catch impossible-to-catch fish with their bare hands, right?

Only...no.

I shake my head to clear it from that silly idea and really look at her.

This girl, she's dressed *her* ultra pale skin in layers of —well—sunburn and dirt. On closer inspection her cheeks are too red, and she's also not wearing any sort of gossamer gown. She's got clothes so tattered not even the thrift store would take them. Her hair isn't bone straight, either. It's braided, but I can see these escaping curls springing all around her freckled cheeks. Elves are not brunettes.

The girl smiles oddly like she was somehow *expecting* me.

When I don't smile back, she raises one of her perfectly arched, yet very mud-encrusted brows, as though she, too, wonders who and what I'm supposed to be. In a voice that's half question half laughter like she finds me amusing, she asks, "I'm here for a little adventure. Fishing. You know?"

I feel like I've been punched. My legs start to shake. She tilts her head to the side and next asks the question that confirms I've just met the girl of my dreams. "Don't you *like* fishing?" she asks me.

I work to close my mouth, suddenly annoyed with myself.

More unexplainably, I'm annoyed with her. Before I can think, I blurt out, "Haven't you been taught not to talk to strangers? It's dangerous. I don't even *know* you."

"Yeah, but strangers aren't usually skinny kids, are they?" Her comeback is so fast. She tosses her long braids behind her, and my eyes are caught on how the wet tips of them are now dripping against where her waist curves in at her lower back. "Besides, I could totally take you out, or outrun you if you turned out to be *dangerous*."

She laughs, and for the second time I get the sensation she finds me strange and entertaining, which only makes me more annoyed, because she's the one who's strange and entertaining—*not me!*

"I'm not a kid. I'm fourteen. A freshman—starting *high school* in August." I pull myself up, hoping she notices how tall I am.

"Oh. Like me." She blinks, staring at me as hard as I'm staring at her.

"You look like a baby." I sneer this time. She's nothing like me.

"I do not. You're really rude."

I straighten my back more, and work to flex some muscles. "Well, you called me a skinny kid when I'm not. I'm also always first on my cross country team, so there is *no* way you could outrun me."

"You're on a running team?" She walks the rest of the way out of the lake so she's standing next to me and scrunches her face and looks me up and down like she's assessing me—my legs—to see if it's true that I can run fast.

"Maybe we can race sometime? I run everywhere. And I think I'm fast, but maybe I'm not—you know —*team fast*. I'd love to find out. I'm hoping to join the cross country team next year, too—or maybe the track team."

"That's in the spring. Cross country is first," I say, feeling all wise.

"Oh. My father and I think it would be cool if I could get all the way to the Olympics."

I try not to stare back at her long, perfectly shaped legs, but suddenly I can't seem to take my eyes off of them, because like her, they're so very well...*designed*. As well as covered in mud. And, hell yeah, a lot of people brag about speed, but I don't think she's doing that. She simply does look like she'd be really, really fast.

She shrugs and crosses her arms when I don't answer again, the movement releasing my gaze so it travels back up to her smiling face where I note the bridge of her nose and the tops of her cheeks are bright with a light sprinkling of freckles.

"Running and fishing are my top-two most favorite things."

I can't answer her. I can only stare and wish the lake would pull me into the water and save me from sucking at talking to a girl.

"I'm Jojo. Nice to meet you." She leans toward me, her expression extra encouraging like she can tell she's turned me into a stuttering fool. "This is the part where you say your name. Then, how about you tell me two of your most favorite things like I just did, and then we won't be strangers anymore. Okay?"

"Okay." I parrot, liking how this amazing girl seems to have on no makeup under all of that mud—or a bra, I'm pretty sure. Either way, I'm not going to stare in that direction again because I'm already so mind blown here. But my eyes keep wanting to dart there—to her wet chest.

She seems not one bit self-conscious compared to me. Nor does she seem to care where the mud is sticking to her, either. I'm also kind of impressed that not one of those usual girly comments about her *"hair being wet"* and *"OMG, so messed up"* has dropped from her wide, bow-shaped lips. And she isn't concerned with the flopping-dying salmon she's thrown on the bank next to us.

She's just ankle deep in water and talking to me as though this is the most normal conversation in the world—which means she just might be the coolest girl in the world, right?

I force my head together and try to just be myself. Be like her.

Be...cool. Be cool.

"I'm Alex. More than anything, uh...my top two favorite things are, uh...I love fishing. And books. I mean, reading." I blink, trying again. *"Fishing* and *reading* are my two most favorite things. Yeah." I shrug. "Look. I'll prove it."

She waits while I turn and trudge back to retrieve my backpack and my fishing rods from where I'd stashed them.

I pull out my lunch first, then lay out the rods next to my books and suddenly, feeling like I may have just shown her too much, I say lamely, "See?"

My eyes feel heavy with sudden embarrassment over my show-and-tell. I'm so lame.

"Wow. Cool. Nice rods. I don't have one. Someday..." Her eyes are glued to my fishing poles, and I feel instantly renewed. I'm not so lame.

"It's why I've come up here. To...you know. Fish and read."

"And have lunch." She's now eyeing my bag with great interest.

"Yes. And nice to meet you, too." I hesitate, testing the sound of her name inside my head first, before adding, "Jojo."

"Back at ya, Alex." She winks like she's testing out my name as well and my heart flips upside down as that smile of hers comes out again.

"Will you teach me how you catch fish with your hands?" I ask as I feel my smile widening to match hers.

"It's not easy." She shakes her head. "Could take all summer. Besides, it's my family's sworn-secret method. I'd never betray my family...so...I don't know if I'm allowed."

"I have infinite patience, and I'll promise never to tell or teach anyone else your family secrets. I swear." I smirk through my words. I'm pretty sure we're flirting. I like this.

She's chewing her lip, looking me up and down. "I'll consider it, but only if you…share that lunch and…" She pauses to eye my books. "Teach me how to read?"

"You don't know how to read?" I gasp a little with surprise. I can see her wince, and I try to tone down my reaction. "How can that be?"

"I can…just not well. Not fast." Her smile fades, and I feel guilty about it because I know my shocked reaction stole it away. "I can do Algebra equations all day long. But reading? Any sentence over three words and I'm stuck. If I try to go fast, or remember what I've read, everything falls out of my mind; nothing sticks. I don't get to hang out with other kids much and my mom taught me. Homeschooled me, I mean. I thought, maybe you could show me how you do it? Give me your tips and tricks and stuff. I've got this thing—dyslexia is what my dad calls it. I just say I'm stupid, but I'm always trying to be better at it."

Suddenly, all I want to do is be this girl's hero, erase her doubt and bring the light back into her eyes—that smile. Please bring back that smile. "It's obvious you aren't stupid."

"It is?" One of her arched brows shoots up. I hate that she thinks this about herself.

"Yeah. People just learn at different speeds. Like, I'm

behind in math compared to others. I'm only in pre-algebra, but it will all balance out."

"I'm starting at West Tacoma High School, so I'm worried it will make me not fit in. I toured it last week. Seems really cool, but *really* huge."

"You'll be a freshman? At West Tacoma? West Tacoma High School?" I blink at her, dumbfounded. "West. Tacoma. High. School?" I blink again.

She nods at me, her expression shifting and I get it—she thinks I'm an idiot to repeat what she's just said so many times, but like—*how could I not know this? Know her? Our town is small and everyone would have been buzzing about this girl had they seen her, Grady especially, because she's interesting and beautiful and...*

"You got a problem with that? Is it not cool there? Is it, like...a trouble school?" She interrupts my scattered thoughts.

"Oh—no, it's very cool. It's just like...so will I...I'll also be—be a freshman," I stutter out, rattled as hell now. "This—that is—you know—so—cool to know you will be, too. And, I mean. Nice to meet you."

"Oh. Um. Okay." She laughs then. For sure she's laughing at me but I don't even care when she adds, "And look at us, not even strangers all of a sudden."

"Friends already." I laugh at myself along with her. My skin feels hot, and I suddenly don't know what to do with my hands or feet. I'm not even sure I *have* feet.

"Well you never answered about sharing your lunch and...reading and..."

"Yes. Of course. I will. Of course."

"I'd like that. Very much." Her grin is wide and beautiful and real.

Damn...is this what love feels like? I think it, breathing out this sigh of breath I'd been holding this whole time. I'd had this idea that maybe she was a summer tourist and only here for the weekend or something, but she's going to my high school.

Better, if she is going to West, and is standing *here*, then she must live nearby, as in close enough to walk to...often. This means she will be on my bus and everyone will wonder how it is I already know the beautiful new girl. I wonder if it's too soon to ask her to every single dance, and to be my girlfriend for the next four years, and hell...maybe she can just go ahead and marry me.

A girl who catches salmon with her bare hands and loves being covered in mud is the kind of girl I want to keep.

"Don't worry about the reading. I tutor kids at the elementary school, and I know all kinds of tricks that might help. If you're allowed to meet me here at the lake sometimes, I'll bring some books that might help you. How hard could it be to teach someone to read?"

"Very. You have no idea." She frowns again. "I'm sort of broken. Very broken."

I shrug. "All we can do is try. We'll start today with what I've got here, and I'll bring books you might like next time. I'll bet you'll be reading ultra-fast before I ever land one fish with my bare hands how you just did." She blinks at me then and makes this face as though she might still not want to show me how she catches the fish.

"Do we have a deal?" I press her.

"Yeah. Okay. What's in the lunch bag?" She nods at it.

"Turkey and cheddar."

I want to pat myself on my back, because I'm pretty sure I've just asked this girl on a date. Hell, she and I are sharing my lunch. We might just already *be* on our first date. Kind of. Sort of. Is it a date if God and the universe and your favorite lake hands the girl over to you out of nowhere? Is this girl part of my best birthday present ever?

I almost laugh at that as I hand her half of the giant baguette sandwich the cook handed to me on my way out the door.

She pushes back her heavy mop of now half-dried brunette curls and grins at me like I'm the best person in the whole world for sharing the sandwich. She takes a bite and talks with her mouth full as she cries out, "Yum. Best sandwich ever!" Then, "You got any desert in that bag?"

"Heck yes, I do. Fresh baked brownies."

"Wow. You're the best friend anyone could find." She talks with a full mouth, and I'm in love.

I reach in and break the giant packed brownie in half and hand it to her. "Back at you," I grin.

Just when I thought it was impossible, she smiles even wider.

As she chews the brownie down, making little *mmm...mmm* sounds while she's swallowing it, my heart flips upside down so many times I think I'm having a heart attack.

And when we're both done eating and she and I are standing in the lake, trying to land trout with our hands, I quickly change the order of my list of *favorite things*:

Fishing and Jojo's wide-eyed smiling face have the top two spots now.

Reading has moved to number three.

Forever.

6.

JOJO, PRESENT DAY.

During the funeral, I caught glares from everyone. From May, of course, but considering our greeting in the parking lot—the years I dated Alex—that was to be expected. What I didn't expect from her were the soft moments, the few times I caught her staring at me like I was a puzzle. It was almost as if she'd been expecting me to look one way, and maybe I was different...or the same.

The looks from Grady, Alex's brother, also were no surprise. His carried the most heat, the most hate—the most hunger.

I didn't need to talk to him to see the boy who was awful had obviously turned into a man who was awful. I shudder, thinking his father would have been so proud at how he turned out.

I waited for Alex to look, willed him to turn to face me, knowing he could feel me watching. But he never looked. Not once. His will is stronger than I had expected. Or maybe it's just as it should be.

As we filed forward to leave a rose placed on a silver tray on top of the closed casket, Grady even went so far as to blow a kiss my direction. Everyone heard the cackle under his breath. When I blew one back, he frowned, and all but ran back to his seat to face the parade of speakers all set to talk about what a wonderful man his father was—a gift to greater Tacoma.

Gift my ass!

I waited long enough to see whether Alex would speak or not. I think I knew he wouldn't. He's never been one to be the center of attention. During school, I was always the one to present our projects, to lead us into the party, to stand in the center of a spotlight.

Before the family rose to walk the aisle and lead the procession to bury the Sinclair patriarch six feet under the very dirt that caused so much strife among our families, I ducked out the back door and rushed to my car with the push of blood and panic that came with the thought that *it's too late* coursing through my body and over my eardrums.

I pulled into the side alley and hid, and an hour later, I sit here still.

Alex is one of the first to leave the ceremony. I recognize the front of his SUV as he approaches the exit, and I don't bother to duck or hide; he will never search for me. He doesn't want to find me. I sit tall and watch as he drives the opposite direction of everyone else, turning left and disappearing into the thickness of the woods, toward the lake.

He always goes to the lake.

He used to call it our lake, but of course, like every bit of open land in the area, now that his father is dead, it's all his and Grady's, I'm sure.

May rides alone. Funny, I've never seen her drive before, but yet the black Mercedes, shining—brand new —the Limited model with gold trim, fits her to a tee. She leaves after most of the guests have gone, but she pauses in her car, her windshield square with mine. And even though there's a great distance between us, I swear she sees where I'm parked. I wait for her to pull her mirror down to touch up make up or to lean into the center and adjust her hair in the rear-view mirror. She does none of that, though. She doesn't look down at a phone or anything else that would require her to pause right here, right in my view. She just stares forward, and after a full minute, she turns her car and pulls away.

I suck in a deep breath through my nose and hold the fullness in my lungs. Something isn't right, but I have too many things to worry over and figure out. May will have to go on the bottom of the list.

When the last car passes me, I shift into drive and follow Alex's same path, slowing to a crawl at the dirt road that leads to the lake. So many memories, so many nightmares.

I hate that lake yet love it with equal passion.

My eyes rake over the gravel, the fresh tire grooves

cutting along the center, the width exactly right to match his car—I know in my heart Alex is there. I could so easily turn and follow. Is he expecting me? Does he want me to follow? I know if I did I'd still be playing into the Sinclair game. He'd push me away so hard that I might not survive it this time, which might actually be what he wants.

But I want something else, and I already know Alex so well that I know I won't be able to save him until he wants to be saved.

He has to come to me. He will come. The attraction between us is still undeniable, and I know he felt it. But is that attraction destiny or is it dangerous? When he comes to me, will it be to kill me like he may have finally killed his own father?

Will I care that he's a murderer if suspicions turn to truth? As long as he can guarantee that it's the last mysterious death that will happen between the Sinclairs and the Wallaces, then I know I won't. I will keep his secret as long as he agrees to keep mine safe.

My chest grows heavy and my head fills with momentary doubt, but I whisper my new mantra hoping that saying it out loud will make it true: "I am stronger than all of you."

My eyes settle back to the dotted center line of the roadway before me, and I press the gas and move on. I know Alex will be disappointed he read me wrong when I don't show up.

I smirk, pulling in a deep breath as I straighten my

shoulders to match the road ahead. Yes. I'm stronger, indeed.

I'm here for a little adventure.

After leaving the area around the lake, it doesn't take long for the roadway to weave through the small canyon, opening up on the downtown that was my entire life—and heart—for so long.

Tacoma, Washington.

My childhood is rooted here—these storefronts, the way the sidewalks rise and fall with uneven cracks the city council left in place to keep kids from riding scooters and skateboards—even the damp, musty, salt-water-shipyard-meets-pine-trees-crisp cool air is familiar.

It's home, all rolled up in the walls of a hell I thought I'd never see again.

If I could find a way to scoop this precious historic square block up and drop it anywhere else on this earth, I would.

The horseshoe sign hanging from the pole outside of my Aunt Shelly's white-washed brick building is the same as in my dreams, and the smile hits my lips out of precious habit as I pull through the alleyway behind the storefronts into the small carriage house garage in the back. I pull my one small bag out with me, tucking it to my side and stepping around the back of the car.

Renewed, I spin on my heels and jerk the metal door down to a close behind me, hiding any trace of my vehicle even though I'm sure just like Alex, the rest of the Sinclairs also know exactly where I am. All it took was for me to show my face at that service for the whispers to begin their trail to curious ears. There's no place left for me to go that isn't tainted with their all-seeing eyes, their murder or my own heartbreak—this tiny room is all I have left.

I'm going to need to sleep with the rifle.

And whether the Sinclairs like it or not, this small apartment above my aunt's antique store will be my home for however long I need it; however long it takes.

Whatever the *it* might turn out to be.

A part of me hopes I won't be here but for a few days, another part of me hopes for forever—because I know if I leave soon, it's going to be because I've failed.

I turn the key and push open the door, a waft of acrid air suffocating me the moment I step inside. There's a layer of dust over most things; my aunt warned me I would need to do some cleaning. But in the corner, there's a bed, and to the side, a small kitchenette and a door I hope leads to a bathroom with running water and a shower.

I take in my surroundings and close the door behind me, locking it on both the knob and the small sliding lock near the top. It's all for show; if someone wants me dead, there isn't anything a two-inch layer of wood can do to stop them. I've stepped back into their arena—and that makes me fair game. I had no choice. Michael Sinclair's murder...it was a calling card too loud to ignore. Too...gruesome and bold.

That murder was mixed with something deeper than money and greed, and I intend to find out exactly what the motivation was.

I have to.

My bag falls to the floor next to my feet, and the thud kicks up a layer of dust. I cough as I tiptoe to the far wall where a small lamp sits on a night table. I'm surprised when the bulb glows after I click the lamp on, but my success gives me hope that more than just the lights will work in this apartment.

I never got to see the inside of a dorm room. Instead, I picked a roommate off of the community center board in the small Ohio town I ended up in. I'd wandered there in my lost, hurt and dizzy daze. I used the little money I had saved to get far away on my own terms. Jeff, my roommate, is gay, which is and was perfect because I had sworn off dating forever. I wouldn't take the Sinclair bribe money Alex tried to send me away with to pay for an education. I refused it, which meant school has been long and slow. I study a little at a time, and I'm close to earning my liberal arts degree. For a girl who struggled learning how to read, the fact that I gravitate to research-related work is rewarding. I've thought about clerking with a law firm, or maybe applying for a government job—I like the idea of steady benefits. I could *use* good benefits. Classes will have to wait this semester though. There's no way I could study with this interruption. And ignoring something as big as Mr.

Sinclair's death wasn't an option either. It's an opportunity.

"Let's see how hot you are, water," I say to myself, moving to the small sink in the kitchenette. I turn the handle and hold my fingertips underneath the chilly stream, counting to sixty before turning it off again.

Prepared for disappointment, I step through the doorway and find a narrow shower stall with a tiny tub nestled next to a pink pedestal sink and a toilet. It isn't much at all, but it will keep me clean. I turn the shower nozzle on and repeat my exercise from the kitchen, which ends in the same result. I can handle a lot of extremes, but the cold water of Washington is not one of them.

I toss my sweater on the back of the lone chair that sits next to a round table pushed against the wall and stove, flip open a few of the cabinets and drag open the matching drawers until I find one with a flashlight. I shake it to sense the weight, and there's a small chance the batteries I feel inside still work. When I click the light on, I chuckle to myself, musing over the great question—would I trade having light for a hot shower right now? Yes. Yes, I do believe I would.

Flashlight at the ready, I creak open the sketchy panel that I pray houses the water heater. Only, when I crack it open I realize quickly what the problem is— there is no water heater. The slight chuckle in my chest blossoms into rich, belly laughter, and I take a few steps back until my legs hit the edge of my bed. I slump, letting the flashlight fall to the floor, and bring my palms to my eyes, pressing on them while my mixture of laughter and whining fades into a mere sigh.

I really want a shower.

I remain statue-still for several minutes, imagining the cold water, gearing myself up to handle it, preparing myself with lies that it won't be *that* cold, when the loud pounding at my door sends my heart through my throat and my fists cling to the old quilt on the bed.

"Open up, JoJo. It's just me," Aunt Shelly shouts.

I rush to the door to let her in, giving her wide eyes as a sign that I don't want her shouting my name. Maybe they know where I am but I don't need Aunt Shelly to paint a bullseye on my door with her loud voice.

"Sorry." Aunt Shelly huffs, a little out of breath as she moves closer to me. "I figured you should just about be gettin' in." Her arms are loaded down with a heavy box plus a duffle bag dangling from her arm. Her hair has always been just as wild as mine is, only now, her color doesn't match mine anymore. It is caught between her old-lady gray and my chestnut brown. Her curls are large, puffy and tangled like she's given up trying to tame them like I do mine. Because our hair grows bigger before it grows longer, Aunt Shelly's bob-length cut also makes her head seem about three times larger than it should be.

"What's all this?" I ask, pulling the box from her arms and taking hold of the duffle to move it to the small table for her. We start undoing the tape she's placed to hold the box shut.

"I wanted to get some fresh sheets in here, and there's also towels and such. And you probably didn't bring a lot of your toiletries, so I packed up a few things from the house..." Her teeth pause over her bottom lip, her eyes on my hands working on the tape, and her breath catches. I see a flicker I don't recognize cross her expression. It isn't like her to be afraid. Aunt Shelly has always been the one in our family who stood up to everyone and anyone. She's been the one I've leaned on most these past years, even though it was mostly through letters, emails and phone calls while I was away. But the way she's watching me—she's so still. And suddenly she looks so old and tired—I get that she's more than afraid.

"Thanks," I say, doing my best to ignore the vibes she's giving off. I focus instead on pulling out her packed soft blankets and a pillow that's so soft that I almost no longer care about the shower. All I want is to push the dingy bedding to the floor and hug this pillow until morning while happier scenes play through my mind.

Eventually, Aunt Shelly unfreezes and begins helping me unpack the remaining items—moving the soap and hair products into the bathroom along with a stack of fresh towels.

"Ya-know, I don't think Walt ever put in that new water heater. I'll get him out here tomorrow." Her voice echoes from the bathroom walls. Walt is her longtime boyfriend, and they've been together so long now that it's practically marriage, only they live apart. My aunt is a little hard to live with. Like most antique dealers, she hoards, but she's also a dealer that likes taxidermy. Add the antiquing every weekend to the taxidermy thing into the hoarding thing, and well...

It was her main floor bathroom that's wall-to-wall stuffed rodent heads that made Walt finally move out. They'd had a fight over her gallery of rare and antique vermin—and some full body rodents that were perched on little ledges—all with glass eyes and hung to be staring at you as you sit on the toilet. For better viewing. Aunt Shelly told me once way back that not many people took the time to fill rabbits, mice, groundhogs, squirrels, moles, minks and even marmots with sawdust —you know—*back in the day*. And now a-days, no one does it at all.

Hard to believe.

This living arrangement and relationship works for them, and somehow Walt shows up at her store every morning, and doesn't leave her side until she's ready to shut her eyes for sleep at night.

Aunt Shelly shouts over the sound of water running into the tub. "I know it won't help for tonight, but if you can handle a bath, I can heat up a few pots for you on the stove." She cuts it off and steps to the doorway, her hand on her hip, waiting for my answer.

I never thought of that. So often the simple solutions

ELIOT SCOTT

fail me. My lip quirks up on one side, and I nod back to her. "My God, yes. Please...can we—you—do that?"

She chuckles as she steps from the bathroom, squaring her shoulders with mine, her hands coming out to cup my bare arms as our eyes meet.

"Pumpkin, I would do anything for you. A hot bath is nothing." Her smile is soft but still tainted with that worry I sense lives behind her eyes.

"I know. I'm so grateful." I step into her arms and squeeze her tightly, breathing in deep when she holds me with just as much love. Though she's my aunt, she's also my mother, my father and the one person who knows all sides of my story, just as I know hers. Family is so important and ours is so very small.

I let my Aunt take over, and during the hour I soak my body and wash my hair in the small bath with the aid of four pots of stove-heated water, Aunt Shelly manages to spruce up my small apartment with the cleaning supplies and small touches she brought from her house. When I come out, dressed in my pale pink pajamas, my head wrapped in a towel, my aunt is packed and ready to leave, and my tongue touches the roof of my mouth, ready to beg her to stay. I close my lips instead and smile, because as much as I don't want to be alone, I know I need to be. It's the only way I'll be ready to face more demons in the morning.

Deep down, I always knew I'd come home again. Even so, I didn't expect it to happen so soon. Somehow, I'd gone from wanting to rush here in an instant to wanting to put this off forever. It's because of the details. Everything needs to work out just...perfectly. If it doesn't, my world will crash—again.

"Fresh sheets." My aunt startles me from my trance and tilts her head toward the bed. "I'll wash the old ones and bring them back so you have a spare. I'll drop them inside the door before I open up the shop."

"Thanks." I swallow, fighting to keep that smile—the one that's brave—on my face.

"Oh, and I had a few extra things in our pantry. I put them in the right cabinet. Just soup and cereal...oh, and a loaf of bread. Put some milk in your fridge, too. But you can join me in the shop anytime for breakfast or lunch tomorrow, okay?"

Her eyes dip as she waits for confirmation.

I smile again. "Alright. But I'll probably be out most of the day." Her lip twists in dissatisfaction at my answer. I fight to fix it. "I'll do my best, though. Breakfast will probably work best."

She still stares me down for a few seconds, giving in finally with a nod as she folds her arms over her chest. I notice the empty duffle bag clutched in one hand, so I turn to the open closet door to see a few extra items hung inside next to the few things I packed for the trip.

"Just brought you some sweaters and a rain jacket. I can't let my favorite girl catch a cold, now. After all, what would little Emily say if I sent you back with the sniffles," she says.

I smile on instinct, hearing my daughter's name, my

eyes fluttering closed and immediately taking in the vision of her before I left.

She stood at the bottom of the steps at Jeff's house, tap shoes on her feet, and a bow in her brown, curling and fluffy hair. I promised her I would be home in time for her dance recital next weekend, but my girl—she senses the truth out like a Foxhound on the trail. She dressed up and performed her part (and everyone else's part too so I could see the whole show) right there next to my suitcase.

I didn't cry until the cab drove me away.

I'm going to miss my little girl. But I couldn't bring her with me, because it's not safe, because just like my parents were with me, I do not want the Sinclairs to find out about my daughter. Would they think of her as yet another Wallace girl? Someone to be destroyed like they'd done to me and my mother? Or worse, would they try to take her, keep her and make her into one of them? Both situations are unacceptable.

Her ultimate safety is the reason I now exist. Here.

I'm determined that Emily will grow up free of lurking shadows, free of restrictions and worry. She has no idea what it means to be a Wallace girl, and she's never met anything as evil and as dark as a Sinclair. If I do this right, as she grows into a woman, her life will not be made up of feuds and the past that haunts our two families.

It will only include her future and love, and whether Alex wants to or not, and even if I have to drag him kicking and screaming—or even kill someone to make things right—he and I will be the ones who set Emily free.

We owe it to her.

And she'll be able to love and be loved by whomever her heart decides it wants. And that boy—he won't be a devil in disguise, that's for damn sure.

"Thanks." My hand finds hers and squeezes.

She grasps back. "You know where the rifle is?" Her eyes dart over my shoulder to the small desk pushed into a corner. I follow her line of sight then look back to her, nodding. "Good. If something feels wrong, don't second-guess yourself—you use it."

"I doubt anyone gives two shits that I'm here. But..." I hold up a hand as I feel her start to argue. "I promise; if something gets me scared, I'll have that thing loaded and ready."

She smiles, then pauses at the door, turning to face me, her cool hands finding my cheeks and holding my face while her eyes rake over my features.

"You look so much like your mama, you know that?" She's biting at her lip again just as she did when she walked in. It makes my heart sick when she looks at me like this, but I know how happy it makes her to see my mom in my features, so I let her have her moment.

"She was something." I hold in the tears.

"By God, yes, JoJo. Yes she was." Shelly nods slowly, her lips curling even more as a breathy laugh escapes.

Leaning into me, my aunt presses her lips to my

forehead while her palms hold onto my cheeks, and I let my eyes fall shut, soaking in her love again as my thoughts go to my daughter. How I wish I could kiss her goodnight right now.

"You lock this door behind me, and when Walt comes, I'll have him add one more bolt, okay?"

I don't argue with that. It's one less project I'll have to do around here.

"Sounds good." I hold the door open for her, breathing in the scent of my last real family member—lilacs and cigars—as she steps out to the wooden porch landing and hurries down the steps.

I wave goodbye, then close and lock the door just as I promised I would, sliding the small card table in front of it for good measure.

The desk by the wall is easy enough to move, and the moment I slide it away from the wall I see the loose board on the floor. Bending down with a pen in my hand, I stab at the crack between the boards until I'm able to wedge the pen in enough to pry the board up. Once in my fingers, it lifts easily—and my daddy's Smith and Wesson is quickly in my hands.

The metal is cold in my touch, and my fingers buzz just from holding it. My father shot many deer in the woods just a few miles from this apartment. But there's an aching feeling in my gut as I hold it because it's one of the only surviving things we own that once belonged to my dad. I also wonder if the bullets fired from this weapon may have hit more than deer in the woods. Has it spilled human blood as well? Not by my daddy, but possibly by the devil's son himself?

I grip the rifle and my mind spins with images of Alex's beautiful angled face, how he looked at me today, and I wonder if the glimmer of the boy I once knew was really there or was it simply wishful thinking?

Alex. Alex. Alex.

I'm not able to push away the memories of our last night together. I think I've thought of that night, said his name over and over again, every day since. That night between us was almost perfection. Pure love quickly turned to absolute hell then so much hate.

I can't regret one second of it. Not really. That night was the end of my life as I knew it, yes. But it was also the beginning of my entire future, of all things I've become thanks to school and life hitting me smack in the face. Alex ruined me, but he also gave me everything I now live for and hold dear. Our girl. My courage. My will.

Alex. Alex. Alex.

As much as my mind wants to hate him—as much as I know this man wants me to continue to hate him— after seeing him today, devil or not, my whole body, my entire essence, longs to be close to him again.

Is this fate? Is this the irresistible feud—the very blood in my veins my parents and Alex's parents said was passed down from our ancestors, pushing me at him, or is this something else?

I flip the rifle over in my hand again because it's

grown hot under my fingers as I've stood here stewing on the past.

My aunt used to keep it in a case. Alex had full privileges to use it any time he wanted, but I don't think he ever took them up on it. Every time it was offered Alex always answered that he only hunted when his father forced him to do it.

After I left town, my aunt told me Alex had come by to borrow the rifle, but instead of giving it to him, she'd told him it was lost. But in fact she'd decided to hide it. I never asked her why—I didn't really want to know, nor did I have to ask her why she'd brought it back out and up into this apartment for me today.

I crawl into bed with the gun, safety on, and tuck it half hidden under the pillow and nestled under the covers on the other side of the bed. My palm rests along the trigger while my mind relives that moment not so long ago when May and I stared eye-to-eye. She's always made me uneasy, but she has me feeling sick right now.

I do my best to shake the weird feeling off. My phone lights up with a picture of Emily smiling out at me as I set it to charge next to me, and I snuggle up, comforted by the feel of hot metal by my side.

I'm done with the feud. I'm done with secrets. I'm done with lies, hiding and being afraid. I'm also done with the Sinclairs. And if Alex isn't, then I'll have to admit defeat and be done with him too.

No matter who he is to Emily.

7.

ALEX, PRESENT DAY.

I'm watching them from my top-floor penthouse of the 1894 remodeled apartment building my father gave to me as a gift after JoJo left town. It was a gift for my *"job well done."*

The cold glass cools my heated forehead as I press it against the tinted windows. I'm straining to watch the lights flick on and off in the two-story building next door.

JoJo and her Aunt seem to be navigating the few rooms allocated to the Antique Shop's back room apartment. It's a small place everyone in my family, hell everyone in town, has all but forgotten even exists, it's been vacant so long. Everyone except me, that is.

I only know about it because it's the place JoJo stayed the few short days before she left for college—after her parents' farm house burned down and left her all but homeless.

Thanks to me. Always...thanks to me.

Back then, I'd watched her from the attic of this building through a blackened window, hiding behind the massive foundation crack that had split the entire front facing wall of this place from ground to sky.

Tacoma was in an economic slump, and this place was an abandoned factory that had been boarded up for years. The facade was tilted, and had been so notoriously dangerous to any who'd entered it that not even the gang members or the homeless would occupy it.

Just like I'd done back when it had become necessary to watch over Jojo when we were in high school, I wait for JoJo's Aunt Shelly to leave. After some time, she does, making her way slowly to her white Ford Focus. I nearly choke then flip my lid when I notice what looks like May—my mother—and my damn mother's car pulling out of the alley behind the antique store fast, as though JoJo's aunt's appearance had startled her.

I know my mother's been tracking JoJo's activities since they met face to face at the funeral, but I don't know why. When we were kids, she did the same thing, but back then, I'd always thought my father had put her up to it. Just how he'd put us all up to tracking the Wallaces. I'm hoping this is just habit for her. Like scratching at an old wound that hurts now that my father is dead, or like some sort of cold and morbid curiosity she has to look at the one Wallace we collectively could not destroy.

But then, I wonder if my mother is just like me—

she's after JoJo, she's obsessed with tracking her because of something deeper. In my mom's case is it more sinister...more dangerous than what I am to her?

In case my mother decides to return, and because I can't fucking stop myself, I stare at the empty alleyway, at the lights and shadows flickering in the windows that tell me JoJo's still moving around in the place. I stare until my back hurts, until my legs hurt because I haven't moved them, and I now doubly track and analyze any car that drives by. I prepare to battle any person who walks down the street, and I wonder what the hell my mother is up to by being in the alley behind Jojo's place. When the windows darken, I wait longer, eyes boring into the last light—the light that must be by JoJo's bedside—to click off. And then, only then, after giving the darkened windows another hour of observation, and though I do not deserve it, I allow myself to breathe fully and head toward my own bed.

I don't often sleep in this apartment because I prefer sleeping up at the lake. I've slept there since the day JoJo left. First on the ground in a rolled out sleeping bag and pad, then in a tent, then in a shed I built myself, then inside a bigger shed, and finally I'd made a home inside what I'd told my father and brother was my fishing house.

A small but beautiful place I'd used my trust fund to create and have been tweaking with additions and ideas since I'd turned twenty-one. Because Grady and my father never went to the lake, how it's developed is one of the secrets I was able to keep from the old man. Had he and Grady shown up, they would never have thought it was my main place of residence. Because who would leave a luxury penthouse like the one I'm standing in to sleep in what they'd consider a weekend cabin.

But...of course like always, I'm not like them and the lakeside cabin they assumed I use only for fishing days is way more than just a cabin now. It's my home, my glass palace and the only solace I have. But with JoJo back in town, it's fitting that I stay here. I do have some affection for this pad, because the project of restoring it stopped me from ending my own life.

I imagine how it was then. The horrific lightning strike cracks inside and out, the ancient defunct boiler that would never throw heat properly again. It's cancerous asbestos layering every inch of it had appealed to me so much. As did it's central, winding yet delicate sea-shell staircase, one that allowed you to stand in the lobby and look up all ten floors like it was the entire spine of the building. The whole place was originally a hotel, designed by an architect from Paris. That staircase was riddled with sections that had fallen out, but it was the empty space that spoke to me more than the staircase itself.

I would stand mesmerized by it, like I do when I find a particularly perfect spider's web.

Because it was the building next to the last place I'd watched over JoJo—and because I was now in charge of watching over her nutcase aunt who spent her days in that antique shop, the building had to be mine.

That staircase I repaired. The cracks I covered but even now I could show you where they were. I've memorized every nail, curve and dent.

Convincing the old man to help me purchase it was easy. I told him just what he wanted to hear so he'd agree to the investment, because it would have been cheaper to tear it down. But once I told him I'd wanted a place that was in downtown Tacoma, a place with class that would honor our *family name*, a place that everyone in town would talk about while we were redoing it and a location that no other would have the courage to touch, he was hooked. He agreed that restoring a place like this would make the Sinclair name be seen in a good light. As if we were benefactors to the town's depressed spirit, not the reasons behind it all.

When I also implied I needed a place where I could bring my women—a place I could fuck them and forget them, and shove them into cabs long before they sobered up—well that was the icing that closed the deal. Grady loved the idea too, only, as usual, he wanted his own project. So, because my father got stuck on the idea that our oil empire would book-end the entire down-town area, a second condemned building was purchased for my brother blocks away by the waterfront. It's a building Grady used to one-up me on design, spending, and fucking as well. He'd even created a secret and discrete bachelor pad for my father to use for his...*indiscretions*, which really earned him the points.

He and father would often pick up women together. I'd go with them sometimes so they wouldn't pester me or wonder too much about my real life. They'd even invited me and the girls who'd thrown themselves at me to come along and party with them. Of course, I never said yes to that. Father understood and never pressed. He knew Grady and I never shared our toys. I always saw my girls home safely. Or, if they insisted on staying —and only after I told them this could only be a one-night stand and they'd agreed to that—I'd bring them back here for a few selfish hours of the physical contact I craved, and the forgetting that comes with good, raw sex that I sometimes needed so I could wake up and go on another day.

As I stare at JoJo's darkened windows now, I allow the memories I've been fighting against since I saw her —smelled her—at the funeral to flood into me with a vengeance.

The force of it is so strong the room tilts and spins as I reel into a chair. Imagining JoJo breathing in, and then out, is what keeps me from blacking out completely. I think of my father next. I try to picture him six feet under a pile of fresh dirt, unmoving, unblinking and permanently still.

I regret not breaking into the closed casket so I could see him like that, but I also know it would not be any sort of solace. Because even stone-cold dead, my dad is very much alive. All I have to do is look at myself to prove that fact.

Even with his face shot off, he's won. Does the man, even dead, watch me and smile? I feel like he does.

Pushing away my father's face, I think only of JoJo. I welcome the memories. I will let them consume me so they will burn out the few heartbeats JoJo accidentally fired off inside my heart today, and when I see her tomorrow, I will be ready.

She won't get in again.

8.

ALEX, SENIOR YEAR, JUST BEFORE GRADUATION.

"I hate when girls cry."

I spit out the first words that come to my head because my mind and my body is still scrambling for sanity because I just had sex with JoJo Wallace like I was some sort of animal, and then I dumped her.

No...I broke her.

How can I ever be human again after tonight? I'm reeling from what I'd just done with her and said to her —already longing for what I'll never get to do, touch, taste, smell and feel ever again.

Why did I sleep with her? I'd resisted her so long. She doesn't deserve this memory. Not this...it had been so important to her.

I meant to set her aside just like I'd done all of the other times. I meant to end it—without things ever heating up. I'd been so damn strong for all of high school, *fuck*...on prom night she begged me so hard and we both had some beers and it was nearly impossible to resist, but I did; I put her off, using her birthday as an excuse.

Now at least...at least, knowing her, maybe she will be twice as hurt, twice as angry with me. That thought doesn't make me hate myself less, but it's too late for any regrets now. After what happened with Mr. Wallace, and now Jojo's mom, nothing will ever, ever make me likable to myself. Hell, tolerable even.

Calmly—which is always her way—she replies, "I'm not crying, Alex. I'm asking you to make this stop. Please. You don't have to do this. We could run away. Love for love, Alex. Come on. It's not hard. We can change everything. "

"My family motto is pain for pain—stop messing it up with your stupid ideas of something that does not exist." I spit the words at her. They aren't a lie; her version of our lives is impossible.

"We're not hard. We are so very easy, me and you. The future can be what we want, not what your father envisions. Love for love. It's going to win."

Fuck, I wonder, gritting my teeth. *What am I supposed to say next?*

I'd planned this so carefully and for so many months. But the plan—my father's fucking plan—never included me analyzing the sexy sheen of sweat shining on her golden tanned and naked skin. The plan never came with her biting her bottom lip and talking about a future I'm not allowed to have. I can't let this long-awaited moment pass me by just because I want to entertain her idea of love being capable of saving us. Saving me, anyhow. This pain will save her. And, because I do love her, I can't derail the plan now just because I long to believe the words that are coming through her sweet, quivering lips. She has no idea what my father—my brother, too—is capable of. I absolutely do.

I glance back at her, hating myself for how she looks like some sort of otherworldly pearl against the bleached out boat tarp I'd hastily thrown to the ground as a makeshift bed. This girl should only ever have silk and rose petals next to her skin, and instead she got me, rough canvas, a few stolen moments in a damp boathouse for her first time—and her second—all after I promised to give her pillows and a bed.

I retrieve my hastily kicked off jeans, working to keep my father's harsh and threatening face inside my head so I can remember to stay on task.

First: Do not look at her face anymore.

Second: Put one leg into the jeans and do the right thing.

Third: Put the other leg into the jeans and do not fucking cry.

Fourth: Say anything you need to say to make her understand. You've practiced this shit every month since you found out your part in the deal. Say it all. You can't run away with her, and she can't ever be near you again or she dies. That's the equation. Do the assignment. Complete the problem.

From far away, I hear my own voice sneer out, "Looks like we rocked this dock so hard my fucking underwear fell in the water because I can't find them." I laugh. Then, when she still hasn't moved, I add, "Shouldn't you be getting dressed? I'm not down for giving you a ride home. Hope you don't mind taking the trail back to your place. Driving to the other side of the tracks feels pretty far out of my way all of a sudden."

I snort out what I hope is a cruel-sounding laugh. "If you can walk at all after spreading your legs so wide."

Keep going.

Say it all like you mean it, because if you mess this up, the girl you love will die just like everyone else in the Wallace family died. Because she has no idea the Sinclairs killed her father. Because she has no idea my mom laughed the day her mother died.

Because she has to leave this town hating you. She cannot have a reason to come back.

"Why are you suddenly being someone I've never met?"

I pull the jeans up over my bare ass and turn slightly away from her so I can slide off the condom. I zip up, working to get my voice colder than it was before. "I've never pretended to be anything other than just me. Maybe you're only seeing me right for the first time. Now that I've fucked you senseless maybe the dreamy cobwebs are finally gone."

She gasps. "Alex, I don't know what you're doing right now but I can only think it's your father making you act like this. I've always been just me with you and *just me* is calling you out. How you are acting is not you. Not after what we just did together. No way."

Her words—which ended with a shaking whisper—are all true. JoJo, *just being JoJo,* is the reason I fell in love with her. She's always been so open. She is light, laughter and everything beautiful. She's being herself even now, working to find a way out for me even after I've said these unspeakable things to her because this girl is also pure love. And she's told me more than once that she loves me.

Love and JoJo.

I almost laugh out loud at myself for going there.

Love and JoJo are two things I was allowed to touch but that were not ever meant to be truly mine. Ever.

She sits up, her movement drawing the moonlight to new places on her hair and skin, drawing my eyes to linger where they shouldn't. "You convinced me to make love with you. And we did it—and I loved it—here and now, with you," she pleads. "We waited so long. I thought it would be amazing." She spreads her arms wide like we've just made love inside some sort of gold-walled palace. "And it *was.* So special," she whispers. "And so amazing. But only because we *are* in love, and we're best friends, and you're my everything."

I turn away, watching her now out of the corner of my eye. When I don't answer her, she starts shaking her head like she wants to wake up from this bad dream she's having. "Alex?"

"That's all you, Jojo. Always making fantasy fiction shit about my actions being all special and heroic. Like the times Grady messed with you. Like the time he broke your collarbone."

"You were there and helped me every time he messed with me. You punched your brother at the hospital. You're my protector and yes, always heroic." She remembers it right, but I have to change her memories somehow.

I shake my head.

"Think about each and every time a Sinclair hurt you during high school. Think about Grady and how I was always there. The shit my mom said to you, the crap my dad pulled? Every time, you cried—and hell yes I was there. I was participating. And every time I told you the truth. That my family meant to hurt you, that Grady was a devil and the Sinclairs enjoyed making you cry and would do it again. Don't you see? I never *helped* you. I only watched and waited to pick up the pieces, every time, because that was the part my father ordered me to play. You should have walked away from me long ago— the first time we figured out who I was to you—but you never did."

"Because we're best friends. Because I wouldn't leave you for pages written down about some stupid story- book feud between the Wallaces and the Sinclairs! Because you needed me to protect you from your father

—you needed me to pick up *your* pieces, as much as I needed you. I'm not stupid. I know Grady and your father would hurt you if you ever directly stood up to them. Despite their plan, I *know* you've been protecting me all along. And I think you're doing it now by making love to me and dumping me in this terrible way. You want me to hate you. I don't know why...but I will find out. They won't win! *You're not like them.*"

I shake my head, willing her to get it. "*I am them.* Oh, and let's just please keep the facts straight about tonight. I didn't *convince* you to make love." I snort, rolling my eyes at her ridiculous words. Painful words. "You begged me for it, and I finally gave in. When you think back on this night, please remember the part where I told you it was a very bad idea, that I didn't want to do it at all. And now that it's over, don't blame me because I enjoyed what went down. You did, too. *Obviously. And twice.*"

That last line had made her gasp—just how she'd gasped when I was pounding into her, taking the air out of her lungs with my thrusts—*and dammit!* That little sound. The way she's stood up and is walking over to me all naked and unashamed—despite what I'm doing and saying to her right now—has made me want her all over again.

Jojo Wallace has always been magnificent. And I've always wanted her so much. I pull in a ragged breath because, damn me if even now in the middle of this, all of the blood I can't control is rushing back into my cock.

"But I love you."

"No! You. Don't. Love. Me." I reel back from her, angry for real now—angry because she won't listen to me. "Think back, JoJo. Think back, and think about you and me becoming friends. Think over how many times you were hurt and I was right there—I was a part of each horrible moment." She shakes her head. "You can't love me. It will be impossible once you realize the truth. A real friend would have confessed what was going on. A real friend would have ended how I exposed you to pain year after year. I'm not even human, because a fucking human would have told you at least to stay away. But I didn't, did I?"

"They made you. You're not like them." Her arguments are weakening.

"But I am. Exactly. I let you come back and come back until tonight when I led you to this boathouse and fucked you here—not in any way that I promised you, either. Where's the bed? Where's the roses and all that romantic shit I promised you? I didn't even have the decency to take you to the lake."

"Our lake…" she whispers out.

"My lake. Not yours!" I shout and point, and those words do the trick. Her face crumples some.

"You don't love me. You only just met me today. Pleased to fucking meet you, *stupid Wallace girl.* You've been pranked. I'm Alexander Robert Sinclair."

I pull in a deep breath and straighten out my shoulders, trying to make myself appear bigger and scarier to her. "Josephine Annabelle Wallace, this whole thing was planned—hell maybe even it was *preordained* when they named us after our great grandparents." I shake my head at her. "You knew more about the feud than I ever did when this started. We researched it together, and then your father *died*, and still you stayed. How did you think this would ultimately work out?"

I bark out a harsh laugh and pause to kick at the sides of my father's boat.

"Did you really think any of this was real? This was simply our destiny. It's been my father's grand plan ever since he found out about you that summer before we met. The lake, you being homeschooled all those years— that was your mom's biggest mistake. It was their game played out by us. Your mom and my dad, and my grandfather and your grandmother. And now that your mom is dead and I've popped your cherry and made good old Dad proud, well, it's done. You're off to summer University for stupid dyslexics who need extra help how you always do—and there will be no reason for you to ever return here. I can guarantee you that, Jojo."

Finally, like it's all sinking in, she blinks and small lines form creases in her forehead.

"Alex, you're talking about years and years of our lives here. All of our perfect moments, all of our firsts together, the lake, the campouts, the school dances, all that you said to me at prom—how you made me wait until tonight?" She sighs meeting my gaze. "So many...best and wonderful days together...no. I don't—I *won't* believe you. It's impossible what you're saying."

"Don't feel bad—it went on so long the entire town fell for it. *Fell for us*." I bark out another harsh sounding laugh. "Hell. Even I forgot sometimes, but only for a minute or two because you're annoying as fuck, and it's a lot of work playing *boyfriend* to your high maintenance bullshit life. Your father dies, and your mom gets cancer again. Christ!" I roll my eyes and run both hands through my hair. I wish I could dig into my skull. I hate this monster that I am.

"The learning disability? All the homework help. All of that farm work I did to help out your family. Stepping in to be the man as needed. I'm sure you can imagine how much I'd rather have been fishing." I snort. "Two funerals, all of the damn needy texting you did. I had to text back and then show up and *talk* to you all the damn time. Sleep over, be there for you and hold you—fuck, Jojo...no dude likes to spoon! And you're ridiculous with all of that that *hold me* shit. It was worse than babysitting."

I roll my eyes again, hoping she doesn't call me out on the part where it was always her holding me, and I forge on. "Maybe when you look back you'll feel sorry for me—because—" I swallow down the sand-brick that's formed at the back of my throat from these lies. "You, JoJo Wallace, were the most soul-sucking, needy girlfriend ever. And, God, but it took your mom so damn long to die. Had she not lingered on so much, I would have been free of you a year ago. But see…" I smile wide, trying to make it maniacal. "She fucking knew! That bitch refused to die. She knew what we were doing. She knew this was my father's revenge."

"Don't ever call my mom that!" her voice wavers and her face crumples more.

I wait, letting her absorb the information, watching as she puts the bits together to form what can only look like a terrible new reality to her. Thankfully, she doesn't make me wait too long.

She whispers *exactly* what I've been waiting to hear. "If it's true, then…I'll have to hate you. I don't care about what you did to me—but if *you*—if your family actually plotted to hurt my mother all those years while she was widowed and *sick*? My mom, who's the most amazing and kind woman in the world—if *one second* of just that part of this is true, then I won't have any other choice." She puts both hands over her ears. "How can I hate you? How can I not?" She gasps out, "But if it's true then…I hate you, Alex Sinclair."

Her eyes connect to mine and she says again, stronger this time. "I really hate you." Her eyes have gone wild.

I close my eyes for a second, my knees growing weak, because if she's already hating me I won't have to play all of my cards and tell her everything she doesn't need to know. My cruel lies are way gentler than the truths I'm still hiding.

"Hate away," I sigh out, almost giddy with relief. "It's

the Sinclair goal." I fake a grin, cruelly raking my gaze down the length of her, noting the layer of goosebumps now covering her skin on this very hot summer night. I'm unable not to let my eyes rest for a moment at the swell of her breasts and on her perfect, rose-tipped nipples as I listen to her jagged breathing.

When I'm certain my voice won't give me away, I recapture her unwavering gaze as I continue. "My father says it's the hunt we Sinclairs love, and what a long and successful hunt your family has been for us. If only there was a way we could each put some sort of trophy on our mantel to prove that I placed first and you lost. But here..." I hold up our knotted, used condom. "You did get this small ounce out of me. Keep it if you want. For your fireplace."

I drop it at her feet.

"Fuck you, Alex Sinclair." Her voice is even stronger as she shouts at me now. "And the day they put your devil-father in the ground I'm going to be here to dance on his grave. I promise I will. I should kill him, and kill you and—and— Grady, too, for this."

I laugh again, this time agreeing with her—because after what I've done all these years, I deserve to die, and if anyone deserves to kill the Sinclair family, it's JoJo Wallace. Only, JoJo is the kind of girl who rescues ugly dogs and stray cats despite being allergic. She won't even kill the spiders and moths that sneak into the house—so yeah—she won't be back to kill anyone, that's for certain.

"Always so dramatic. I'm sure Father would want you to come back and try to take us all out. See how the feud is in our blood? It's irresistible, even to you, isn't it? " I refocus my glare on her because what I need to say next is the most important part of this whole conversation. It has to stick. "My father is too evil to die. But if we both get lucky and he croaks, please don't come back. If you do, Grady and I will kill each other fighting over who will get to finish destroying you."

She crosses her arms over her bare chest and nods. "Oh, I'll go. But I suppose you know that. You're so stiff and fake right now, I bet you're reciting from a script your father made you memorize!"

"I'm glad you finally understand." I smile, making sure my voice is condescending yet approving. I point to the throbbing lump in my jeans. "You standing there still naked is making it hard to talk. If you don't want to have another go maybe you should cover yourself."

I toss her the flannel shirt I'd tied around my waist. As she puts it on and draws it closed with shaking hands, I add, "Like I already mentioned, this was generations before you and I were born. I simply executed the *final...strokes.*" I snicker.

JoJo doesn't even flinch at my words. This time her voice is as cold as mine. "The scholarship you helped me to apply for—all the way in New York City?"

"Farthest point on the map away from Tacoma."

"The generous offer to 'help' me with the sale of my

family's property that your father ruined with that oil spill?"

"Stop calling it your property. It's Sinclair property now. Sold to pay for your mother's medical bills and to ensure you had no reason to return here. We bought it as a favor even though your mom had willed it to us already, you ungrateful little bottom feeder. I could show you the legal documents that highlight the details of that deal, how much money we lost on it." I hit her where I know it will hurt her the most. "Considering you wouldn't be able to read it very easily, how about you just take my word for what it says this time?"

She winces and my chest constricts with a wave of regrets. She's standing there in my shirt—my fucking shirt. This is killing me...killing her is killing me.

"How about you go straight to *hell*," she calls out, but all of the fight's gone out of her voice.

"Already been there awhile, JoJo."

From the way her hands are shaking more now, and how she's got them clutched into my shirt, I can see she's all the way where I need her to be.

Finally, just make it through. If you waver she will waver. If she stays, she will die.

"That land deal goes way deeper and darker than even our fucked up relationship. Should that throbbing between your thighs fade away and you forget how all of this feels. Should you get sentimental or stubborn, like you always are and decide to visit, your Aunt Shelly for example, or even think you should come back home to rehash any of this, let me be clear. You or she might end up in some sort of terrible accident. Like the kind your father had."

She puts her hands up to her ears. "What are you saying to me? Alex. What do you mean by *accident*? What are you saying to me right now?"

I don't give her any more details.

She's smart enough. Long after she's gone from here I know she will connect the dots and those dots will tell her everything.

I only add, "For the first time since your father died, I'm allowed to tell you the goddamn truth about me, about what my father is capable of and what he will do. So, if you need to see your Aunt Shelly make sure she comes to visit you. *That's what I'm saying.* Be happy it was me that got assigned to fuck you over. Grady wanted to get you drunk and have his way with you the first day he saw you when you were a freshman. Do you remember our first fight?"

She nods, eyes wide and body still shaking like she's going into shock.

"Grady's plan was to get you to a football party, get you loaded, and loan you out to his friends. He'd meant to send you home bloody and crying to your daddy after anyone who'd wanted to had their taste. My father almost went for it, too. But then your father ended up in a grave, and we found out your mom was sick." I shrug like that memory isn't about to make me vomit. "And suddenly my father didn't think dealing with you quickly would be as lasting or as extreme as what we ended up doing to you and your mother. What do you think? Was I a better choice than Grady? Or worse?"

Her eyes flash and she tilts her chin toward the skylights. "You were better. So much better. The best," she whispers and I wonder if she's calling my bluff right now or trying her hand at sarcasm.

Her voice is so soft it's threatening to crumble me, so I avoid looking at her face at all to make my own words come out harsher. "You want to know why I waited so long to *fuck* you?"

"No." Her voice is stone cold.

"There's paper in my father's desk drawn up between *our parents* that actually states I couldn't touch you until you were eighteen. Family honor and all that shit."

"Our parents?" She's shaking her head more now.

"Yes. My father. Your mom."

"My mom...what do you mean...*my mom?*"

"They made an agreement at the end of sophomore year just after she was diagnosed. Apparently, your mom understood how gone you were for me and made a deal with my dad that I had to wait until you turned eighteen. Your mom assumed you'd grow tired of me, move on—wise up, maybe. But really...who would you move on to? Your mom got scared I'd accidentally plant a half-Wallace, half-Sinclair abomination inside of you. A baby like that would try to strangle itself inside the womb, I'm sure, so I don't know why they were so worried." I shrug at her horrified expression. "Guess my father didn't want to add drowning newborns in buckets to the list of secret felonies we each seem to collect."

"You're so sick."

"Like I said. Just one of the monster clan, and it all runs deeper than you could imagine. Which is why I had to wait all of this time until your *birthday*, because had I fucked you sooner, the land my father bought off of you would have reverted back to you—though I would have denied touching you. And you can't really afford an attorney, can you? So, even though I tried to talk you out of this, in hindsight, I'm not sorry I took your V card after all. Oh, and if I didn't say it yet, with emphasis on the word *fucking*: Happy Fucking Birthday, JoJo"

"Don't say anymore...*please. Stop. Stop.*"

She brings one hand up to cover her heart as if that move could block more of my words from pelting into her. And now she's trying to ruin everything for both of us. With one small sound, she has pierced my heart, drawing my gaze to exactly where I didn't want it to go.

Back to her big, wide, beautiful eyes, to tears I'd never seen fall from them before that day.

Oh, my JoJo. My sweet JoJo.

You don't ever, ever cry.

Not when her father's body was found.

Not when she'd been bullied and laughed at around town after everyone found out who she was, the *secret girl hidden away*, the unwanted Wallace baby because she was born so dumb—a rumor my brother started and my family perpetuated. Not after each of Grady's cruel pranks and frightening threats, and not when the mean girls or even the teachers taunted her for being slow or unsophisticated.

Not when her mother died a mere two weeks ago.

I can't look away.

I track every tear pouring down those flushed cheeks. I match my breathing to her shallow-fast breaths. I note exactly how her shoulders slump like her lungs are collapsing in on her heart. I watch in silence as she trembles—not from cold, but from *pain* clawing at her from the inside out. The moonlight from the glass-sided boathouse streams over that damn delicious skin. It brings a hint of color to the small smears of bright red blood now drying on the insides of her slim thighs. Her lips are still kiss-swollen sexy. Those long, tangled strands of hair I'd unwound myself from her braid both hide and highlight her curves, framing her face. I'm caught on the marks I made on her neck. I should have been more gentle.

For her first time.

For her birthday.

Today...yes. I am now the kind of man my father hoped I'd become.

I stare while she cries, because though she'd just vowed she'd hate me forever—*and God I'd hope she will*—I know her well enough to understand that hate won't come easy for her. Which means the pain on her face proves that she did in fact love me as much as I loved her to push her away like this.

My last words: "Eye for an eye. Pain for pain, and-what-the-fuck-EVER, JoJo. Don't come near me again."

Her last words to me aren't words at all. Just terrible sobs, but ones she only lets loose after I step outside the door.

I wait in a dark shadow around the side of the boathouse until she's emerged, fully dressed, without my plaid shirt. I silently follow behind all the way up the six-mile trail behind our house, through our estate and past the lake—*our lake*, though she or my father still don't know it's really hers. I'd given it to her.

She pauses, sniffling a few times at the fishing hole where we met. She wipes at her eyes then straightens her shoulders how she always did when she was acting brave. I follow her more until she walks the last mile home.

I wait until she washes her face in the pump, and I hold on long enough to hear the front door lock of the farmhouse click. As I back away, I see her move through the house, turning off the light her crazy Aunt Shelly, who'd moved in to care for them both as her mother lay dying, always leaves on for her.

I pause until her bedroom light illuminates the upstairs, and the hallway bathroom light goes on, then both lights turn off again.

I sit out here for another half hour or so, straining to hear if JoJo is still crying, because if so, well then I'll add a whole new layer of self hatred to the noose of despair I'd already placed around my own neck freshman year when I realized I had no way out of this life of "privilege."

Thankfully, JoJo seems to be done crying. I walk around the house three times to be sure I'm the only Sinclair in the area and that for tonight she can sleep safely, remaining alive.

When I get home, I tell my Dad and Grady the deed is done. I lie about how much it sucked to be with a fucking virgin. I nod in agreement and smile in fake anticipation when they tell me they'll make it up to me with strippers and prostitutes. And soon.

They both slam my back with their hands, sliding me the shots they've saved as they'd waited up drinking a whole bottle of Father's good, thirty-year-old scotch together, knowing I was playing my final card. I drink trying to drown the guilt while they drink in celebration, and when the bottle is empty, the harsh impact of the alcohol keeps me from killing the two people I hate more than I hate myself. I cling to my reason as to why I won't kill myself.

Jojo. Jojo.

Together, the three of us watch the sun come up—a father and his two perfect sons—Sinclairs working together. For the first time not one argument went down between me and Grady.

That's because Father and Grady are happy, and I am determined, resolute and still too devastated to feel like fighting any of it. Soon, we begin to talk about the Wallace farmhouse, the only thing Jojo's mother and father had left her as an inheritance, and how it must burn to the ground.

I, of course, am tasked to make it so.

And, as always—as proven—I won't fail this task either.

I can't even pass out from drink. Nothing kills monsters, I guess.

9.

JOJO, PRESENT DAY.

I'm used to sleeping with the gun now. I almost don't think I could sleep any other way. It only took seven days for this new norm to set in. I smirk at the thought as I tuck the cold metal gun back into it's safe place, an upgraded case buried under the fourth floor board from the wall—another addition Aunt Shelly insisted Walt take care of for my safety.

I love how they love me, but I can see the worry in their eyes. Shelly does her best to hide it, her eccentric ways and bravado amped up when she's around me. I love her for that even more. She's showing me what brave is supposed to look like. I don't have the heart to tell her I don't need it, so I let her go on and pretend she's the stronger one of the two of us. She's not. I'm fearless. I've spent years training myself because I knew this time would come. I know what brave looks like—it has wild, curling brown hair and bright, blue eyes, and it can shoot a dime being tossed in the air from more than fifty feet away.

My rifle locked securely, I drop the key in my handbag and check the safety on the small pistol I bought from the pawn shop. I couldn't very well carry the rifle around everywhere I needed to go, but I damn sure wasn't about to walk these streets unarmed.

I lock up my apartment and scan the empty alleyway on my way to the garage, lifting the door quickly, backing out, closing and driving away in under fifteen seconds. I've gotten faster. I'm not fast enough.

It's a Saturday, so the streets are filled with the weekend tourists. Shelly's shop will be busy with people in search of artifacts from *the real Tacoma*. She used to tell me she sold people visions of the past. When I was a kid, I thought it was magical. But I know she gets a lot of those things from a catalogue, or picks them up from Goodwill and refurbishes them to make them look older so she can sell them for five times what she paid to the weekend crowds from afar. The only past people get that's genuine are the parts of her taxidermy collection she places in the store, stuffed and mounted on her walls to stand guard. Those pasts share very common ends—bullets through the heart and head. And luckily, very few people offer to purchase them, because when one sells, Aunt Shelly mourns its loss for weeks and weeks.

I'm grateful for the gullible tourist crowd today, though, as I zip unnoticed down the main drag through the downtown. My rental car blends seamlessly with the

THE WALLACE GIRL

others, my hair tucked inside a ball cap and my over-sized sunglasses shielding much of my face.

The Tacoma Planning and Zoning building is on the opposite end of town, and I can't help but chuckle at the irony as I pass rehabbed building after building on my way to the dingiest one near the end, its bricks missing from the corners, tarnished metal framing the windows and mismatched paint from patches and years of wear and tear.

"If they wanted to hide secrets, they should have hidden them in a less obvious building," I muse to myself.

I scan the roadway in front of the building, looking for the alleyway Will Adair, the records clerk I spoke to at least a dozen times this week, promised me would be there. I'm not asking him to do anything illegal. I'm a citizen who wants public records, and Mr. Adair is employed to provide those records. Now...the fact that he's accommodating me on a Saturday falls a little outside the norm, but Will Adair is not in the Sinclair pocketbook, at least as far as I can tell. And if he is, this is all a big trap, and I'm screwed anyway.

It's nondescript, the passage barely wide enough for my car to fit. But it does, and I find the small opening tucked at the rear that leads to a ten-space garage underneath this building that I'm starting to think should be condemned.

I pull up near the steps that lead back to the front of the building and park, honking my car with the lock and cringing at the sound it makes. The tourists don't come to this part of town. There are no fancy bread factories and coffee shops to visit; only business gets done here.

Business.

Secrets.

Plotting.

I notice the small, white sedan parked in the far corner, pulled in backward as if it's poised for a fast getaway, and my feet stumble underneath me as I can't help but wonder if I should pull in that way, too. That thought flees to make room for my next one: "Should I even be here?"

My legs work on autopilot, and in seconds I find myself at the door, my finger pushing a buzzer twice, just as Will told me to do.

He's exactly as I pictured him—a bit of a professor-looking type, but not one with money. His hair is combed from one side of his head to the other, covering the massive gap of baldness in between, the thin, brown strands like strings on a guitar. His glasses balance on the edge of his nose, and there's a bit of a limp to his gait as he digs in his pocket for a set of keys, somehow picking the right one out of what looks to be more than twenty keys, and unlocking the door to let me in.

"You must be Miss Wallace," he says, peering at me atop his glasses while his hands work to re-lock the door again. It's strange that he can do this without looking.

"I am. Thank you for meeting me on a Saturday."

Will only grumbles, then stuffs his keys back into the crinkled pockets of his tan Dockers and begins walking to the hallway he emerged from only a minute before. I follow.

"I'm really grateful for your time on my project." I'm striving to hide my pounding heart beats by filling the silence as we move down a corridor, the wooden floors beneath our feet uneven, and the walls discolored from years of dust.

He pushes a door open near the end of the hallway and steps back for me to pass. "I don't want any trouble." A chill hits my spine as I enter, and I press my bag a little closer to my hip so I can feel the little gun—a Beretta—at my side, wishing I'd popped the safety when I parked.

"Now, why would there be trouble?" I say, maybe a hint of flirtation in my voice. Will looks to be in his late fifties, and his lip raises a hair on the right when I speak, but falls just as quickly with a grumble, his eyes following suit as he takes in the wide-open, polished concrete floor between where he stands and where I've set my purse on a desk pushed against the opposite wall.

"Those are Sinclair documents you're looking at there, are they not?" he says, pulling his now fogged glasses from his face and pinching the bridge of his nose before opening his aged blue eyes on me.

Through a faint smile, I scoot back the chair near what will be my desk for the next several hours, take my seat, and cross my legs like a lady should.

"I suppose that's up for debate. Depends on what

exactly these documents say...you know...in the fine print?" I mean to laugh, but it comes out in a puff of a breath through my nose.

I don't distrust Will, but I see the fear in his eyes, so I can't trust him either, because I can't trust anyone who's afraid of the Sinclairs, and he seems to be afraid. I don't blame him.

"I hope you're good at looking at fine print then, Miss Wallace," he says, his glasses pushed back in their place, halfway up his nose. He pulls a wallet from his back pocket and slips out a dollar bill. "There's a soda machine one flight down. I'll be in the office next to it."

"I'll let you know if I get thirsty," I hum, spinning in my seat and sliding the heavy box of documents in front of me, lifting stacks and plunking them on the dented metal tabletop before me.

"A'right then," Will says.

I catch him before his steps fade completely around the corner.

"Oh, and Will?" I look over my shoulder to see him looking over his, and I smirk again, my own black-rimmed reading glasses now in place. "When it comes to reading fine print...there's nobody better than me."

His belly jerks with a chuckle, and I watch as he shuffles the few more steps out of my view.

Fine print.

Lies. Lies they used to trick me back before I even knew what a lie really was, because my family raised me to tell the truth. My father expected me to mean what I say and to say what I mean.

But not the Sinclairs, they're the opposite. Even with all of the signs given to me, even with all of the warnings Alex spoke, trying to make me stay away from him —them—I wouldn't listen. And now I'm like them.

Lying. Lying. Lying to everyone. About what I'm doing here.

About Emily.

Lying is what makes up the Sinclair blood, but it still tastes bad on my tongue and is taking it's toll on my sleep and on how my stomach won't stop hurting ever since the day of the funeral. It's because I miss Emily so badly it's slowly killing me, but it's also because all of this deviousness and secretiveness is not my natural state. I'm used to walking in and saying what I want, what I need, and going after it directly.

But I can't do that here. Not yet—because I'm still unsure of where I stand, and what exactly I need.

I suddenly get that even my Alex lies to everyone he meets, yet I don't know if he's doing it for good or for evil like the rest of his family does. And for Emily, I need to know. I also need to understand why the Sinclairs want us Wallace girls to all be dead and gone.

Most of all I need to understand where Emily fits in this twisted puzzle, and what exactly will keep her safe for the rest of her life. If that's at all possible.

I feel like my mother's last few words hold the key.

"Search for the documents. The deeds. There will be answers in the boxes—the *Sinclair* boxes."

It was meaningless rambling when she spoke those words years ago, but over time they started to hold meaning. She had a secret, or she *knew* a secret. And this secret was the key to everything. It's in this room. I feel it. I feel her spirit guiding me. I just need to listen so I can find it—whatever it is.

10.

ALEX, PRESENT DAY.

My phone buzzes, the caller ID letting me know it's the Tacoma Building and Planning Commission, and my only friend, Will Adair.

"You better be serious about paying me for my time. I didn't expect Jojo to take so damn long in here. She's as sweet as I remember—and for some reason spying on her hour after hour is making me feel bad. Should make you feel bad, too, because you owe me like five hundred bucks already."

I'm instantly annoyed that I can't just ask him for the favor. That I have to pay him.

My only friend. Fuck.

"Christ, I'll pay you double if you'll stop whining about it and make sure she wasn't followed here by anyone. And remember, you're more bodyguard than spy, got me?"

He laughs. "Followed by anyone other than you, you

mean. Stalker. I see you out front in that cheap rental car."

"Damnit. Busted."

"You'd make a crap-ass cop. You must still want a piece of that—if not, what's the point of both of us spying on her?"

His snark and the fact that I have to pretend Will is funny right now is irritating me even more. "Protecting my...interests, that's all, and stop psycho analyzing me. What is she looking for—which files has she been pouring through?"

I know in my gut. But I also know she's not going to find what I've been hiding all of these years. Father never found it—and Jojo won't either.

"She's into the county property deeds from what I can tell, but the hasty remote camera I set up isn't as clear as I'd hoped." His voice is tinged with stress. "My name is on as much illegally signed shit as yours is down there. I'm just saying with your father gone, I don't feel safe with anyone digging around. Makes me want to put my house on the market and move before the next person comes digging. Or the fucking feds show up."

"She's not looking for any of that kind of stuff, asshole. Besides, Jojo's the most trustworthy person I've ever known. She'll be looking for information about her family; that's all she's ever cared about." It feels right to say something good about her out loud. Everything I've said about Jojo since that day I ruined her has been cruel—part of the act—and it's always felt like acid on my tongue. The truth is soothing, if not brief.

"You sure about that? Your father didn't have a bullet between his eyes until she came back around. Who's to say she didn't come back for the sole purpose of doing him in and fucking with us all?" His accusation is laughable, but also credible.

"Didn't we all have the right to murder him? Even you, Will. Even you."

The line crackles when Will doesn't respond to that.

The way my father ruined Will's family to keep them in line, like he'd done to half of Tacoma's families, is something he and I don't talk about ever.

"Call me if she does anything interesting—or if she makes for the door—in case I fall asleep out here, would you?"

"Sure." His response is curt. I reminded him of the past.

As I hang up and try to slouch in the uncomfortable seat, my thoughts spin with more fucked-up memories. I don't like the way Will's words have filled me with shreds of doubt about a girl—now a beautiful woman— who I think I know.

I shouldn't be worried about her digging through county records. I've hidden the one file that would be of interest to her—hidden it for years. I also can't afford for her to find it just yet, even though the document means I owe her a shit ton of land and money now that my father is dead. A shit-ton of explanations, too.

It was impulsive on my part to ever set that document in stone. Brave. And stupid. My one great and secret rebellion against my father. My whole family.

When my father found out, he nearly beat the life out of me but even then, I never told him I still had the original deed. I'd sworn to him that I had no clue where it had gone—told him that maybe I'd put it into the mail along with the copies the night it had been signed.

The only thing holding him back from striking that last blow was the fact that if I died, the Wallaces—Jojo—would own what my father never wanted them to own. My impulsive and childish gesture would mean to him that *they* won the feud, and because that document is filed not only in the county, but in the state as well, my father had no way of buying his way out of what I'd done. So he buried it. Lied about it. And to keep Jojo alive, I played along. But that original copy I'd kept hidden.

For insurance. For those long nights I thought I might give up and kill myself.

Jojo was never going to find that copy in this building.

As soon as I can shake this paranoia that my father might still somehow reach up from the grave and get to Jojo—once the will is read and a few months have passed—I'm going to tell her about it—make it right. Pay her off or hand over half of what's rightfully hers. However she wants to handle it.

Will's words about Jojo being my father's killer spin

through my mind again. *Could she have done it? Could she know already what belongs to her when no one else does? Could she have slipped into town, killed my father and stayed for the funeral, secretly laughing at all of us, even now?*

It's possible. I suppose anything is possible. My whole life has been evidence of that. Awful things happen to and around awful people like us.

I picture JoJo holding a gun at my father's head and my throat constricts—not with fear or with regret, but with how that image feels right. In my mind, it is right. It would be pure justice finally served. Until Will brought it up, I had my bets holding on my brother Grady doing the deed. Even my own Mother would be justified.

But...Jojo.

Could she...?

Would she?

Could her return all somehow still be part of the feud? Is she here for revenge? Last time we saw each other, the Sinclairs were up a whole bunch of points on the Wallaces. Did all of it change her? Make her into a monster, too?

Damn my thoughts and damn my father—and even damn Jojo's mother to hell, because she may have been the biggest monster of all in this.

Back then, I didn't know.

And Jojo didn't know.

But Mrs. Wallace knew everything. My father, too.

Jojo and I were simply players in this fucked up game they'd created. We were pieces on a chessboard, constantly moved back and forth. Before Jojo and I knew, we were so pure and innocent, rising above what we thought were only simple town rumors of this feud that ruined our lives. *Folklore,* that's what we thought it was. Ancient history.

We were the biggest joke of all. Jojo Wallace and Alex Sinclair, rising into this beautiful future we both imagined would be ours.

Together.

I CAN STILL SEE the exact spot where she told me she loved me on that big flat rock—the rock that later became the cornerstone of my lake house.

It was well after school had started Freshman year, during one of those endless-summer kind of days before daylight savings comes and ruins everything. The kind of day where the air is hot and the sky is blue and you think summer will never come to an end. But all of the leaves had turned yellow—and our book bags were full of assignments to turn in and books that were too heavy.

I remember watching the leaves fall that day—and being annoyed that they were fluttering on top of the glassy water, scaring the fish. I was even annoyed that Jojo's reflection in the lake was competing with this massive trout I'd spotted, hiding in the deep pool beside the rock.

"Alex."

She'd been pestering me to stop fishing for the last ten minutes. "Alex, come on. Please put down the rod and come watch this beautiful sunset with me. *Please.* I have to go soon."

When the wind blew another wave of dry leaves so they floated like pretty little boats that skittered on top of the water and the trout disappeared, I gave up and waded out of the water.

"Okay, Jojo. What?" I huffed out, thinking I was going to stay annoyed, but then I couldn't because she was smiling at me so darn wide it was like getting face-punched by the setting sun.

And damn, she was right to call me in. What a beautiful sunset it was.

"Well…" She blinked those wide-set eyes at me while I secured my fishing gear.

"Well, what?" I turned to look at her.

"I think—no. I *know*, Alex Sinclair, that I love you. And that I'll always love you. There. I've said it."

Overwhelmed by her wider smile, and that declaration, I moved to stand behind her—to wrap my arms around her—to breathe in her warmth, her lavender scented hair, and get as close as possible to her body so I could remember every bit of how she felt while I made myself a memory of this—her—us in this moment.

I turned her to face me, and my eyes trained on how the lake reflected in her eyes, how the setting sun made the edges of the blue in her iris go light and clear and look like glass.

I smiled and stroked her face, the sides of her neck, and watched the wild tendrils of her brown hair as they swirled in the breeze, also lit by the sun's rays.

"I love you." When she said the words again, I thought it was me saying them to her. Or that maybe I'd dreamed them. And when she suddenly looked concerned because I guess I hadn't responded yet, her brow furrowed with worry that I might reject her.

"Is that okay?" She asked, voice draining of confidence, those eyes drinking up my face, my lips—my soul.

"Is it okay? Jojo...*yes*. Hell yes. And you know I love you back. You know I do, right?" I felt my chest break open, and it was like the bones had gone out of my legs. I took both of her hands, brushed a fast kiss across her smile and added in this choked up voice, "I love you, too. So much. I wanted to tell you before school started, but I also didn't want to scare you—or—whatever."

"Thank God," was her laughing reply.

I was a stumbling mess as she stretched onto her tiptoes, but she didn't care. My lips found hers, and her lips were on mine—and *fuck*—we were swept away as we both dropped to our knees.

11.

ALEX, PRESENT DAY.

I remember how I could span her waist with both of my hands—how it turned me on to push my hands up her curving sides. How, when she'd moan low and quiet sometimes when I'd graze the underside of her breasts, the sound nearly did me in every time.

I remember the sound of the crickets in the grass, and the feel of her smile against my lips, something she did whenever we kissed. I can still sense how we tasted like the warm, gooey chocolate chip cookies we'd shared out of my bag—a treat that was becoming a staple. Chocolate, and crumbs, was something I now associated with kissing, and her, and with utter happiness.

That day, the sun had gone down and made a streak all the way across our lake and spiked into us like a laser beam, just as though nature decided how and when we'd go from our knees to lying on the rock together. Our making out was always timed by some higher power.

And I remember our joy. The unforgettable joy.

So much so, that even now I swear, for that day, and for so many after that, I thought we were magic. Because we were together and in love; we were nearly able to fly. I had this idea we were untouchable and so different from everyone who'd ever fallen in love before.

Problem is, I didn't know that last bit was true in such a horrible, terrible, devastating way.

We'd created quite a stir, Jojo and I—stepping onto the school bus that first day. We were holding hands and had eyes only for each other.

Hell, even now I lie to myself about it.

She had eyes only for me and I had eyes that tracked how everyone was reacting to me being with her. I was too proud...I was too sure of myself.

I had filled out some more by then, and days spent at the lake had lightened both of our hair to a rich gold and tanned our skin. I remember, even though we were freshmen, holding onto Jojo's hand and knowing we were beautiful. Entering the bus as *one* also made me feel more powerful and alive than I'd ever felt. I was a notch above. I had *someone.* And together, we instantly became more interesting than Grady and the new crop of seniors who thought they were so cool because of their newfound status. People loved it—*us*—but they envied us, too. Especially my brother.

My father, in retrospect, must have been laughing his ass off. He must have known that JoJo Wallace and I were more than friends at that point.

Grady was already reporting everything to him—because Grady, well, he'd been in on it from the beginning.

Jojo was my girlfriend, and I was her boyfriend—and we belonged to the feud. We thought we'd just had the best summer of our lives. But my father, and my mother...hell, they must have watched my elation and my growing love, day after day, rooting for it with palms rubbing together. They let it falsely fill me up like a helium balloon, one that had been planned for years to simply—*pop.*

Freshman year, I was so proud each day to ride that bus. I'd been so conscious of Grady behind me, staring from where he always sat with his friends in the cherished back row. I was up front with the other freshmen, and all eyes were on us. Grady had let me know he'd taken note of Jojo day one, just like the others had, but for such different reasons. I feel sick even now thinking about it.

And, damn me, I was so guilty of wanting Grady to be jealous. Jealous of my girlfriend, of my relationship with Jojo, and my growing relationship with my father.

I egged him on, and flaunted my girl—and the lake—in front of him so hard that when the time came to bring me in, my brother could only be on my father's side. I didn't leave any room for him to be on mine. There was zero motivation for him. But that's how my father had planned it all.

When I told a few people her name, that she was *Jojo*

Wallace, that made everyone whisper about her more. It made *us* all that more sensational.

A Wallace girl, dating a Sinclair? Is it true? Can it work?

Ha.

We showed them that it could...until I proved for my father that it couldn't.

I had this idea that it was the first time Grady looked at me with any sort of wonder and respect. I could see his wheels turning, feel the jealousy radiating off of him. I also sensed a sort of panic in him that I didn't quite understand yet. But that was because I was self-centered. I never noticed our father turning the screws on Grady too.

I should have known. I should have sensed that when my brother met Jojo for the first time, he would feel how I felt the day I met her. Enamored. Spellbound.

Despite my father, he'd fall fast and hard for her. He'd want her too. Everyone did.

When I look back on all of the carnage, I can't help but beat myself up about it. Yes, I was a kid—only fourteen when they started all of this—but Grady was a kid too. And I didn't even notice what our father had done to my brother to seal his proper place in the Sinclair family, not until it was way too late, and not until Grady hated me more than he hated our father.

Accidents...set ups...games, fear, and people hiding the truth all to execute the feud. All to hurt—and to end —Jojo Wallace.

I know my part in it was forced, but I can't forgive

myself for it. I still think that somehow I should have fucking known. I should have done better, been better, protected her and her family more.

Even now, I'm watching over her, hiding in a fucking shit rental car because I don't want anyone to know she's here and vulnerable. Even with my father dead in the grave, I feel like he might just hurt her all over again.

I know that's impossible. But I have also learned not to count on things like that.

WHEN I BUILT my lake house, I fully intended to cover the big rock where she and I used to hang out, but I couldn't do it. Jojo was gone, but the rock witnessed all of it—all of *us*.

It was where we first kissed, where we first said "I love you." And it was where Jojo, so sweetly our junior year, seduced me. I lied to her continuously that I didn't think we were ready to have sex yet because I knew my father wouldn't approve. More than that, he forbade it.

Jojo was awakening, though, and so curious. The way she wanted me was impossible to resist most of the time, so when she got on her knees and unbuttoned my jeans out in the open air, where we could be discovered, I gave in. Hell, I asked for more. And she gave more.

I'll never forget how my eyes rolled to the back of my head in pleasure, or her, catching her breath while telling me that she studied blow jobs by searching for directions online. *Fuck.* The thought of her watching porn for tips to please me made it hard to hold on for long.

She was so sweet that day, but she wasn't sweet when she was like this. In a sudden decision, she became a vixen—so goddamned sexy that I was ready to forget all reason and take her virginity fast and hard.

The memories pound into me, and I try to push them away. Seeing her just brought them rushing back, though. Especially her beautiful mouth. It's hard to forget the way it stretched around the width of me—her big eyes peering up, sheepish at first then hooded and wanting more. I always lost control and would push deep into the back of her throat. That is seared permanently into my core, and I can come now just thinking about it.

She would ask me if this is what sex would be like, and it was all I could do to not simply just show her right then and there. She would wonder if I was being sweet or rough, and if I'd be like that when we finally slept together. It was a question I could not answer, because I was being all of the above.

And then, like she couldn't tell I was in a coma-of-release and new wanting, she beamed proudly over at me and bragged about how she made me lose myself completely. She added with an impish laugh, *"I took all of you in my mouth, and I like the control."*

My response to that was again a loss for words. At that age, I was a star-struck dumbass. My inability to communicate was directly connected to every time Jojo and I were naked together—as would be *any* high school guy who was lucky enough to look at Jojo Wallace's small, high, rose-tipped breasts and have his dick sucked by her on top of that.

That first time I saw her bare skin. It was impossible not to stay hard at the sight of her, which I think is why she stripped for me. She put her mouth on my cock until I was so hard that I begged her to make me come again. And she did.

As the weeks passed, we did a ton more *studying* on that topic. And she got better and better at taking me in. She would popsicle-lick the sides of me, circle her tongue around the tip with way more flair, and those plump lips would swallow me whole every single time. Later on, she preferred to stroke me until I came, loving the way my warmth landed on her lips or her breasts. I would always wash her off in the lake afterward as she stared at me with eyes wide, heavy with her own desire.

I wasn't selfish about what she was doing for me, either. I learned expertly how to return every favor she'd given to me. Always going first, though. That was only fair. My tongue, even now, has a memory-map of her soft, tight clit. My fingers could easily find the spots on the heated insides of her. I learned how to stroke the hidden, satin button at her center. I knew when to go hard, when to go soft, when, where and how to suck to make her go insane. On that rock, she'd moan and beg— cry and even scream my name. I can close my eyes now and my pulse hums with the feel of her heated skin against mine, the memory still so strong of how she'd buck against me, gasp, and then come against my tongue, or my hands.

Tighten and release. Again, and again.

What we did on that rock. What I did to her. What she let me do to her as we got older. The image of Jojo with her legs spread wide for me—not like that last night, but those days we were really and truly both in love—almost does me in.

I shift in the seat of the rental car because *fuck me* for letting the memories crowd in here. "What the hell is wrong with me?" I mutter, shaking my head. One glimpse of her and I'm a teenager again.

I know what we did together, though, and I know it was because of how much she truly loved me. She felt safe on that rock, out there with me. At our lake, we were free. My dick drains instantly with those last thoughts.

Safe and free are two things she and I have never been.

WHEN IT CAME DOWN to doing covering the rock up so my home would hide the memories, I didn't have the strength.

I sent the architect back to the drawing board, and that rock is now built into the edge of what is a long back deck that connects to a sliding door off of my master bedroom. We decided to build no railing so the edge of the rock ends with the steepest side of the rock dropping off into the lake. For years, when I remember too much, the rock has been the perfect place to dive in —to hold my breath and stare up through the water and try to forget.

Sometimes I get into the mood where I like to torment myself by sitting on the edge of that rock. I picture her there with me, hovering near, whispering in my ear while I stroke myself. I'm so basic in my needs, but it's the only way I stay focused on the mission. If I don't indulge the few fantasies I have left, then I'll act in reality. I'll break my promise to keep her safe, all because my body wants hers too badly.

To keep my sanity, I'm careful to only go out there when it's pitch dark outside. I don't bask and relax on my back deck or anywhere near that rock. It sits there for the occasional glance to remind me of what I lost, and what I protect. I've avoided warm chocolate chip cookies, too. Any cookies, for that matter. And I avoid all lavender, both the color and the smell. As for sunsets, I never really look at them, because why would I invite hurt like that and unspeakable longing into a space that is already too filled up with my own personal self hatred?

And when I'm in my house on those nights where the moon is too full and too bright, and the small waves on the lake remind me of the sparkles in Jojo's eyes, I close off the blinds or drive away fast into Tacoma so I can watch the view of the soulless shipyards then go to a bar and take home a woman who's willing to bring me some release. Mostly, I drink myself into a stupor and pray as hard as I can that Jojo's holding out, safe and alive, and hopefully not thinking about the days we were young and in love, just like I always am.

12.

ALEX, ONE WEEK AFTER MEETING JOJO.

"I told my father about you. Told him you're a Sinclair," Jojo says, her hair a tangled mess, freckles hidden by a new sunburn, and wide eyes glowing with reflections of me inside of them as she moves closer. I can't look away because I love being inside those eyes. "He wants you to come to dinner. Can you?"

Jojo and I are lined up, and we've been diving off of what we've now deemed to be "our favorite rock." It's a long flat plate of smooth and ancient sandstone that, on the lakeside, has a small cliff drop off that juts out and shades part of a very deep pool.

She dives in before I can answer, and the beautiful clear water momentarily swallows her up whole. I watch her curls fan out around her as she does a few underwater strokes, and wait for her to resurface safely before I line up to go with my toes curling over the sharpest edge of the rock.

As I leap to her left, she locks on me and grins when I surface. "Did you hear me? I told my parents about you, *Alex Sinclair!* Will you come to dinner?"

I swim up to her, loving how drops of lake water always stick to her long lashes and reflect off those kaleidoscope eyes. "You told them my last name?" We tread water together, as though it's as natural as taking a walk together. "I don't think I mentioned that to you?" I frown, feeling my heart sink—feeling nervous that she knows who I am—that it may taint her opinion of me somehow. My dad isn't well liked by a lot of people around here. "How do you know it? And for that matter, what's *your* last name? Unfair."

"Mine? It's Wallace." She grins, and I feel my heart sink even lower, then slow some with a feeling of dread and worry. I've got this odd gut wrench happening, because her name, it's a name I know well. "Your last name was on your books. Each one has a fancy sticker inside of it."

"Bookplate," I correct her.

"Bookplate, then," she repeats, flourishing her hands wide out of the water for a moment. "From the Library of Alexander Sinclair. Very impressive." She jerks her head to my forgotten backpack. "Do you have a real library in your house? With sliding ladders and marble floors."

"My father does. The floors are wood, though. Grady and I have one wall of it."

"Wow." She processes that for a moment. "So then... you are from the Tacoma *founding-fathers* Sinclair family? One of *those* Sinclairs"

"Yes...I am," I answer, praying that it doesn't matter —that it won't change things between us.

She shrugs.

"Well, how cool is that. I'm from the founding-fathers *Wallace* family. One of those Wallaces that's featured in the museum, just like you," she finishes, sounding proud about that. "Though...we have no library. Only one big bookshelf. All mine. If it helps, we also have wood floors. Recycled barn wood. Based on our family history and all, though, it sorta feels like destiny that we are hanging out now."

"It does?" I shake my head at her, trying to process what she said, but I'm distracted some because I love the way her wet hair looks when we're swimming, the water taming her curls and making her usual brown color black as coal. The effect makes her wide blue eyes pop even more than normal against her pale, freckled cheeks.

I also love way her two-piece Speedo clings to her curves and stretches thin across her breasts where rivulets of water stream in every direction. I force my gaze away and flip myself to float on my side so I can be a gentleman and not openly stare at her chest, even though, these days, that's all I want to do.

I wish I could get the courage to kiss her. I know that one week of being friends is probably too soon for that, or for me to even ask, but still...I want to kiss her.

I try looking up at the sky, wondering if she thinks stuff—crazy longing, potential making-out-kind-of-stuff—about me? It's probably so obvious to her that I've got zero experience.

I wonder if she has any experience. I toss her another sideways glance and almost crack up because she's doing this goofy underwater flip she calls the dolphin spin. Yeah. No. She's probably got no experience either.

When she's out of breath and facing me again, I ask, "What did you tell them—your parents? About me?" I've sunk myself lower in the water and have been repeating the word *parents, parents, parents* in my head, because nothing kills endless boner-spikes like the word *parents.*

"Everything. That I've got a new friend. A great and smart and maybe a new *best f*riend to start school with. Do I? Are we?"

It's the cutest bunch of questions. Her eyes are steady and hopeful, and I get why they call it a crush—because it's crushing my heart and lungs flat every time she looks at me.

"Damn, Jojo. Hell yes. I can be that. Sure. Best friend, signing on. No problem." I'm so pleased by this request that my heart's flipped more than once, and of course I'm now wishing even more stuff about her—or about me. And I'm talking like some kid from one of those sixties TV shows. I almost said *golly.*

"It won't make anyone else—jealous? Push off another best friend...or girlfriend, or anything?"

"Oh. No." My heart thunders with worry that she's going to find out that I don't have any close friends. I don't want to lie to her so I answer honestly with, "Until you...I've been a bit of a loner."

I wish I had the guts to say more—say that I want to be more than friends. Much more, but for that, I'm going to need time. I have to figure her out, and work on how the hell to make some moves so I don't look like an idiot.

"Have you told your parents about me?" she asks.

"Nope. Not yet." Another honest answer.

"But you will? You'll tell them you're teaching a girl, you're *best friend*." She beams, trying on my new title. "How to read better?"

"Eventually. Yes, I will." I evade her eyes, willing her to understand that I don't talk to my parents. Not about things that are important to me, and she, in a few short days, has become *way* more than important.

"Well." She side-strokes around me in circles, and I, to defend myself from her beauty, begin to side stroke in the opposite direction because she's clueless of my efforts to control what's going on in my swim trunks. "We're really open with each other. I give my parents daily updates on our activities, too. They want to meet you. So...*can* you come to dinner—like tonight?"

"Um...I don't know." I shake my head, wondering what it would be like to have family meals where people talk honestly about their days. Where people might laugh and actually enjoy each other's company instead of just get through it, which is how I approach going to dinner with my family. Sinclair family meals are a study in the judgmental surveillance of my parents, who pick apart everything from my hair, my choice of outfit and my manners, all peppered in with glares and snark coming from my brother.

"Is it because you're worried about the rumors—about the history between our families? *The feud?*" She swims up to me, blinking comically.

"What? What are you talking about? That's ancient history. Folklore."

Because the urge to plant a kiss on her is too huge, I dunk my head underwater and pop back up.

"Well, my dad wondered about it. He told me to tell you he swears he doesn't care about stuff like that old feud either, that you are very welcome in our home. So I'm a Wallace, and so you're a Sinclair. So what! The major stuff between our families was a million years ago, right?"

"Or...a hundred and fifty years ago, considering a million years ago nothing was here. But, Jojo...I don't know what you're talking about. What *major stuff* was between our families?"

"I'm not exactly sure, but there was a very real, and very bloody, feud between our families." She flashes her eyes wider to show she's serious.

"I've never heard of it being...*bloody*. I know there

was some competition, maybe some oil and water rights, or land stuff. Typical history junk." I shrug. "And like you brought up, we both know the museum has the display about our families founding the town, because our last names are part of the history here. But no one in my family says the word 'feud' or, for that matter, speaks about the past."

"My parents do. They kind of freaked when I told them your full name—thought I was playing some sort of prank at first. My mom acted kind of crazy; she threatened to lock me up and homeschool me forever. I heard her beg my father to move away from here. But she does that sometimes. Freaks out? She does it more now that she's been sick. She just flies off her rocker and hugs me so tight, begs me not to go outside. Cries a lot, too. I think it's the medicine she's on for the chemo-therapy, that or the pile of pills she has to take for the cancer. It all makes her act off. *Way off.*"

I sigh, feeling sad as I watch the light fall out of Jojo's eyes as she speaks of her mom. "I'm sorry she's going through that, Jojo. Will she be okay?"

"So far, so good."

A short smile fixes on her lips. It's a brave face.

"My dad says she's heading into remission, but only time will tell. She acted so extreme last week that now I want to go to the museum and ask the curator about this feud. Are you down for a little digging and investigat-ing?" She waggles her brows in invitation. "My father says my mom and your dad were friends once, back during high school. I've never heard her mention that to me, though. Dad said it was her story to tell, not his. One day soon, I'm going to get the nerve up to ask her. Should I?"

I've become so curious about what she's said, I have to agree. "Sure. Why not? Let's at least ask at the museum, huh? Maybe they know. We can also dig around the high school archives. Could be fun. And if it's true, then my father just doesn't bring it up on purpose. That's how he is. A closed book. He always gives speeches about *going forward*. They are the most boring, endless speeches."

"What do you mean?" Her cheeks lift when she questions me.

"He's always preaching." I pull in a breath and copy my father's serious face as well as low-low voice. "*Your job right now, Alex, as the youngest Sinclair son, is not to dwell on the past or on any town rumors, but to focus on being a good Sinclair, on making me proud, and on making a mark for the family.*"

I laugh when Jojo cracks up, adding, "He says because we have money, people are bound to talk about us badly. Maybe because of who we are, or because they're jealous of what we have. He constantly says that I should only care about the present and the future, and making him proud."

"That's good parental advice actually. My father would say the same to me. Look ahead, not back, right?" Jojo's so sure when she speaks.

She swims another lap around me, and as I follow her, I can't resist bragging to her a little more.

"He even told me I'm on track to learn the family business better than what Grady's done, and without trying." I splash her as we pass each other. "I think that means he thinks I'm smarter than Grady."

"You probably are." She agrees. "But wait. You'll have to work for your father, doing his business, like…forever?"

I nod.

"Do you want to? I've never heard you talk about it." She frowns, pausing to tread water again before kicking her legs to float some on her back. I do the same, staring up at the cloudless blue sky.

"It's just what I know will happen. It's what's expected. I guess I've never thought about it. I'll go off to college, study business, and then I'll run the business with my family." I look over at her, wondering at her odd expression.

"But what if you wanted to choose something else? Like…I'm going to study liberal arts—that means you study a little about everything. Everything! I have my eye on those 'Colleges that Change Lives' schools. The ones where they expect you to think outside the box and make art, or come up with something that changes the world. Find your true passion, I say, and then you live that passion *forever*." I can tell by the light in her eyes that she can truly visualize this future.

"Uh, my father would never go for that," I say with a

hard chuckle. "We, including my mom, are supposed to focus our efforts for the Sinclairs as a whole. And we all do what my dad tells us to do, down to the letter. It's not like we're not all allowed to go off and do our own things. Like, I have this lake and all of the surrounding lands to…uh…steward."

She laughs. "Nice SAT word, Alex Sinclair. Steward of the land." She laughs again.

"And I get to fish, which is my greatest passion. And Grady, he's into football. I think he's got dreams of playing some college ball, but whatever we're into, we both know we're going to return here to Tacoma when it's all done. Our future is to learn the business. Be…you know…good Sinclairs."

It's not lost on me that without my father's voice layered on to drive that last bit home, my imitation made it sound lame.

"What does your mom say about your dad deciding everything?"

"Nothing. But…my mom hardly ever says anything to me anymore, except how to comb my hair and what to wear to political dinners—that kind of stuff."

"Your family sounds so cold. You don't seem to match them at all. I'm sorry, but…" JoJo and I have made it to the shallow water by the rock so now we're standing and she's shaking her head at me. "It—*you*—sound kind of sad."

"Don't be sorry. I don't know anything different. It's just my family, and I'm not sad. Not one bit." I hold back my tone, not wanting to sound defensive. I'm not. Honestly, before Jojo, I never really thought about something different.

"Okay. Good." She shakes her head, as though clearing her own mind. "Then dinner. You'll get to see how *my* family is. We'll feed you things like cobbler and meatloaf, because I'm sure you've never had those served up on your white tablecloths by that fancy live-in chef of yours, have you?"

I shake my head, but don't answer to that, because just like how I may be kind of sad—she's pegged me hard on this point, too.

"You can walk me home. Then you'll know the way to my place." She hops on the rock to wrap her bikini-clad body into a towel, and I don't tell her that I already know the way to her place. I was curious about where she lived, so a few times I followed her to the edge of her property. "We'll ask my parents about your dad and my mom, and *the feud*. We can ask them how they used to be friends. I'm sure she'll tell us if you're there. It has to be quite a story—something about how my mother left your father's riches and fancy offers of diamonds and yachts behind, all so she could be a poor farmer's wife."

"You won't do that to me, will you? Leave me for some poor farmer?" I ask, hopping out on the rock myself and taking up my own towel. I'm frowning at her, jokingly of course, but only slightly. I've been so caught up in our new friendship that…well hell, I simply can't imagine it ever being over.

"I will if you try to make me wear stupid diamonds, or if you make me get on a boat any bigger than a fishing raft, then yes. I will." She folds her arms in punctuation.

I laugh, smiling back. "Good to know. Very good to know."

She grabs my backpack and pulls out a bag of cookies. "These are still warm from the oven."

We pause to each take two, and I smile, watching as she folds the soft baked cookie in half and then takes a bite. "I bet it's such a romantic story, how my father won my mother," she says, mouth full. "We Wallace girls—we love honor and kindness above all else." She sighs, staring up at the sky. "My mother, stolen away from your father by my romantic dad. The more I think on it, I think maybe this feud idea could really be true. My mom is the kind of woman people would fight over."

"Please. Your imagination is going wild again." I laugh, trying to picture my father losing at anything. "No one has ever stolen away anything from my dad. Because if my father wanted something, he would never give up on getting it. So I'll bet he wasn't into her like that."

"I'm going to find out. Or better yet—you start digging around your house. Ask your mom!" She winks. "She would be the girl that came *after* my mom. Girls always know about their competition—or in this case, according to you, who they beat out."

"Ha! You're hilarious." I grin. "And my mom probably

does know. She's the jealous type to be sure." I laugh, but this time it's sort of harsh and horrified. Her suggestion that I just ask my mom this junk has made the cookies swirl with nausea inside my stomach.

"Look, Jojo. All joking aside, let's not bring this up at dinner. My family, we're not as free as you are. At my house, we have decorum and protocols. I'm sure no one is ever, ever allowed to discuss my father's ex-relationships. Ever. And…like I bet it will be just terrible and awkward if we bring this up at your dinner table when, for me, it's going to be awkward enough."

"Fine." She pins me with her gaze. "But this means you're coming then. Right? You've just agreed?"

"Yes. But what if your mom and dad try to poison me at the table. What if this is all part of some big scheme to murder me." I joke.

Laughing, Jojo stands and chucks the last of her cookie at me hard, but I catch it without a blink and eat it fast, happy with the thought that her mouth was just on the edge of what is now inside mine.

"Please." She rolls her eyes. "I wouldn't need my parents to poison you. I could drown you right here in this lake all by myself. You have no idea of my true, inner strengths."

She suddenly rush-leaps on me with all of her might and pushes her entire body weight onto me. I'm so startled to find her chest pressed up against my back that I stumble into the lake, taking her with me. My arms have instinctively wrapped around her so she wouldn't stumble and fall onto the rock.

I kick us back up to the surface and we're both laughing. I don't want to let her go.

"Wow." I sputter, working hard to act cool. "Okay killer Wallace girl. You do not need your parents to destroy me. Point taken." I loosen my arms to give her a way to swim out, but she doesn't swim away, instead she moves her hair aside and levels me with a steady gaze. She licks the water from her lips, and it does me in— hard. She throws her arms around my neck, locking me into her embrace.

"What else will you tell your parents about me… when you *do* tell them? *Really*," she whispers. I feel my crush for her.

"I'll tell them that you're beautiful. That you're awesome. That you're the coolest friend I've ever had."

"*Best* friend," she corrects.

"Best." I agree. "And I'll tell them that you make me happy."

13.

ALEX, LAST DAY OF SUMMER, BEFORE FRESHMAN YEAR.

"**W**hat? You only told them yesterday? No. Impossible." Jojo's eyes are wide, her voice sounds mad. She's flat on her back next to me, and we're drying off in the sun from our latest swim. She's also looking over at me like she doesn't know me at all. Like I've hurt her. I don't like how this feels.

"Yes." I push on with what I've revealed to her so I can make her understand—make her smile come back. "Yesterday was the first time I mentioned you to my family but I have my reasons—very good reasons."

While she's rummaging around in my bag for the cookies I've brought, I silently consider how father was also equally pissed off that I'd kept Jojo a secret from him for so long. I could tell her that he was oddly pleased about my announcement, but for some reason, I feel like I shouldn't share that either.

Unlike when Jojo told her mom and dad about me, her last name *Wallace* had hardly raised the brows on my father's forehead.

But Grady— he freaked about it. He started popping off at the mouth, immediately trashing anything beautiful I said about Jojo and the Wallaces, and started up a whole bunch of bullshit-tantrum-style rantings by shouting out that I'd been *"fucking a Wallace chick up at the lake all summer while Father had him in an endless SAT study course,"* and how *"It just wasn't fair!"* Just like it wasn't fair when Father gave me the lake.

I barely survived telling them more about Jojo after that. Because even Father had started making cracks about me *sticking it to a hot little number up at the lake.* He asked pointed questions, sneering and egging Grady on, about how I was "more of a man" than Grady. He joked that the leaf, which I guess is me, didn't fall far from the tree. He said I was just like him, and that he'd fucked a whole cheerleading squad, one by one, like picking apples off a tree, during his summer before high school.

At that point, both my father and brother made my summer with Jojo suddenly feel so wrong, so dirty— everything that it wasn't. I was red-hot pissed off, and I almost punched both of them in the face, starting with my dad!

Thank God all of my training about being a "good Sincliair" kept my shit under control. I managed to defend Jojo's honor with politely said words and a heart full of rage—not with my curled up fists screaming let go.

I know if I would have hit my father and then gone after my brother's face—or worse, hit my father *in front* of my brother—I'd be in the hospital right now and not here, swimming at the lake, that's for sure.

These are all things I don't ever want to reveal to Jojo, but also things I think I need to eventually tell her. Because now—now that school starts tomorrow, and even though she's the most badass and toughest girl I've ever met—I feel like she's somehow twice as vulnerable because my family knows about her. I feel like she's not going to be safe with Grady circling around, and with my father thinking she's some sort of fling or fuck-buddy stepping stone on the way to the next girl. Or worse, that she's a Wallace.

"Alex. Why didn't you bring me up earlier? For real." Jojo shakes her head, pausing to dip into the Ziploc baggie full of cookies, breathing in the smell of them. "I've spoken volumes and volumes of beautiful words about you, like how cool you are, the amazing things you've done for me. I'm so wide open with my parents about how much I like you. I say it in front of them—in front of all of you—to you even, as you've heard me do more than once."

She pauses to lick her fingers free of some melting chocolate, and my chest has filled up with pride and amazement because of what she's said. She goes on, "You've been over to my place dozens of times. I thought that by now you'd at least have shared the same stories at your place."

She shakes her head as I shake mine. "You assumed… but *no*. I just couldn't," I say.

She frowns. "Are you ashamed of me? Because I'm… poor? Or not smart enough, or not getting the reading thing fast enough, or...*why*?" Her eyes grow wide. "I know we joke about this, but is it the Wallace-Sinclair thing holding you back? The lady in the museum said there was not much to go on after the turn of the century…but maybe it's true and you haven't told me? I feel so freakishly paranoid right now."

"No! No to all of those things!" I don't let her entertain those ideas. "Never, ever think any of that. *Ever.*"

I swallow, trying to make her understand by joking half-truths to her. "It's because of my family—like I always tell you about them. They're just so different. You're right when you call them cold, because they kind of are. You'll meet them one day soon, and then you'll totally understand."

"I've been hoping to meet them all summer. I'm ready when you are."

"Well, maybe I'll never be ready for that. They're so…invasive. They're beyond helicopter. For example, if they found out I was hiding a beautiful girl up here…" I blink, scouring my mind for more words while trying to put her off of this conversation some. "Then they'd show up and interfere, because they can't help themselves. And if I told them how you were magical and mystical and so wonderful to me—and that you truly are my very best friend now—they'd somehow get jealous or act all strange because of who they are. They'd investigate you from your toenails up to your last hair follicle. They'd show up here at this lake to try to trap you like wild game. Forget about your paranoia, I'm terrified they'd make me stop seeing you."

There. I said it all. My worst fears—the unsayable, unthinkable things are out in the open now.

"Could they do that? Would you listen to them if they said for us not to see each other?"

I gaze over at her intently, wishing she could know all that I just said was so true, even though it's fantastical, too.

"I would never listen to them. Not about that."

When she frowns at me twice as hard and cocks her head to the side like she thinks I'm crazy, all I can do is stare at her lips, which, thankfully, are quirking up as she digests everything I've said.

"Magical and mystical?" I breathe out a huge sigh of relief that she's understanding how hard my family is, forgiving me for keeping her a secret, and that she's changing the subject off the deeper stuff and keeping it on the surface. "You have *got* to lay off the fantasy novels, dude. But at the same time...thanks for the cute compliments about me."

"All of them true." I laugh at her eye roll, relieved she's not mad or insulted anymore.

"What made you finally mention me now, then?" she asks, quietly.

"The first day of school tomorrow, mostly. My secret will be ruined the second you step on the bus. Please understand, my dad and Grady, they have this way of taking away things that make me happy. They make these dark-sided cracks and like to tease me about anything I adore. And I've just...well..." I sigh out. "I've adored this summer up here with you, and I adore you if you must know—I didn't want to jinx any of it. "

"Wow. That's...so nice of you to say." She sighs out long. "And I guess I can understand. My dad was worried about me hanging out with you at first, and I never told you this, but...after he and Mom met you the first night I'd dragged you home to dinner, Dad was kind of a mess."

I nod, trying to remember how Jojo's parents were that night with me. "They didn't let on about any distress. As far as I remember, they were simply kind and polite, and nothing more."

"After you left, they got really worried because they could tell how much I liked you. The saw that maybe I liked you too much." She pulls her gaze away from my face as if she's suddenly embarrassed. "Dad was ready to come down to the lake the next day and give you a piece of his mind that first week, but I talked him out of it. Mom started threatening again to not let me start traditional high school. But I made them both trust me. And I asked them to trust you."

"And that was enough?"

She nods. "Eventually, yes. They love you now."

"Well, good. And you—they—*should* trust me." I smile. "Because I'm very trustworthy where you're concerned, and I'm glad your parents know that."

"I know. But, I swear, Alex, you're sort of too trustworthy. You're so…" Her eyes skate away from me. "Frustrating. And it's getting awkward, and I want to talk about it. Do you get me?"

"No, I do not get you." My brows shoot up as does my pulse rate.

"I talk to my parents about how you're always so attentive, and how you chronically watch over me even when we're sitting still. How you've really helped me catch up and be ready for the upcoming year because you want me to fit in but…"

"Hell yes, I watch over you," I agree, sitting up when she sits up. "But what's the *but* about?"

"Well." She sighs. "I swear you think I might drown in two inches of water or trip every step that we're hiking or, heck, even when I'm turning the pages of your books, you're so watchful over me that I swear you think I might get a paper cut from every page."

"I am *not* like that with you," I lie, because I am. I can't help myself. I hover too damn close to her. I know I do it, but it's not like I can stop. "And if I am so concerned with you, what's the big deal? Is it…*wrong*…or…"

"No. Kind of. I don't know." She cracks up. "It's not a big deal…unless it is a big deal? You know?"

"*What?* What are you talking about?" I shake my head, horrified with the realization that I've been a dork around her when I only want to be cool.

She shrugs and locks gazes with me.

It's so intense I get even more worried.

"When I was alone with my mom last night, I asked her if she thinks I'm not normal. And she told me to ask *you* what you thought about me. Is there something wrong with me? Something that would make me seem too different to be able to fit in at school, or something that makes me not relate properly to people or anything? Like, do my signals not send, will people not…get me? Alex, do *you* think I'm…*off?*"

"What?" I ask her again. "Nothing's wrong with you. It's the opposite of off. You're—so *on!* You're beyond beautiful, and special and more amazing than any girl at our school—in this entire town even. You're going to be a superstar when we start tomorrow."

She draws her brows down but keeps those eyes intent on mine. "Then why don't you ask me out? Why don't you try to kiss me, or ask if I'll be your girlfriend? If all the amazing feelings I have for you are real, and if all that special stuff you say about me is true, then don't you want to go out with me? Kiss me at least, and break my heart before school starts, like the plot of that insane movie *Grease*? Is it that I'm not pretty enough? Because Alex, I'm attracted to you, and I want to kiss you."

"Oh my God," I stutter out. "No. No. And No! Shit. Jojo...*shit*, really?"

She looks down at the water. Her shoulders go visibly limp with what has to be embarrassment at my crappy response to the questions I'd been hoping to hear and dreamed to ask her since the day I met her.

"Don't say anything more. I get it. I'm not your type and you want to just be friends. You don't have to say that it's you and not me, or whatever."

She dives into the lake then and I follow her fast, capturing her retreating form before she has a second to swim away from me.

"Hold up. Please. I'm so sorry."

"You are? No...no, I'm sorry. I shouldn't have said all of that." She looks at me, her face is all freckles and water droplets that might be tears, plus all the shades of burning red that flush her cheeks when she's mortified.

"Yes. Listen to me. Please." I easily hold her weight and tread water for both of us and suddenly, I'm not sure if it's her pounding heart I hear or mine.

"JoJo, please don't misunderstand me again. Of course I like you. But it's not fair of me to even assume that I could deserve a girl as amazing as you when you haven't seen the other choices out there. Do you really want to kiss me? Because that's all I've ever wanted to do. But like...I felt like I should wait. Let you have other choices because you've been homeschooled. You haven't met any other guys yet. And if and when you do, well, you may find me lacking...or, whatever."

"What?" Her flashing blue eyes skate over my face and stop at my lips. "What do you mean? I've worn chapsticks of every flavor. I even bought lip gloss last week and slathered it on just hoping, and you didn't even notice it."

I'm trying not to smile, or worse crack up in the middle of her being so upset, but I do defend myself and say, "Oh, I *did* notice that lip gloss. Oh, yes I did. Had to cold shower it that day two times, if you must know. Damn your lips, Jojo Wallace. But they're gorgeous— with or without gloss."

"Well then, you suck." She pulls out of my arms and treads water in front of me; I do the same. "Then why don't you make a move? I can only think it's because you're so handsome and composed all the time, and I'm stupid and too much of a tomboy and not for you. I keep thinking it must be because my hair is always wild and tangled, and because I don't have the right clothes. Or maybe, because like you said, you have other girls to compare me to, and all along you've found *me...lacking.*"

I swim pull her into the shallows so our feet can both touch. "You're JoJo, the girl with the dreamy, sky blue eyes. JoJo, the girl who's smarter than all of us. JoJo, the girl with the smile that makes me wish for unobtainable things. You make me want to own the moon just so I can give it to you as a gift, because you don't want anything fancy, and because the moon is all I can ever think of that would be a match to show you just how huge I feel about you."

I put both of my hands on her upper arms and give her a gentle shake because she's shaking her head like she doesn't believe what Im saying to her. "You're the girl I couldn't share with my family because I'm jealous of anyone who knows about you, and you're the girl whose laugh I will never get out of my head and whose voice has been in every dream I've had this summer. You're also the best friend I've ever had—and I never ever want to lose that. Ever."

"So...why? Because—I—want—you—"

"No. Let me finish. Please." I gather the courage I've been trying to find all summer and blurt, "The why is— I'm scared to lose you because you're so far out of my league and you don't even know it. Tomorrow you're going to meet new people and new guys who might be way more handsome and smarter than I am. I don't know a lot about girls, but I do know you should have this right to choose. I also know no girl has ever liked me on the boyfriend level, and I mean at all, *ever before.* Girls like handsome football players, and hockey players, and guys with muscles way more than guys with backpacks full of books and a craving for more fishing rods.

She nods to my biceps. "You have muscles. They're perfect and you even have an amazing six pack. You're generous and kind, and you're so flipping gorgeous. With those warm brown eyes of yours and that curling mop of hair that does need to be cut, to me you're the most awesome and handsome boy I've ever known in my entire life, and that counts all book heroes and movie stars. Your face and your heart does it for me, and I don't think that's going to change tomorrow. I also think you know me well enough to know I'm not one to change my mind. I want *you*. I have the world's biggest crush on you, Alex Sinclair, and I'm hoping you'll be my boyfriend after this. And I'm about to choke to death on the shivers going down my spine and the butterflies that go into my throat every time you smile at me."

"Every time I smile? But I never stop smiling when you're in front of me, because *you are* what makes me smile." To prove it, I smile and smile and smile—how can I not?

She rolls her beautiful eyes to the sky. "I know. Sheer torture. That's what you've been doing to me."

I pull her close and she wraps her arms around me as I place my hands gently against the sides of her face. I pull her face to mine softly. Somehow, I don't screw this up, and my lips fall into the exact right place against hers.

Her first sigh wipes out all conscious thought, and her second sigh nearly does me in, because I am also breathing out an entire summer's worth of relief.

After this, all I will remember is how perfectly she fit next to me mixed in with the feeling of comfort. Tomorrow, while at school, I will have every right to continue to keep her safe, to hover inside of all of her beauty. My most perfect summer with my dream girl will not have to end.

14.

JOJO, PRESENT DAY.

I haven't peed in four hours.

My throat is dry, and my stomach is whining with pangs. It's all tolerable compared to the cracking sensation I feel growing in my heart as I pull the final stack of deeds and override documents from the boxes Will set aside for me.

47.67841. USGS & Surveys.

That's what this one starts out with. Riveting stuff.

Its tiny numbers and letters have made my head pound. The sticker below that says more is nearly peeling away. I have figured out from going through the others that the numbers are some sort of map thing—a latitude, or a longitude—implying there's going to be more indecipherable maps in here that don't apply to me.

Absentmindedly, I sip my coffee and bend the part of the sticker that's curling away back in place. It holds for a moment, and I read the faded words that were hidden from my view: *Sinclair Aquifer, Deeds and Contracts,* just as the sticker pops off and curls up again.

My stomach drops—*I know* that this box contains information about Alex's lake, because nothing else I've sorted through has mentioned it.

Alex's voice—the one that used to be in love with me—creeps into my mind: *Our lake, Jojo. It's...our lake...our lake...*

A lake that's never, ever been mine. Never was.

I glare at the box. Damn that lake and how much I loved it, and damn the clear water I swam in when Alex first kissed me, and damn the sunset we watched together when I admitted to myself that I loved Alex out loud for the first time. And damn him one hundred times that said he loved me right back! He shouldn't have said that to me.

The sound of my own voice coming from the past hits me next.

Why, Alex?

The tears threaten to return to my eyes faster than the words and the memories have, as I think of the very last day Alex trashed me with his words—the day he made love to me finally.

Damn the memory of his too-tender kisses and his hands on my skin. It was the night we made Emily. I wouldn't know for weeks. It was the night he said all the words I've told myself year after year were not his words, but his father's. Grady's. May's. *But not Alex's.*

Years of resolve, but now I'm starting to slip—maybe they were his after all.

He never looked in my eyes again after we had sex—not once. I didn't see into those golden eyes of his until I saw him at the funeral. Not at graduation, and not even when I caught him red-handed snooping around my burned down house. By then I was so hurt, so broken, that I didn't even try. I couldn't even cry anymore. He'd already turned down the pathway to the lake—*his lake*—when I spotted him. It was easier to just drive away.

Damn my inability to let him go.

I came to the funeral—to look for *what?*

I've read countless documents searching for—*what?*

I've scanned page after page of Tacoma-based documents that all mean nothing to me, because yet again, and as always, maybe I'm too stupid to understand all of the big words my eyes can hardly read anyhow.

I have to admit to myself I've wasted more than five years of my life on this burning feeling of vengeance I swore I'd come back here for. Only, now that I've seen Mr. Sinclair's coffin with dirt on it, I know I'm never going to wreak havoc out on anyone or anything. I've also now wasted days here in a place that doesn't want me—with people who hate me.

Not counting my aunt, of course, and Walt.

At least I saw what's left here, and I've faced some demons. It wasn't for nothing.

My eyes flick to the last box again.

Sinclair aquifer. My heart is full of scorn and bitterness about what was written on the label. It's so very *Sinclair* of them to inflate what that lake was—to call it what it's not—*an aquifer.* Please. It's just a lake…it's just *the* lake.

I let my mind wander around the images that will forever be with me. I think of the rock we lounged on while planning to take on the world, the shining gold and pink and yellow rainbow trout we'd scare out of pools as we swam. The pebbles I'd let slip through my fingers while he and I were studying or making out. The fishing—the kissing—the way he used to make me crazy, and the way I used to unzip his jeans and he'd flash his brows up high.

How many times we lay under the stars there or swam—our hands always unable to get enough of each other's skin, our lips always unable to stop trying new things. We would kiss until raw, then touch until our bodies were exhausted from every new sensation.

The memories. Our happiness, and my devastation. Plus all of my love for a boy who threw me away, yet who gave me everything, who made me the person that I am today.

A mother.

I think of Emily missing me, of how she calls me mommy and how her warm brown eyes look just like Alex's, and my head starts spinning.

The pressure to answer all of my stupid questions suddenly seems like a ridiculous, petty and horrible reason to be away from my sweet adorable daughter.

Alex doesn't want me; he's made that clear. And maybe he shouldn't know about Emily, because if he did, perhaps he would he try to take her from me.

My heart races with fear. Maybe I need to just step away, as advised all along really.

When I found out I was pregnant, my courage grew leaps and bounds, but it was equaled by my fear. I knew there was nothing I wouldn't do to protect my baby from these horrible people she shares blood with.

I also knew that if they found out about her, they would stop at nothing to corrupt her and make her their own...or worse. I don't let myself finish the thought of worse often, but I know it's death. The Sinclairs don't have much care for life unless it's their very own.

Aunt Shelly forbade me to contact any of them. When Emily was born, after hours of exhausting labor in an Ohio county hospital where I pushed and screamed and cried all alone, nobody but a nurse I'd just met that day there to coach me through the most joyous and terrifying moment of my life, something deep inside me shifted. Fear turned to resolve, and eventually strength. I began formulating my plans then, really. Everything was just going to take time—time I spent with the most beautiful little girl heaven had ever created.

Parenthood was harder than any hard work I'd ever done on the farm. There were days, raising Emily alone, that made me question my sanity, and days that made me happier than I'd ever felt. There were moments where I smiled and cried at the same time because I was so in love with Emily and so afraid all at once. So…tired.

We were always searching out the next apartment, and for a while I was stuck in a crap motel until I finally met my roommate Jeff. My hero. My friend. The kindest soul in the world who took us in—a random girl who called when she found his name on a community board posting. He made Emily and me feel welcome, and every day he says we fill his heart and his life. Jeff's happy-with-life attitude kept my despair at bay. And after what Jeff had been through in his life—kicked out of his house when he told his parents he was gay at just seventeen—he gave me a mirror of strength to look at when I didn't think I had it in me to carry on. He reminded me that giving Emily up wasn't an option, and most of all he gave us what I crave: a sort of family when mine was so very lost.

But Jeff, he's moving on—he has to. We aren't his, and he's not ours. He got a job in another state, and though he will always be close to us, he's not someone I can lean on anymore.

Nobody will ever keep my little girl as safe as I can.

At least…nobody besides, I hope, her real father Alex.

Safety—and family—that's who Alex is deep inside, at least to me. He's a protector, *my* protector. And he's going to be good for Emily no matter how he feels about me. I just know he's going to lose his heart when he sees her. He has to…he has to, or all will be lost.

I swallow down some fear, hoping and praying that he is still inside of himself—that he is still him behind the huge mask he's been flashing at me. Hoping, of course, that everything will change.

It has to for Emily.

Emily deserves her father. A real dad.

And Alex...well, he deserves Emily.

15

JOJO, TWO YEARS AGO. OHIO.

E mily called Jeff *Daddy* today.

I made eye contact with him the second those words escaped her lips.

She's three, so he did the best he could with his answer: "Your daddy lives far away, but I'm your best friend. And I love that I get to be in your life," Jeff had said.

Sometimes I wonder if it would be better if Jeff could be her dad.

Only, I know I'm not his type. My gender is the first turn-off for him. And the second. And the third...

I feel bad because I know Jeff would love to meet someone and have a relationship. One that involves more than just the few dates he goes on with guys that he never brings home because he doesn't want to risk having Emily form attachments to someone who won't be around long. He doesn't want to mess up the love and the consistency he and I have found here—as friends—and with Emily's love shining on both of us, making each day worthwhile.

Jeff's as damaged as I am, and was hurt even worse by his ex-boyfriend Jacob. I hide out, waiting for a relationship that will never happen, and Jeff hides with me, both of us wondering if our broken hearts will ever heal.

Jeff, for years, has been content to play house with me while he searches for his next fling. And me? I don't even bother with dating apps or flings. I know what I want, what I miss and what I long to get back. Jeff says I'm a sadder character than he is because I spend extra time in the bathroom, or playing with some toys I've put by my bedside, but always for the sole purpose of remembering how Alex used to touch me, how he used to move me—make me feel.

I can make myself come with a dozen different battery-filled things, and it's never the same. Why would it be? There's no warmth to fall into, just my cold and lonely sheets.

It's fine. Jeff is my rock, and I am his. We've built a new definition of family for now. It's a careful ecosystem of kindness and non-judgment. Jeff's generosity turned into an unconditional love between us. His schedule lets me take a few college classes while I work pieced-together jobs in retail and at restaurants. I make sure he's always got food in the fridge and zero excuses to feel lost and alone. Together, we've been able to keep Emily at home—safe. Jeff is happy to be both father and mother to me and Emily, two states of being that is simply his essence. And he lets me fill up all the holes Alex punched in me when he sent me away by letting me be mother, and sister, and new best friend to him.

Jeff took Emily to the park an hour ago so I could study. Those two are such great friends—such parka-holics—that sometimes I wonder who likes the swings more.

I haven't moved beyond the first page of my humani-ties book, though. My mind just keeps getting drawn back to everything that led me here, to this moment...right now.

I did more than leave Tacoma after the way things ended with Alex—I ran away, and I said I hated him, when of course I never could.

When I found out I was pregnant, I made what felt like a million decisions all at once. I dropped out of the scholarship program Alex had set up for me. I realized by then that Alex's help on the free ride to NYU was simply a way for him to keep me as far away as possible from Tacoma, and also probably a way for all of the Sinclairs to keep tabs on where I was. I would have been fine with that if the only person I needed to protect was myself. But once the baby was growing inside me, I knew, without a doubt, that I would need to run. To hide her.

Not from Alex. Never from him. But from Mr. Sinclair. From May. From the people who hurt my parents—who had an obsession with anything running around with Wallace blood.

I also realized very quickly that I couldn't let Alex know. It would make him lose his mind, for the one simple fact that he wouldn't be able to help keep me safe if he didn't know where I was living. And Alex would want to keep Emily safe. But he would still be under his father's terrible rule. There would never be a way out.

So I bolted. I told no one about my plans, or my baby, and I left as planned for college Back East, only I never made it that far. I didn't even tell Aunt Shelly where I was for the longest time. I left no way for the Sinclairs to find me. To them, I was simply...gone.

I stumbled into Ohio with less than a gallon left in a gas tank, in a car that was already on its last bits of tire tread when Aunt Shelly gave it to me in high school. I'd sold it off for fifty bucks and no title to some dude who I'm sure was high, who told me he was heading toward California, mostly because I just needed the car to disappear as fast as I did, and because the guy had cash.

I didn't even consider another job option when I saw the HELP WANTED sign in the corner diner just outside of Toledo, I just told my future boss, Ellie, and her husband that I'd work hard. Harder if she could recommend a good weekly rent hotel.

That first month she rented me the small closet-like back room of her cafe. I worked there two months before she suspected I was pregnant. Thankfully, she loved me, and wasn't pissed off to discover that I was heading into my second trimester. She was a kind woman, whose kids had never given her grandchildren. She even let me keep Emily in the back when she was an infant. She helped me with her in that rough beginning and let me keep the job.

I didn't trust Emily in anyone's care—which is good, because a good daycare runs easily a thousand dollars a month. But babies grow fast, and soon Emily was crawling around too much and getting into trouble in her portable crib. She was developing a temper that matched Alex's, and a short patience that matched mine. Those two things weren't going to work in the back of a restaurant once she'd started to walk.

I was reaching a new state of desperate before fate brought Jeff's posting into my view. I was visiting the community center looking for possible daycare options when I read his short but sweet note: *I'm clean and neat, and very quiet. I need a roommate because I love my house but can't afford it on my own. Please help me stay here. It has real-wood floors!* His number followed, and I was dialing it without moving from where I stood.

He was desperate for a roommate; and I was desperate for a moment to breathe. My boss, kindly, laid me off so I could get unemployment for a while, and I moved in with Jeff that weekend. Emily has been under our watch every second of her life since, and Jeff found out he loved being a stand in parent. I plan my schedule around Jeff's job, and the classes he's taking for his doctorate, and he plans every holiday and weekend around hanging around with us. My small jobs here and there supplement our rent. It's exhausting but it works.

It works because it has to, and so far, no one from the Sinclair family has made an appearance staking any sort of claim to my daughter. Now that she's almost three, I've done the paperwork to make sure they don't. They're called *absentee* relatives. I don't stake a claim to them, and now legally, after these years of not providing for her, they don't have a claim to her. When she was born, I thought about not putting Alex's name on her birth certificate—mostly because I didn't want to write the word *Sinclair* next to the name that represented my family. My father—and my mother.

Dirty next to clean. Honor next to lies. Darkness next to light.

But I operate on the truth, and one day Emily will know that her father was different. That he is like us. Clean, honorable, and light...though he used all the tricks in the book to make us think he's not. He is good. He always was, and I get that, especially now that I'm raising his daughter.

I will see Alex again when his father passes away. He knows I keep my promises. In the meantime, I will keep Emily hidden here—hidden out of sight and hopefully out of their minds, for as long as it takes, until the moment Michael Sinclair takes his last breath. But the day that man dies and that family's grip on Alex loosens, I will get what's mine.

I will get the man who gave Emily those honey-brown eyes—who gave her the world's biggest and most protective heart. She will melt any ice that he's formed in his chest, and she will be the bridge that gets us back together. And if not...at least I will have tried. At least I will have kept my promises—been who my father would want me to be.

"Mommy, look. *Look!*" The door slams closed in the main room, so I walk out of the bedroom I share with Emily just in time to catch her body before she slips over the pillow fort she left in the middle of the floor.

"This is why we clean up," I say, not really mad. I could never get mad at this creature.

Ignoring my mom-lecture, she barrels closer. "I need to find my bug cage. Look! Look!" Emily holds her cupped hands up, slowly opening them until I can see the moving green inside. "It's going to be my pet."

"I refused to touch it. She keeps trying to make me hold it." Jeff shoves his hands in his jean pockets and shirks back a step, squeamish. My girl is so much like me, and it makes me giggle.

"It's just a little hornworm caterpillar," I say, chuckling, the sight of the green squishy insect making me miss Tacoma and my parents more than I have missed them in a long while. "We used to have them on our farm. My father hated them because they ate the tomatoes, but I thought they were cool."

"It's just a little disgusting is what it is," Jeff says, moving one more step away until his back is against the front door.

I let some of my laughter spill through.

"Jeff isn't as tough as we are." Emily's eyes lift to meet mine as I wrap my hands around hers. I'm hit with every piece of my past in one breath. Those are her daddy's eyes for certain.

She smiles, sloppily, her lips revealing the holes where teeth still need to come in, and I take the crawler from her hands and carry it to the kitchen.

"Your bug cage is in the laundry room," I say, walking over to get it for her.

"We're keeping that thing? No...I just...*no*. My foot is down. How about we get her a real pet. A kitten?"

"Yay!" Emily shouts out. "Or how about we get both."

"Not happening. And we will only keep the worm for a couple of days, because he will die if we don't let him out eventually." I shoot Jeff a look and he raises both hands in one last protest before finally waving them at me and going to his room.

"What should we name him?" I ask, distracting Emily from the kitten idea more. One day, when we're more stable, we'll have a real pet, but right now I don't feel stable enough to care for anyone or anything beyond my daughter.

Emily slides the bug cage on the counter, peering into the screen mesh at the little worm as she considers the right name. I move to the fridge to pull out a few spinach leaves for him as well as one cherry tomato.

"Ajax. His name is Ajax."

I bunch my lips and turn to face my daughter,

because Emily has a hard time saying some of her letters so it's come out sounding like, "Ayyeex."

"Ajax?"

"Uh huh! Ayeex." Her mouth stretches into her cheeks, dimples sinking into each side.

"Ajax it is then," I say, stressing the letter 'j' while adding in the food. I hand the caterpillar over for her to dote on for the rest of the night.

"Is the creature contained?" Jeff asks.

I turn, laughing, to face Jeff, who is clinging to the corner as if he may need to escape at a moment's notice, but I know him, he can't stand to be left out of something as huge as *us*, and getting a family pet.

"Yes, Ajax is safe in jail."

Jeff's reaction is a lot like mine at the name. "Ajax? What's that from? A cartoon?"

"Emily picked it." I shrug. "I have no idea what it means, but she was insistent."

Jeff's mouth slips into a tight line.

"What?"

"Do you think she meant *Alex*. Not Ajax, Jojo?"

My heart turns to lead, the beats pounding against my ribs with slow, heavy thumps. I feel sick, and I feel stupid—and I deny it. "No. No I'm sure she didn't make that connection...no way."

"Should I make her change it?" I say, turning without moving my feet.

Jeff's hand wraps gently around my elbow. "No..." his eyes meet mine. They reflect my worry—they share my pain. "I don't think it's worth it. She's little, and it's all subconscious stuff, right?"

I nod.

"She doesn't know," he adds.

"But maybe she does..." I sigh, keeping my eyes on my daughter as I swallow the thorns and the hurt and the fear down—these emotions that had formed in seconds. All I can do is nod because there's no way to make someone truly understand without them having lived what we have.

"You're right," I croak, my chest stinging now with poison from the past and the hate I will always feel when I think of Mr. Sinclair and the evil that man spread.

I let her have this, but my mind screams my rejections.

Everything is in a name. Everything...and nothing.

16.

JOJO, PRESENT DAY.

I push back a few feet in the rolling chair hard to stop the flood of memories—to stop the fear—and as I do, I accidentally knock over the stupid box marked *Sinclair Aquifer*, and send the contents inside into a waterfall of mess.

"Fuck," I utter out, feeling suddenly too exhausted. I'm so done.

I'm angry at myself for coming here and dredging up all of these old memories. It's making me feel stupid, like how I used to feel in this town. It's making me miss Emily and my parents so badly it hurts every inch in of my soul right now.

God, what I wouldn't give to have been able to introduce Emily to her grandmother. Emily matches the three generations of strong, unrelenting Wallace women. Whenever I think that, though, I can't stop myself from acknowledging she's also a Sinclair. I seek solace in the idea that the Sinclair women are as tough as the Wallaces. They're women who had to be strong. I hope that deep down, despite this stupid feud that darkened both houses, that they had the same ideals, same goals for their children.

I think of how that didn't quite work out for my mother. How it may not work out for me, because certainly the last six years of being alone doesn't feel better than the amazing love shared by my mother and my father. I also can't help but hope Emily is more Wallace than Sinclair, in more than just her name. And I hope to live long enough to meet my own granddaughter, because I'm driven to at least do that. Whatever happens to me, I also mean to make certain Emily's life gets to be way happier than mine.

"What were you expecting to find?" I mutter out, scolding myself as I drop to my knees to scoop up and try to sort out the spilled papers. "A smoking gun, a red-flashing light? An arrow marked *look here JoJo Wallace*." I laugh—because I know that if I don't laugh here and now, I'm going to start bawling or go mad.

I'm done. I'm not looking at one more paper, and after I dance with a few more of my ghosts, I'm going home—to my real home with Emily and Jeff. I promise myself, bending down to gather up the flow of documents I've spilled on the floor, trying to put them back into some sort of order, when one tiny word—then two words—catch my attention.

Ann.

Ann Wallace.

It's my mom's name!

My heart pounds wildly, and I scoot into the desk with the papers until the metal edge is flat against my ribs. I find my glasses and pull the stack of papers close.

I scan past the top section that's all drivel. Attorneys' names and addresses, dates and tiny print. I move through numbers until my eyes catch on the words: *600 Square Acres. See attached maps.*

I flip through the pages. It's a puzzle, but not one I can't piece together. Six hundred acres is a measurement I know in my heart. I find the map that outlines miles and miles of Sinclair property and find the exact points where this six hundred acres lies.

It's our old farm. I knew it.

The lines stretch from the tip of the borders of Alex's lake up to mile marker 145, stopping where county roads twenty-seven and twenty-eight cross.

I'm chewing my bottom lip and my fingers are tingling because I'm gripping the papers too hard. I wish I could somehow discover what this means faster. Pulling in a deep breath to calm my chest, I go back and flip through pages once more, then again, reading each and every tiny word, looking for legal jargon I might recognize, when I realize a repetition of the use of these certain words: *water, and water rights.*

I read this part out loud.

"This agreement includes the full transfer of ownership of all physical standing water and all water rights to the deep underground aquifer, hereby designated the Sinclair Aquifer. Whereas all water and water rights to the underground natural spring that feeds said aquifer, as well as the entirety of Sinclair Lake which is the surface actuality of the entire aquifer shall be deeded to Michael Sinclair henceforth. Depth and volumes recorded in documents 14.a and 16.b. But let it also be recorded here because of the size and depth of said aquifer, the actual recordings of volume have not been truly measured. Current estimated scientific guesses are 35 cubic miles of water underground with a surface elevation of 3,498 feet, and the surface lake diameter of 17 miles. The underground aquifer portion is guessed by the Williams Hydrology and Geologic Company, out of Seattle, Wash. at nearly equalling the amount of water stored in Lake Tahoe, California. It will be known here that this transaction will create the nation's only privately held underground pure water aquifer. True value is unrecordable at this time, but for the purposes of this document the parties have agreed to establish current market value for the lands at $35 million, knowing this number is an underestimation because of the aquifer below it."

I read it through twice, my voice fading out the second time through.

I don't want any ghosts hearing this. This discovery, it's dangerous. This land, it's the entire property above ground and underground that, for the past 107 years, was otherwise known as the Wallace Farm Holdings and

Estate. Only this document shows the sale of my family's lands—riches they'd never told anyone about—to the Sinclairs!

My mom sold the entire thing to Mr. Sinclair for only— fuck—for only one dollar?

"Why?" I choke out.

My heart hurts deep inside, as though it's having trouble keeping blood beating into my veins, as though it's falling apart. I'm covered in goosebumps, and I feel like I'm going to vomit.

"Where's my father's name?" I utter, while reading on: *As per stated in the attached letter and bill of sale, written by Ms. Ann Wallace, this contract confirms such sale.*

All   Lands   Zoned Residential/Agricultural/Mining/Wetlands

On the bottom it's all caps:

LET IT BE RECORDED IN THE CITY OF TACOMA, PIERCE COUNTY RECORDS THIS IS A REVERSION OF A GIFTED LAND DEED THAT WAS GIFTED FROM MR. MICHAEL SINCLAIR TO MISS ANN DYSTEL now known as MRS. ANN WALLACE, from the year 1989. Said lands and aquifer were originally given away as an engagement gift from Mr. MICHAEL SINCLAIR.

Signed, Ann Wallace, Michael Sinclair.

The date this document was signed matches our time in high school, when Alex and I were falling in love.

Alex and I had asked my mom point blank if she had a friendship with Alex's dad back in high school. She admitted to it, and said that they were *schoolmates*. But she and my father never told me that my mother was once engaged to Michael Sinclair. All along, my parents lied to me. Maybe it was to protect me, or perhaps she was ashamed. Or maybe it all comes back to the feud that I can't help but believe may have killed both of them.

To conform my mounting fears, stapled to the deed is a handwritten letter. I know at a glance it's my mother's handwriting.

I pause, missing the hand that wrote this letter so much, fighting back a surge of anger that she'd never told me about this—not even when she was on her last breath and dying.

Let it be known that I, Ms. Ann Wallace, am of sound body and mind, and willingly give this deed of ownership for the Wallace Family Trust to Michael Sinclair. I waive my rights to the property, the well, and the aquifer waters discussed in these documents with the understanding that I will be allowed to live out the rest of my life in my home.

My daughter, Jojo Wallace, will also be allowed to live in this home after I pass. She is to be funded an anonymous scholarship to the university of her choice by Michael Sinclair. As well as guaranteed access to the land and the farm properties until 30 days past her high school graduation so she has an appropriate time to move out of Tacoma, Washington with no harm done to her.

As discussed, the farmhouse and all surrounding buildings are to be burned to the ground, in an attempt to keep Jojo Wallace from returning to Tacoma. Michael Sinclair promises no harm or plans that would interfere with Jojo Wallace's safe and happy future as long as she remains away.

In return for this transfer and protection for my daughter Jojo Wallace, the Wallaces will no longer be responsible for any fees associated with the land. By giving this land to Michael Sinclair for the price of $1, he takes on any and all future debt and promises to maintain adequate power and water supply for as long as a Wallace lives here.

Should there be any direct descendants from the Wallace bloodlines, this contract shall never allow them to dispute it and they will have no future claims. In exchange, these descendants will be left alone by the Sinclair descendants, and all lands hereafter shall belong to the direct Sinclair descendants of the stated and legal and appointed head of the Sinclair family. And no other.

The head of family descendant shall instantly assume 100 percent ownership of all properties, entities, enterprise, and any future use not currently zoned or foreseen, for as long as this document stands. As such, beneficiary retains right to transfer ownership to any person at any time he or she sees fit.

Signed, Ann Wallace

Signed, Michael Sinclair

It's not lost on me that the scrawling signatures are tangled up together as I wipe away some tears, then let my finger trace the lines carefully etched by a dead man and my dead mother. I follow the curve of the M in Michael Sinclair's name, stopping on the letter 'e' at the end of my mother's name. It's a letter scribed years ago, and I wonder if any of this was innocent, if the love letter I found from him to my mother while hastily packing my belongings and fleeing town years ago was sincere, or just one more domino he lined up as he patiently waited for life's clock to tick on so he could sit back as an older man and watch my family be thoroughly eradicated. Exterminated. By him and his sons.

Only he never thought there would be a *descendant* that could take this land legally *and* be of Wallace blood, too. Or did he think of that? Is that why Alex waited so long to sleep with me? Was he afraid of that? That we would make a child?

My blood runs cold.

We did create the Wallace-Sinclair child.

Our child.

Alex's and mine.

My head floods with confusion as to what I'm supposed to do next. My first thought is no one can know Emily exists…or *shit, maybe they can?* Now that Michael Sinclair is dead perhaps everyone needs to know. I can't remember for certain what was said at the funeral; words flew in and out of my ears in a blur of panic and hate and terror. I'm pretty sure someone said it was Alex taking over as head of the family and CEO of all businesses. Someone mentioned Grady, the older brother, was to be the CFO. But did that mean there was a swap in power between the brothers? Alex was always the smarter brother. If he took over the reigns, then Emily's the heir—the heir to *everything.*

I swallow hard at the sound of Will's heavy footsteps

in the hallway and wipe away all of my tears. I work hard to hide the shaking as he comes closer, and in the last second I compose my expression.

As he enters the room, I clutch the paper with one hand and reach for my chest with my other, my palm pushing and begging myself to create a steady rhythm in my heart.

"Well? You find what you were looking for?" he calls out from behind me. "I hope you're done—I need to head out of here."

Quickly gathering the top stack into a bundle, taking care to include the letter and the deed agreements, I slip everything into my bag, deciding that if Will sees that I've just stolen pages, I will fight to keep them. I just need more time, another look, and then I'll put it all back.

"Not really. I don't know what I'm looking for anymore, honestly," I say. It's true because I don't.

I face Will, trying to hide how my legs are still wobbling.

"You'll be back then?" he asks.

"Maybe. yeah. I don't know. Probably," I add, wondering how I'll get the documents back in here. I need to at least keep an open door policy with Will.

I've irritated him just enough to cinch up my bag and feel certain that the documents are hidden away.

"I'll need to know as soon as possible. I don't have a lot of extra time." He mumbles the last bit.

"Neither do I," I mutter, cryptically—already

deciding yet again that it was a mistake to come back here. I almost wish I didn't find out what I just found out, because it makes me feel vulnerable. This twisted feud makes me want to protect Emily more, and it makes me so uncertain about Alex and his current part in everything. Before the funeral, I'd been so sure.

THE NAUSEA RETURNS, and I notice every tap of my feet on the floor as I exit. I make sure they stay in step with Will's behind me. I'm thankful that he didn't stay in the room where I'd left all of the boxes, because what if he notices something is missing?

He won't. He won't, and he doesn't seem to care about anything other than himself. It's going to be fine. As long as I can drive away from here today and never look back—this is all going to be fine.

He unlocks the door exactly as he did before, and I slip out, careful to keep my bag closed tightly, tucked under my arm and against my breast. I don't think Will would reach for it, but on the off chance, I want it to be as awkward and uncomfortable as possible.

He doesn't bother to say goodbye, and the locking sound rattles behind me as I walk down the pathway, following the curve back into the garage.

My heart kicks, and I whimper a release, happy to see only my car and Will's below in the lot. *Fine...this is all going to be fine. I've found a document that records ancient history—it doesn't mean anything other than there was a bit more lies and a ton more heartbreak that my parents sheltered me from, right?*

Thanks to the Sinclairs...I'm very good at heartbreak and lies. I got this. No problem. Nothing wrong.

My nerves want me to jam the keys into the ignition and pound my foot onto the gas, but I leave calmly, buckling the belt and pulling out slowly, making sure I don't leave a trace that my tires were ever here.

I don't notice the shiny black Mercedes pulling around the corner—going way faster than it should be going—until I'm headed in the other direction. Paranoia socks me in the gut. It was her car, that ostentatious gold trim package is unmistakable. It's May Sinclair, and if it's not her, then it's one of her people. She's watching me. It's how they always do it. What I'm not sure of, though, is if she knows I saw her. My heart skids and skips with worry—and anger—and so much fear.

I get now that May Sinclair has been lurking around everywhere. Smiling in her over-polite way, insulting me with her eyes, while telling me to get out of town. I didn't think much of it but after today, after what I read about my mother and her late husband being engaged, her ongoing interest is beginning to make sense. She must hate me more than I ever thought she did. It's personal.

But then, it's not like I showed up to the reading of the will demanding funds or retribution—not even close. She can't know that I'm here for myself and, hopefully, for Alex. Though after today, I'm not so sure I want Alex anymore, because…who is he really? There's no way he doesn't know his mother is watching me.

Maybe he's watching me.

My trust in him, which I've always believed to be real, is wavering. I can't be certain he's safe, and that he won't hurt Emily. My head spins as much as my stomach. All that I thought I knew starts shifting around, and I'm imagining crazy things like Alex and May as a team, plotting against me. Grady and Alex are friends, running the Sinclair business—stewarding this valuable aquifer together.

I already caught May driving by yesterday as I stepped out of the Antique Shop to shake out an old rug for Aunt Shelly. I thought it was just coincidence, but then she'd locked eyes with me, rolled down her window and slowed her car as she called out, "Be careful, Jojo Wallace. My husband was shot on this street, very near here…shot dead, you know?"

I wondered if she'd lost it. Then I wondered if she was the one who shot Mr. Sinclair between the eyes—a lot of people had whispered it. A lot of people had motives.

It's out of character for May Sinclair to approach me at all, to be so out of control she'd bring up her husband's unsavory death. She's the woman who prided herself in having utter control over everything—manners and composure were a must. Unsavory topics were never discussed. She was the model wife to her perfect husband—a pinnacle of Tacoma society. She'd never let anyone see her talking to someone who wasn't a member of her golf club. But now...I'm wondering if her words to me were a straight-up, personal threat.

Maybe once you kill your own husband and don't get arrested for it, you lose your own mind and think you can kill and threaten whomever you want.

And maybe, just maybe, when you have inherited billions along with your two sons, and you're finally free of Michael Sinclar's cruel-abusive rules, you don't care about anything anymore. Dangerous or not, I'm sure she must feel liberated.

I almost feel better thinking of her as the murderer. The other path lends to reasoning that she would be out for revenge. An eye for an eye, as he always said.

The feud she participated in for so long has to be real for her even now—as real as it was to my mom back when. It was real enough for her to throw away millions for one dollar just to keep me safe. Maybe May is so entrenched she just can't stop herself.

This is all too big for me all of a sudden.

My heart sinks with the reality of it, and my head starts to pound with what feels like my own failure. Because the fear is now winning out—because I have a daughter to protect, I know I may have to just go away from here today.

Go away, without my Alex.

17.

JOJO, PRESENT DAY.

As I drive, I'm tense. I'm caught between my feelings of shock and utter desolation, nearly buckling by the waves of tears and memories I'm trying to quiet. I've also stared so long in my rearview mirror, waiting for May's car to re-appear behind me, that I don't know how I've made it past the first four lights that got me out of town.

Thankfully, I'm tailed by no one, and my panic, fears, doubts and total paranoia about May fades enough to let me breathe. While my world has flipped upside down, here in Tacoma, everything seems normal still.

I work to re-rationalize what I've found in my bag.

Yes, it's horrible, and yes, it's a surprise to discover my own mother was engaged to Alex's father. I wonder if Alex knew, and as much as I fight the thoughts that keep trying to creep in, I have to consider the possibility that he lied to me more than I thought he did.

I try to seek sanity in the idea that the documents are very old, and that Michael Sinclair, the devil in all of this, is dead. As are my mother and father. But if they're dead, and no one else is going to play games with lives anymore, I think the possibility is real that this ongoing battle could finally be over.

The feud, and the documents, are things from the past. Contracts between dead people that I have no plans of challenging or disrupting. I need to get my fears locked back up and focus again on *why* I came here. I'm here for me. I'm here for Alex, and for Emily. We're alive, and we're real, and we need to make our own contracts with each other.

Away from here.

The panic and the paranoia rushes back, thrumming in my head.

There's this nagging doubt that I can't seem to shake. I'm not certain I can trust the one man I came here to save. I blame his mother for a lot of that doubt, the way she keeps showing up. They've been watching me discover details of my past, letting me research through the county documents. I wonder if they were laughing about it, because they know how much it's hurting me still.

That's the poison talking, though—the horrible thoughts that Michael Sinclair forced Alex to put in my head. I remind myself that my gut is never wrong, and it pushes back at that doubt for a breath or two.

I find that in my state of confusion I've driven like

I'm on autopilot, and I suddenly recognize every tree and turn in the road. Subconsciously, I've been heading back to my childhood home. I pull my little rental car off to the side of the road so I can think and pull myself together. I peel my hands off the steering wheel and look around me, taking in how the outskirts of town have changed. Farmlands have been traded for strip malls and condos.

I've been wanting to go see the Wallace Farm, or what's left of it anyway, since I showed up here for the funeral. I've been just as afraid to bring up the memories of how my childhood home last looked before it was lit up with flames. The fear has won out...until now.

I squeeze my eyes shut for a moment as I try to get my mother's handwriting and her command that our home be *"burned so that I won't have a reason to come back to Tacoma"* out of my head.

I try to make peace with the document stating there's been a valuable underground aquifer under my family's farm this whole time. And I attempt to cope with the revelation that I've been kept out of more than sixty years of family secrets. It makes me want to show up there now and face it all, look at it with the eyes of an adult—not a scared high school girl.

My gut also still says I need to find Alex, show him what I've found. I should tell him exactly why I'm here, tell him I love him and want him back. I want my family to be whole.

Because I want to ask him to leave with me.

My body shakes when I think about the confrontation. These doubt demons have crept in and they seem so right. The image of May's Mercedes and her threats to me are making me feel even more like I've made a mistake, and the thought of me not being here to protect Emily makes me question my instincts all over again.

The image of Alex's angry, cold and closed off face—and the horrible words he said to me at the funeral—now bullet and ricochet like sharp rocks around my head. I'd thought that it was all a mask. For the past six years, from the time we had sex in that boathouse and he sent me away, I was sure he was wearing a mask, he was just doing his duty to protect me.

Maybe it was real. Maybe my dream to have this happy family has clouded my judgement all along.

Maybe I'm the crazy one.

"No...no...no!" I scream that out loud then wonder at my own sanity again. I force away my thoughts. I just need to get to the farm, re-read the papers in my purse, and *think*.

I tell myself that my mother is there, and my father—he's there too. And though they lied to me, their love and good intentions for me was absolutely real. They both died at that farm, and I want to believe that they will still be there for me now. Somehow they need to be there.

Their souls. Their ghosts.

By the time I cross the first bridge heading towards our property—*our old property*, I correct myself—I've got the tears under control. The rocks are dislodged from my throat, and the damn horrible doubts have been pummeled down again. I've already decided that whatever the outcome, I will face Alex. And I will pry his mask off as hard as I can. And if he's the same cold man underneath, at least I'll know the truth.

And I'll go.

I focus on a farm truck hauling an autumn harvest of apples in the other direction. The next one, a bigger truck, full of golden wheat, heads off to be hulled then stored. God how I've missed seeing the wheat. The silvery gold husks of the new harvest fly up off the truck bed and glint in the sun like glitter. The freshly tilled fields of pure dirt where the wheat once stood are now waiting for planting next spring.

The waterways that parallel the road glisten, catching my eye, and I begin to speed because I know I'm almost there.

Minutes later, my lungs fill more than they have in years. I taste the fresh air I know better than my daughter's name, and I eye where my house once stood. Most of the charred debris has been cleared, and it looks like the foundation has been graded. My throat hardens and burns at the thought of anyone else touching this land.

The car slides to a stop in the loose gravel that was once my driveway, but even that has been churned into the dirt. I kill the motor and step out of the car, taking my bag with me. Because as good as being here feels, I still know it isn't safe.

A riot of blue blossoms catch my eye, and I spy my family's old mailbox all but hidden in the overgrown flowering hibiscus bush my mother planted years ago. The blue flowers highlight the remaining blue paint my father used to layer on the mailbox every year. Now it's all rusted, but the red flag is turned up as if it still takes deliveries.

Tears well in my eyes, but I have to smile as I whisper to myself, "Hello Mom...hello Dad," because this is them. This is all that is left. They're here. My heart is here, and even though everything else has been stolen from me, this space is still somehow *mine*.

I stand and pull in another huge breath and take a few steps toward the spot that feels like where my old front door used to open and shut.

My eyes close, and I can almost hear the screen door spring creak. I can feel the metal of the handle and the stickiness of the cedar door catching as I shove it with one leg to step inside and announce that *I'm home! I'm hungry and I've made a new friend. He's a boy and his name is Alex! And he fishes as good as you fish, Daddy. He's going to be in my same high school class, and Mom, he's very handsome.*

And I like him. I really, really like him.

Looking back, I get now that my parents were such great actors—as good as Michael Sinclair and Grady, maybe Alex, too.

My parent's eyes lit up that day. And in their way, despite the fear they must have been feeling, they made my happiness their own, even though it must have been killing them all along.

I never knew their hearts were breaking. I never felt their hatred toward the Sinclairs. I know Alex didn't feel it either. Or maybe he did, but like them—like my father most of all—he never let on.

"Alex." I speak his name to the sky, wondering if our love really could have been such a huge lie.

I think of homecoming our sophomore year. I was already in love with him, but it was the night he made me love him more. That was the night Grady and his football friends attacked me. My heart slows at the memory, and I swallow painfully, trying to recall each and every moment of that homecoming day.

Even that could have been a set up. I see that now.

18.

JOJO, SOPHOMORE YEAR, THE DAY OF THE HOMECOMING DANCE.

I've dragged the bags from the last-minute shopping trip straight from the car into the kitchen, shouting, "Daddy. Where are you?"

Finding our house empty, I count two plates on the table. My heart swells and I grin, noting the milk glass is still cold and half full next to one of them.

Alex must be here helping my dad fix the inside granary railings. He loves milk. Drinks it nonstop.

Mom's just coming in as I bolt out past her. "I want to show them my dress."

"Don't you get it dirty, young lady."

"I won't. I won't!"

Making my way past the stout, short, older stone granary, I sprint to the bigger one that goes up in a tall round tower. It's got to be about a hundred feet tall—all metal with a poured concrete foundation. We use it now instead of the older one because it holds so much more. They recently painted the whole thing white with red trim. I think it looks like a windowless lighthouse.

Dad always says proudly how it's the *best of the best*. He saved for years to get this building bought and constructed. He's always bragging about how it's two-layer construction keeps things airtight. It stays warm or cool inside depending on the season, and it never lets moisture or bugs into our valuable wheat harvests.

Each year, all of our upper fields and acres of land my dad farms boils down to this giant tube that gets filled with wheat grains. For me, it's still difficult to grasp the concept that this one building, now full almost to the top of the walkways, will turn into money and support us for the entire year.

I watched them build it. It's like someone took two tall paper towel tubes and stuck them inside of each other, one just a little skinnier than the other. The second tube layer is the one we use to go up inside. It's the fatter one. It's even got little windows going up each side along with matching staircases. Dad says they only put the windows into the nice ones, so you don't get all claustrophobic while going up. It's just wide enough to hold the stairs.

There are shoots and loading spaces, but really…it's a tall, majestic but dark building. I used to pretend it was like a castle tower. Fine, I still do, but the older I get, I find I don't like going in here so much. It's too high and too dark for me.

But if Alex is in here with my Dad? I don't even hesitate.

I'm so in love with Alex that this moment feels like I'm running up a cloud and heading into the sun. Tonight, Alex Sinclair is taking me to the school's homecoming dance. It's going to be our second school dance. During last year's, which was our first, I was all nervous and unsure about being the new girl—*about being someone's girlfriend*. But tonight, I'm so sure. And it's because he's so sure of me.

After the heat of the summer, and because this tower is metal, the fist-sized bolts that hold the circular walkway around the inside of the top of it tend to loosen as winter sets in. It takes two people to tighten them up safely.

I follow the sound of metal pounding into metal, and when I locate the door above the side they're working on, I dash around to the opposite side of the building. The walkways are really thin, and if they're in the middle of working on a bolt, there might not be any room for me to lay out my dress. Plus I wouldn't want to startle them into dropping a tool or something over the side. If something falls into the grain from up top, it gets sucked in, and emptying the grain out too soon would ruin the harvest, so it's never to be found again until the beginning of the next season when it's sunk to the bottom and we clean and dry the whole thing for the next harvest.

When I reach the top of the staircase, I'm panting so

much I can hardly breathe, so I pause just inside from the walkway on the small landing to catch my breath. I also pull out my phone so I can fix my hair and check if I look halfway okay before seeing my boyfriend.

Boyfriend. I smile at myself in my phone just thinking the word.

"Homecoming." My father's voice sounds worried. "Son, you're already dating Jojo. I don't think you need to ask my permission to every dance."

"I know that, Sir, but I guess it just feels right to do so."

It's all I can do not to hug myself. Alex's words are so sweet.

The tools and the pounding start up again, and I hold my spot on the landing because I don't want to startle them. My Dad calls out, "Alex, pull here. Good. Two more turns and this side is done. You're a hard worker, son. You make me very proud."

"Thanks. I'm honored to help you, Sir. Honored that you asked me to help. Means a lot that you trust me." Alex's voice wavers a little with emotion.

"I do trust you. My daughter has good judgment, and we're pretty open with our feelings around here, so every damn day all of a sudden, the girl feels the need to tell me that she loves you. I want to thank you for being worthy of that love, and for taking care of her. And if you and she—should you two ever part ways—I guess I'd like to ask that you be very careful with her heart. Could you do that for me? I know high school doesn't last forever and things can change. But if that comes to pass, be more than gentle with her heart, please? She's giving you all she has; I see it in her eyes when she talks about you." His voice drops and gets all scratchy sounding. "Can you please not hurt her."

I nearly die, straining to hear more. The sound of the bolt-pounding stops. I picture the two of them—my two best guys—having this man-to-man talk, one that's so serious now that they have to put down the tools.

"Mr. Wallace, with all due respect to your request, Jojo and I are never going to part ways. In my family we don't ever talk about our feelings openly the way Jojo does, but I can say to you here and now that I do love your daughter as much as she loves me. I'd never, ever hurt her, and...I can't speak to you about parting ways with her because it's an unfathomable idea to me."

I hold my breath, trying not to let nervous laugher escape, but a small one slips from my throat when my dad does finally chuckle. Alex is nervous, and I can tell by his quickly said speech. When he is being serious with me, he always talks the way people do when they pretend to be all badass and grown up.

"Nice choice of words, Alex. You're very smart, aren't you?"

I clutch my hands to my chest and silently agree with my dad. Alex is *so-so-so* smart. I work to mouth the big word he used.

Unfathomable. Breaking up with me is unfathomable.'

Alex finally chuckles too, the stress of having this

serious talk with my dad breaking him down. "I like how you can laugh at me, sir, yet you aren't mocking me at all. How do you do that?"

"I'm not sure what you mean, son. It's just natural camaraderie, isn't it? Who would mock you?"

"No one. Not really. I'm just making an observation." Alex stammers. "I mean that I wish my family had the same skills you have in conversation, that's all. Natural kindness, I guess."

My smile drops slightly as I stay hidden. Sometimes there's so much sadness in Alex, and I know that sorrow comes from how he feels disconnected from his father and Grady sometimes.

"It takes kindness, yes, but it also comes from true genuine friendship, son," my father adds.

"Right. Well, maybe to you all of that comes easy. You're like Jojo. And you're smart too, I think, Mr. Wallace." Alex says, his voice still heavy with doubt. "But you—your family—seem to be *born* being so very nice and genuine. I don't think my family...we aren't like that. At least I don't think we are. Heck! I don't know what I'm trying to say. Never mind."

It's so quiet that for a moment I wonder if they can hear me breathing nearby.

"Okay." My father says. "Let's go tighten that other side. I heard a car pull up, and I'll just bet my daughter is up in her room tearing up that make-up drawer that's full of gunk and slathering it all on her face. I'm also sure she's expecting you to change into something that isn't covered in dust and oil for tonight. Do you have to pick up flowers?" He chuckles. "I feel for all guys on dance night. How I hated getting those things worked out. Corsages and neckties are the worst. Do you need advice on any of that?"

"I think I've got it, sir." Alex grunts through his words, and I can tell they've gotten back to work. "I'm lucky because Jojo's different. She doesn't like the usual stuff."

"Neither does her mother. Care to enlighten me? I can see if you're heading in the right direction."

"I got us matching fishing lures. I know it's silly but I had them engraved, and I'm pinning it to the center of a wrist corsage."

"Damn, Alex. You *do* know my girl well." My father's voice is full of admiration. "She's going to love that. She'll love to have something to keep forever as a memory of the night."

Tears spring into my eyes at the sound of his words. My heart's beating so fast because I'm going to love these fishing lures with all of my soul.

Feeling terribly guilty that I've overheard Alex's surprise to me, I wait until they're gathering up the tools and clambering down the stairs on the opposite side to make my escape.

Alex's gift is so very…perfect. It's perfect, just as all things he does for me are. My hands will be empty when he gives me my gift, and that doesn't seem right.

I'll make it up to him in kisses. Kisses and more, so

much more. I'll wait for when we go to the lake. Or maybe, because it's getting colder, and it may be raining, I'll do something in his car. We've never ever done stuff in his car before. Either way, I'll give him his own *forever* memory. I blush, thinking of me and Alex and all that we do when we're making out. I know he's been wanting more. He would never ask, so I'll surprise him.

My feet fly down the granary steps faster than how I went up.

I'm flying across the yard on butterfly wings now, and my galloping heart is setting the pace. Tonight, I don't want to be the girl Alex is used to being with. I'm not going to be Jojo the tomboy, Jojo covered in mud. I want to be beautiful and maybe a little glamorous—with hair and makeup, and this dress that I hope will knock him off of his feet.

"Mom!" I shout, elated and excited when the screen door slams behind me. "I'm going to need some help getting ready."

"Sure, honey." My mother comes out of the laundry area. "Did they like the dress?"

"I decided to make it a surprise. Can you help me? Make me look like one of those magazine girls, sexy, and beautiful and—you know—like you?"

My mom's low laughter rumbles out of her chest as she hugs me. "Jojo. You already do look exactly like me."

19.

JOJO, PRESENT DAY.

Kicking my feet into the dirt and crumbled concrete, I wander the old kitchen floor plan in my mind, reaching out and turning as if I'm walking through my past, smelling my mother's stew and looking over my father's catch of the day on the imaginary paint-faded table that used to be next to the hose, way behind the back porch.

I know I've lingered too long, and my tiny fantasy world falls apart as it's interrupted by the sound of tires crunching slowly along the gravel.

My house, my parents, and my bliss fade away until it's just me standing alone and unprotected in an empty lot in a place that was once mine.

A long whistle cracks through the silence. "Well, look what the cat dragged in..."

I don't turn to see who it is. I know it's Grady without looking. His voice and those stupid phrases he says, and the way he always thrives playing the villain—my skin is crawling.

I kick myself for not expecting him to make an appearance in the *Sinclair-stalking roster*. May signed off, so it must be Grady's shift now. Spying aside, I should be used to this—him. Grady's always had an odd obsession with me.

Since the day Alex and I first rode the bus together, Grady's always been there, lurking around, trying to curse anything beautiful in my life, to ruin it or take it away.

I think, just like his father, Grady's always been searching for opportunities to torment me. Somehow he was wronged in life, and in his twisted mind, I'm the way to get back to even.

"Get off my land, *Wallace girl*, or I'll have you arrested," Grady barks out, his meaty elbow hanging out of the window of his giant SUV.

I don't answer him. I know he's dangerous, so I'm plotting the best route back to my car.

Safety.

"There's a lot that could happen to a woman alone out here. That's why I've posted all of those NO TRES-PASSING signs. Maybe you didn't see them. Or maybe...maybe you're still so dumb you just couldn't read them."

His voice is cold, and I don't look over at him as a string of harsh laughter barks out next. I hear his vehicle door open, followed by the sound of his heavy feet slamming into the ground.

"I get it. I'm leaving, Grady." I hide my panic and swallow my anger. Just like him to rub it all in my face like this by calling me a *trespasser.*

"I think you need to be punished for breaking the law. And since we Sinclairs *are* the law, I feel it is my civic duty to step in." His words scare me.

When I turn toward him, I notch my chin up high and keep my face impassive, because I know Grady loves it when people are afraid of him. He gets off on it. "You're not going to hurt me. I said I'm going now. You *will* let me."

He shakes his head, and his eyes elevator up me and back down. He puts his hands to his chest as though my words have offended him.

The sound of his hitched breathing, like he's suddenly out of breath, snakes into my ears. "I like how you said the word, 'please' to me just now, Jojo. So…if you want to *work* back some of your land starting right now?" He motions to the grassy area by the mailbox. "We could come up with a program where you could earn back, say, half an acre at a time. All you have to do is say *please* to me while on your knees. Then flat on your back. Then sitting on my face."

I lose all composure and control. "Fuck you, Grady Sinclair!"

His eyes glitter, and he steps forward a few feet, sneering at me in that way he always has, like I'm fast food and he's really hungry for it, but he doesn't understand why I won't serve it up to him just because he wants it.

"Such language from that pretty mouth of yours, Jojo." He shrugs like he's not offended and steps forward again. "It's a turn on."

I move back, my heart racing faster as he continues with, "Since you're the one who brought up the word 'fuck' first, I think I could oblige you."

"Grady, seriously. Just shut up." I shake my head and try to skirt toward my car while he lets out a long breath of air.

"Jojo, you don't have a choice, I think. Unless you can outrun me." He glances around the empty lot. "My father's dead. And my brother seems to be finished with you based on how he ignored you at the funeral and after. It's about fucking time, if you ask me. I don't have to get anyone's permission anymore, either. So you can step into my car if you want to make this easy and more comfortable. Or you could run how I hope you do, and you could try to fight me." He wiggles his brows up high and says words I never wanted to hear again. "We Sinclairs love girls who fight."

If I didn't have my daughter to think of I'd reach into this bag, pull out my gun and shoot him dead for making this same threat he's made to me since the first week we met, but I don't dare let on that I even have a gun because Grady's huge and he will be able to overpower me. If he's serious, I'll have to be smart, but I hope he's just fronting. Grady was a master at threats and fronting in the past, and people don't change that much.

Because I'm so scared right now, though, I tell my mind that's what this is—a front on the face of a coward. I just need to be smart, keep cool, and get to my car.

Just in case I'm wrong, I grip the gun inside my bag as I try to push past him, saying calmly, "Again, Grady. I'm leaving. You won't hurt me."

His laugh grows more sinister, so I spin to walk backward and face him. He tilts his head back and laughs hard, bending at his belly. His body is still thick, fit like the meathead athlete he always was. But somehow his size feels even more suffocating now. His eyes are wild—dark and possessive.

"Oh you dumb little girl. Golden boy Alex always got first dibs, got the better shit, got our mom to fight for him, always got his way. But my plans for you, they were always better. It's my turn, Jojo. And I've waited a long time for it."

He spits at the ground, leaning forward and taking a lumbering stride toward me. I continue my slow and careful path backward, waiting for my time to zig-zag bolt to my car.

"Alex know you're here?" I ask, like what he's saying isn't scaring the shit out of me. I could always use his brother's name to push Grady's buttons and send him off kilter.

Grady shrugs off my question, but his face darkens with annoyance, so I know it's worked.

"How the fuck would I know. I'm just finishing out our father's plans for the place. Whatever that will says —and even though Father made Alex the CEO—I have just as much of a right to what's under here as anyone does. More. I'm the eldest heir. I worked for it—did all the dirty work in the past. I'm still doing it, too." He pauses and smirks at me again, his upper lip sneering like a bull as he adds a kick into the dirt. "Bet you still don't know what's under here—stupid, stupid Wallaces, living like paupers for no reason."

"I know all about the water! A lake as big as Tahoe. I always did. You were the idiots who fell for *our* games— not the other way around." I shout the lie at him, hoping to throw him off more with my newfound knowledge. The Sinclairs get off on their secrets, and if I can act like I knew all along, maybe, just maybe, I'll make it to my car.

"Bullshit." Grady's brows sink lower and crinkle while his black eyes go blacker. A tuft of his curling brown hair falls across his forehead. I'm backing up toward my car, and trying to process what he's said about Alex being the CEO, but I'm still feeling too unsafe to bring that up directly, so I push him by pretending I know even more.

"Hell yes I know about it. And I'm mentioning it to you right now because I don't care about the water, Grady. I don't care about the money or what's in the past. I just came here to have a look around, get a last look at my home, visit the past and prove how strong I am. This visit is for nobody but me. That's all. I know it's all yours now, and I'm good with that. I don't want or need anything from your awful family. But I can guess that during the last six years, Alex was made CEO because Alex will know what to do with it—and you don't. That must hurt, huh?"

Grady jerks his head back at his car. "Alex has no clue! He wants to keep it as it is. But under the aquifer there's an oil deposit bigger than what they were finding in Northern Alaska back in the eighties. And I will get that oil out before a fucking earthquake drains it—or before the water gets into it and ruins it. It's an inevitable fact that eventually that quake's going to hit this region, and I will have both the oil and the water drained out of here long before."

I raise my brows high. I know Grady will read my shock and surprise as some sort of admiration, but I can't help but whisper out. "Oil…"

"If we do it right, drain and bottle the water first and sell it, because it's pure, and we simultaneously get the oil out, the Sinclair family will be set for hundreds and hundreds of years ahead. I will live like a fucking king! So, who's got the brains now?"

He's smug, but I'm relieved he's no longer threatening in a physical way.

"What about the environment—there's no way you can do what you're planning without trashing the lands around here for hundreds of miles. It will become a wasteland. Both the water and the oil has to be millions, if not billions of years old. You're talking about disturbing a whole ecosystem."

"It's all our land." He shrugs. "Who the fuck cares how it looks after."

I shrug, but inside I'm livid, even more horrified by the signed letters and the transfer of property form hiding in my purse. I manage to keep my shrug as careless as his was, and bluff out, "Like I said, I don't care. Like you said, it's your land. But, I'm holding with what everyone knows. Grady Sinclair has the muscle...Alex Sinclair has the brains. That still stands, so whatever happens, it's gonna be your brother's call—not yours."

His nostrils flair with my punishing insults, which is when I startle him by bolting.

I'm almost within a hand's reach of my car when his hand circles my upper arm and yanks me back until my head snaps.

"I'm going to show you some *muscle*, you pretentious little bitch!" The words stench as he grits through his teeth. "I'm going to stick it so far up into you that you'll never say something like that to me again."

20

ALEX, PRESENT DAY.

Once Will told me which papers Jojo had taken out with her, I didn't have to follow her to her next location. If she read the letter her mom had written, then I knew exactly where she was going. The farm.

And this meant I needed to meet her there. On her own turf, in a non-threatening way, which is why I thought I'd walk in on the pathway from the lake how I used to meet her.

I speed like a maniac to my house and park the car by the lake. I picture how it will go...how I *hope* it will go. She should have been just a bit ahead of me driving in directly, but she'll need a minute or two on her own alone to process and to be quiet with the memories she has of that vacant lot. That is her way.

For me, it's a short hike to her place—and I've already started running it, because now that I'm heading toward her, I don't have the patience to walk. I'm ready to talk to her. I *want* to talk to her, and maybe now she's going to understand just why I want her to leave here again. There's nothing left for her here except the carnage our parents left for us to clean up.

As I walk along the path, I have this idea that I want to be nice to her—to come clean, which is an impossible idea. I want her to forgive me, but that's selfish. I also don't know if I'll ever be man enough to tell her all that I was involved in on behalf of my father.

I don't deserve her forgiveness. I never will. I'm too evil, done too much.

At least she knows now that her mother was responsible for the farm house burning down. I know she thought that it was us, completely—more specifically, me. Which, hell...despite it being her mother's plan, it was me executing it.

Father didn't care where the idea had come from, he simply wanted it taken care of. He wanted me to do the job, then lord it over Jojo. In Father's mind it was the dramatic type of huge-yet-cruel closure that he loved.

I'm sure he also saw me lighting up the Wallace farmhouse as a symbolic and appropriate gesture. It made me *just the right kind of Sinclair*, because by then, I'd been lying to Father about how much I hated the Wallaces. I played the part and gave him what he wanted to see and hear.

I talked about how much I couldn't wait to be rid of Jojo. That, in a twisted way, was also true by the end of senior year. I was so full of self-loathing, nearly sick every day with it, that I couldn't wait for her to be out of Tacoma. I couldn't wait to have her far away from us, where I hoped, finally, she'd be safe.

At the very least, safer.

Mrs. Wallace knew her daughter better than any of us did when she wrote the command to burn the house down in her letter. She understood just how sentimental Jojo would be about the farm house. She knew in her heart that her daughter might leave the farmhouse for college, but every quarter she'd want to come home. She'd want to make a life here and stay after. She would be attached—*endangered.*

I suspect Jojo didn't take the document to report it to the news or anything. She's also not the type to discuss it with anyone she doesn't trust. So, for now, that means she will probably only show it to her Aunt Shelly. But what Jojo doesn't know is that even her dear and beloved Aunt is not innocent of all of this.

My father and I made sure Aunt Shelly knew everything that was going down years ago. Jojo's mother sealed it by confirming it all on her deathbed. Aunt Shelly knowing but remaining silent is what has kept Shelly and Jojo breathing. Jojo's aunt would have moved away along with Jojo, but my father made it impossible. He made her a prisoner here in Tacoma.

She was our father's collateral.

He locked up the woman's money by trashing some of her investments. And he threatened her so badly, all she could do was breathe in, breathe out, live her quiet life, and sell antiques. She wasn't allowed to visit Jojo, and Jojo wasn't invited here. The deal was, if she did all of that with a straight face, she would be left alone to live a decent life while her one surviving relative, Jojo, also stayed alive.

No one could be happier about my father's death than Aunt Shelly. She also was the first one investigated by the police as the most probable murder suspect.

None of us expected Jojo to slip away from school and run how she did. Even Shelly didn't know exactly where she'd been because Jojo made a point of not contacting her for more than four years. Nothing—not until a few months ago, and right before Father was murdered. I'd heard something about him having tracked her to Ohio, and I know he had been trying to locate her address. He even told me straight up once that he was getting close. He was obsessed with the idea that she would challenge us and somehow fight for this land. Even more, though, he was obsessed with finishing something he started.

I wasn't going to let the man show up and surprise Jojo, that's for damn sure. I was so relieved that he died before I finally got the balls to spy on him. I'd been ready to go to Ohio myself, but then Jojo surfaced here, keeping her promises. Looking at me with those damn beautiful blue eyes. Fucking my head more than it already is fucked—and sending my soul all the way down into hell where it belongs.

I know Jojo will be devastated all over again today.

She'll feel betrayed, confused, and she'll be hurting. But once she cries it out, she's going to understand that her mom planned all of it because she loved her daughter more than anything in the world. She wanted Jojo to leave here. For good. Forever. So she could be safe and get to live her life. So she could be free of the past—our families' past.

When Will told me she'd actually *stolen* papers, the letter, and the entire transfer of deed documents, I was shocked, slightly saddened, but maybe relieved, too. That act meant that the good JoJo I once knew has changed. She's gotten wiser—bolder.

But hell...we've all changed, haven't we?

My stomach clenches as all of my parts in this—all of our parts that made this girl change—slam into me.

If she only knew; she would have never come back.

I picture her, stewing and pacing around her old farm lot. She's probably burning with questions and hating us all right now. At least she'll finally understand I wasn't lying that night in the boathouse. When I told her about her mother and my father, she screamed at me to stop, and her eyes told me she would never, ever believe me.

I hear her voice from that night again in my mind: *"Why...why...why..."*

Back then, even I didn't know about the water, or the oil. Now, like me, she knows why. It was more than a feud. It was soulless greed.

I pause my run to catch my breath and to pull some

needed air back into my lungs because the pathway, as it gets closer to the edge of my woods and Jojo's old property line, has become nearly completely overgrown. I've let the path disappear with neglect. But now I'm regretting that because this entire section is blocked with felled trees, massive ferns and these wicked, thorn bush weeds.

I pick my way through it all, annoyed at the delay, and worried I'm going to miss her visit here. I finally carve my own new path in order to exit the grove of trees, my last shelter before crossing into the wide open dust bowl of the once fertile wheat fields that used to make up the edges of the Wallace holdings, when I hear a shout—Jojo's shout.

My eyes land on my brother's truck, parked all haphazardly, but in just a way to block Jojo's rental car. My pulse thrums with agitation and fear and even more annoyance.

What the fuck is Grady doing? How could I have missed that he was probably tailing Jojo, too? How could he have known she'd come here? Is he trying to hurt her? Fuck. Fuck!

The shouting escalates, and that's when my head flips to slow-motion and fast-motion all at the same time.

I don't quite hear much beyond the sound of my heart thumping into my skull and my feet churning and pushing against the dirt as I start running again toward Jojo. I know Jojo shouted at Grady again. I also recall the way he didn't shout back, which really isn't like Grady at all.

Because neither of them were facing me, their exact conversation stayed lost on the wind.

As I approach, JoJo looks calm enough. She's clutching her bag and Grady has his arms crossed in front of him, making his usual *smug-son-of-a-bitch* expression.

In a beat, though, everything changes. JoJo backs away one step for every pace Grady walks forward. And suddenly, the world speeds up. Jojo starts to run, and my brother changes his stance. He whips toward her like a python striking at a mouse, and grabs her arm. Her cry of pain mixed with fear nearly does me in, and when Grady shakes her hard, I make my legs burn faster because I am still too fucking far away.

Jojo manages to squirm momentarily out of Grady's grip and fumble a hand into her bag. That move is to yank out a gun! A gun that's in JoJo's hand and now pointed at Grady!

I can barely contemplate that, because that bastard is suddenly all over her. Helplessly, I'm running and watching as he hits the side of her face with his fist and the gun tumbles out of her hand to land in the grass. I'm almost there, and he's got her pinned against him, and the fucker is laughing while finally I can hear Jojo's screaming at the top of her lungs. "No. Let me go, Grady! I won't. You can't make me!"

My brother's response is, "Oh, but I think I can—

you're going to need to shut the fuck up." He tears at her blouse and yanks her hair hard so her head snaps back as she falls onto her knees.

She's twisting and scratching and fighting him with every ounce of her might, still screaming louder than ever for help.

My brother gets another good grip on her hair, and seeing that makes my whole body hurt. He drags her effortlessly around until he forces her onto her back despite how she's digging her legs straight into the ground and twisting away. "Stop touching me!" Her screams are muffled.

I become white-hot fury, and I close in just when he's managed to pin her down by using all of his weight to grind her into the dirt while still tearing at her blouse.

"I'm going to do way more than touch you right now you conniving, Wallace whore. And because you won't stop your screeching, I'm going to shut you up by shoving my cock in your mouth."

Some of the fight goes out of Jojo's limbs because Grady's weight is pushing the air out of her lungs, but I hear her say: "I'll bite it off if you try. You know I will— I'll rip it in half."

"Fucking bitch. You would, wouldn't you?" He punches her face again, way too hard. And then he tears the rest of her blouse all the way off. "Unbutton your jeans, Jojo. Unbutton them, and do as I say!"

"No. No. Don't—don't! No."

Grady stretches to the side and reaches for the gun and trails the tip of it over her breasts.

"No," Jojo sobs out, breaking finally.

I can't believe my brother doesn't hear me coming, but maybe he's just as amped up on head-pounding adrenaline as I am.

He clocks her with the gun so hard she crumples under him like she's made out of paper, and he starts yanking at the button on her jeans himself. But before he can have his way, I'm there, and I send him flying off of Jojo with a powerful thrust.

Wordlessly, he and I tangle like two rabid, wild dogs fighting over road kill.

My fists make contact with his face, and the asshole actually fires the gun at me while I'm wrenching it out of his hand! The bullet misses me, but I already know there'd be no way, even if it had pierced my heart directly, that I would have stopped breathing until I'd made sure Grady had died for this first.

"Alex. Don't kill me. *Please.*" Grady's voice, now that I've got the gun pointed at him, is whining like a baby's. From very far away I hear myself growl and I land another punch.

"I'm sorry. Fuck. Don't kill me, Alex! What would you say to Mom if you did?"

"I'd say you deserved it." I front. "Everyone already suspects you killed our father so you could take over the business early. I'd say that it was true."

"I didn't kill Father. What the fuck! Why didn't you

say anything at the funeral—stake your claim to her then and there? This is all actually your fault for not doing that." Classic Grady, blaming everyone else for his fuck-ups by using the same logic as a third-grader. "You wouldn't even look at her. I just figured she could finally be mine. Father always joked that if she came back to town I could have her."

Beyond triggered by that line, I nearly start choking —they used to threaten me with that joke. Because it was never a fucking joke! But I don't utter what I would have screamed at them back when I was in high school. Things like, *"I love this girl—you hurt her, you keep hurting her, how could you have done this to her?"*

Back then, I hadn't learned my lessons yet. I didn't understand that Grady, my mother, and my father fed off of phrases like that. This is why I will never let anyone in my family hear me utter words that would hint at the ongoing depths of my feelings about Jojo Wallace. Those words would make me their target again, and make her more vulnerable than she already is.

The feud, I learned the hard way, is not about Jojo being a Wallace and me being a Sinclair. It's really a Sinclair *being in love* with a Wallace. That's how the feud survives. That's the blood that feeds it, forcing people to do terrible, terrible things.

Pain for pain. My family's motto, in retrospect, means more than I ever thought. And it had been working. Keep the love hidden, she stays safe, and I get to hurt. I'd thought it was a fair price all of these years, but now Grady's hurt her anyway.

"I didn't think I had to explain, you asshole. Father *gave* Jojo to me!" I bite out. "Gifted her to me, as my own personal torture—for life. Just like how he gave you that fucked up broken shoulder to carry around for your entire life."

I look away from the flash of true-hurt in Grady's eyes as I bring up his shoulder and how my brother once dreamed of playing college football—maybe pro— but when he resisted our father's plans to work for Sinclair Enterprises, our dad smashed Grady's shoulder with a crowbar. Father paid for the top surgeons in Seattle to fix Grady's "terrible accident." Then he *let* Grady stay on the team. He was benched for all of senior year so he could still have fun with his friends. But Grady could never play again. He was so dejected he never even went to college. And after a lifetime of being called the dumb one, Grady started to believe it.

To keep my resolve, to make it so I don't feel sorry for my asshole brother, I make myself flick a hard glance to Jojo's crumpled body. She's still blacked out on the dirt. I check again that she's breathing, because that's what's most important to me here, then I turn back to Grady.

"I don't share my toys, Grady." I clip out the words. "And you can't just rape random women. You're supposed to be a lead partner in the company now. We're the bosses, dumbass." I say only words Grady will understand—words about the business, and about our family, and money and saving face. Greedy, selfish words. "We can't fulfill Father's legacy and the massive list of directions he left behind from prison."

"I wasn't going to go to jail." He stands up, also flicking a glance to Jojo, his expression remorseless but still full of sick desire. "I would have cleaned up my mess."

He wipes his hands on his slacks, thinking wrongly that it's over between me and him. My heart has stopped cold. My throat hardly lets air in as I speak. "Do you mean you were planning to *kill* her after? Murder her? Truly?"

He shrugs like that idea is no big deal, and wiggles his chin back and forth as he adds, "I can't believe you hit me so damn hard."

I shake my head as my fury increases. Bile has lodged in the back of my throat at this latest example of my brother's complete lack of humanity.

I'm still holding the gun, and I feel my index finger tighten and press against the smooth trigger. At this moment—and for the first time in my life—I want to be like him. Be my father. Because if I could leap the tiny thread that still separates me from them, I know I'd be able to shoot Grady. I think I'd find incredible joy in it, too. I know I would.

All of this makes me hate myself more right now, because I simply can't do it.

I lower the gun, gripping it to my side, and step

closer to him, acting like *yeah, it's over, we're just chatting like this is fucking normal.* Because for Grady, and my father, this shit is normal.

Grady has no idea, with our father dead in the ground, this new game—one he doesn't even know about, and one that I'm going to lead—has only just begun. For now, I need this asshole to be clear about a few things, and the only way to do that with Grady is make him believe my bullshit, and of course to draw some blood.

I eye him up and down. He eyes the gun. "Is this where I say to you that I can't believe you tried to shoot me?" I say to him, cooly, stepping even closer, gripping the gun tighter just in case.

He blinks, acting all innocent, and lies to my face. "Dude. That was an accident. The thing just went off. You were wrestling *me* for it."

He never sees it coming when I hit him on the side of his head with the gun, just exactly how and where he hit Jojo, and hopefully just as hard. It sends him to his knees, but unfortunately it doesn't knock him out how it did her.

"Fuck. Alex." Grady clutches his head, and then leans the weight of it onto his vehicle. "What the fuck? Ahhh...damn that hurt!"

Because I can't say what I want to say—or still do what I want to do—I stand over him like he's an insect on the ground, just how my father would have done.

"You would shame us, risk the Sinclair legacy for a

mother-fucking hard-on you've had for a girl that you've only ever wanted to fuck just because I fucked her first. Think about it, Grady. You know it's true. It's time for you to finally grow up. You have a fiancé. One that I've heard loves you—God knows why. A nice girl, and one I thought father had deemed 'of privilege enough' for you to marry. Don't you have a date set and she's already bought the damn dress? What would *she* have said about this?"

I gentle my voice some next. My father also used to do this. It made us feel as though he was on our side, when he never, ever was.

"I'm going to assume temporary insanity for you. Maybe we can even rationalize things more to say that you lost your shit here today, because you are *grieving the death of our father.*"

That last line was said sarcastically because he and I both know that's not the case. We haven't talked about it, but Grady has to be as elated as I am that Father's gone.

"You won't go near her again. The feud—this fucked up vengeance against anything and everything *Wallace*—it's over now. I've been named head of this family, whether you like it or not, and I'm assuming not. But that's the way it is, Grady. I'm calling the shots now."

I lock gazes with my brother, trying to find a person behind his angry black devil's eyes, and I add, "If you have any shred of soul left in your body after what we've been through, you'll understand that it just has to stop.

We've done enough to hurt this poor girl—and fuck, you and I've been fucked with enough. You have to decide who the fuck you are right now, and who are you going to be now that our *dear-old dad* is gone."

I point at Jojo's prone form. "You nearly raped her— even hinted to me that you were going to *kill* her. *What the fuck*, Grady!" I shout. "We've participated in some dark shit because of Father. We've been forced to field some big-time, horrible, fucked-up fly balls because of Father. But we've never actually been up to bat personally. Not on the level you just took it. Rape and murder. Grady. In one fucking day? Father still warm in the grave, and you're going for rape and murder? Really?"

Grady tightens his hands over where I've struck his head and at least has the decency to look away from me as I finish, "For you and I to go forward at all...for me to let you live," I flash the gun again. "Tell me you lost your mind here today. " My voice accidentally comes out rough, showing too much emotion. "Please. Even if it's a damn lie. Tell me what I need to hear."

Grady brings himself up to his knees; the fact that he looks like he's about to pray for forgiveness in a church makes me feel one notch better.

"Yes," he utters, eyes on the gun in my hand. "Yeah. I —I didn't think it through. *Shit.* Maybe you're right. I lost my fucking mind." This time when he glances at Jojo there is some regret there, and the lust has gone out of his pained expression. "I did lose it. I did, Alex. But Jojo —I know you know. I've just always wished..." He swallows. "*Fuck*...it wasn't fair. Understand that I only ever wanted Jojo, too."

I almost laugh then, because unknowingly my brother has just said my whole essence. My whole heart. My whole reason for being.

I only ever wanted Jojo, too.

Fuck. Why do I feel sorry for my brother all over again? He's right. It wasn't fair.What happened to him, what Father did to him, to me...to Jojo, to her whole family—none of it was fair.

Even more fucked up than that? This moment—this day—is the first conversation my brother and I have ever had about all the messed up things and all of the longing—the hurt we have in common.

We talk in shouts and grunts while Jojo Wallace's wrecked body is broken and immobile at our feet.

Fuck! Father would have loved to watch and hear all of this unfold. He'd smile that pleased smile of his and be so proud that Grady and I were somehow bonding at the foot of a broken Wallace girl.

He did always want us to do that.

I want to scream. I want to sob. I want the earth to swallow me, Jojo and Grady whole with fire and lightning right now. That would mean the hurting—the horror of who we are and what we can't help but do to Jojo Wallace—would finally stop.

As though even now her mind is connected to mine, she moans and turns on her side away from us. She reaches a hand into the dirt and scoots a half inch away before falling limp again. Even like this she's still fighting, still so very afraid.

My chest twists so hard with that last thought that it's easy for me to punch Grady again. He crumples back into his car, cursing and nearly sobbing.

"Jojo's truly off limits, got me?" I say again, waiting for him to open his eyes before I say the rest. "You try to touch her again, you're dead. You try to kill me again —*ever*—you die first."

"Got you. Shit. Alex...*okay*. I'm sorry. Dude, I'm sorry. I said it—just stop."

Grady must really think I've stepped into Father's boots. At the reading of the will, they announced me as head of the family. He couldn't believe it even though father had been hinting at it for years. I didn't want it— something Father knew. I hinted to our mother that Grady and I could swap roles in the company eventually. I thought of stepping down from Sinclair Enterprises completely.

But based on my brother's behavior, it's best he doesn't have everything at his disposal. I'm where I need to be right now. I need to make him believe that I mean to carry on Father's legacy to the letter to protect Jojo, because after reading Michael Sinclair's plans to empty the aquifer—including my lake—just so he can have access to the oil underneath our feet, I'm going to need to stay head of this family while I try to figure out how to reverse the horrible wheels that are already turning at Sinclair Enterprises to make that happen.

"Just do your Goddamned job and be a good Sinclair, would you?" I finish with familiar words.

He glares up at me. "You might be the smart one, Alex. But I've always been the better Sinclair, no matter what your new job title might be. I am, and always have been, the best Sinclair son." He smirks.

I hate that he's not as submissive as I'd hoped. Yes, Grady is, and was, the better Sinclair. The fact that he's still proud of that after what he's just done to a 125-pound girl—after how I thought maybe he'd listen and try to change—triggers me even more.

It takes only one more punch to finally knock my asshole brother out cold.

Fuck me.

Fuck my life, and fuck my damn fucked up family.

AFTER I'M sure Grady's truly out and no longer a threat, I get to Jojo's side and try to rouse her. "Jojo. Jojo… you're safe," I say again and again when she doesn't wake up. She only moans more.

"Safe…okay? No one is going to hurt you. *Safe*," I repeat, hoping that somehow my words are getting to her. I try to speak softly, but I swear she still winces.

I wipe a small trail of blood from the wound on her temple where the gun broke the skin, then I pause to move her bag under her head. I still have things to do before I can pick her up, and I can't bear to see her cheek ground into the dirt. I also can't focus as I look at her tattered blouse, or note the way the shredded bra she's wearing was once more lace.

Feeling guilty for even having that thought inside my head, I quickly peel off my shirt and cover her with it. "Hang on, Jojo. Hang on, you're safe...*safe*," I whisper again.

Looking around, I first pocket the gun, vowing to throw it in the lake so neither of these two idiots can ever use it again. Then I carefully pick up all of JoJo's belongings that had scattered out of her bag. A lipstick. A whole mess of different colored hairbands. A small pack of tissues. What looks like a tiny photo album. Her phone and the deed papers she just worked so hard to find. It all goes into a pile and then back into her bag.

Scooping up the rental car keys, I think I have everything, until I catch a glint of metal out of the corner of my eye that's attached to a scrap of Jojo's pink blouse fabric.

I reach for it, but instead of it being lightweight like I'd expected, the thing has weight to it. A weight I recognize.

It's the lure. The sight of it makes me break out into a cold sweat.

It's the wing-shaped, engraved lure I gave her for a homecoming gift sophomore year. It's the lure I gave to her on that last day—that last day before I knew what Father had been planning, before I was brought in to it all against my will. This old piece of metal symbolizes the last day she and I were truly in love, the last day my love for her was innocent and so beautiful. I flip it over and read the word FOREVER engraved on the back of it along with our initials.

Forever.

I'd made one for her and one for me. I pinned this one on her corsage and gave it to her just before the dance. God...how fucking free and happy and in love I was that day. How stupid I'd been...with father and even Grady laughing at me behind my back for two years. They were just toying with Jojo, and all the while laughing at me.

She was wearing this. She's *been* wearing this, but how? It's been tied onto our old fishing rods for years.

To get it, she must have gone to my father's boathouse, because this lure is something I have stared at, at least once a month since she left.

My heart slams more pain into my chest as I place the lure into her purse then stand to pop her trunk, my heart nearly stopping at the sight of our fishing rods bent and intertwined together inside.

She stole these. She went to my father's boathouse, and took this part of our past. Somehow she did this and I didn't see. Why would she go there? And why didn't I know about?

Will's accusations come back into my mind. If she could sneak up to my parents' house and take these, she could have easily snuck up to my father on a Tacoma street.

Did she show up here to pop a bullet in my father's head? Is Jojo as much of a monster now as the rest of us? Has she changed that much?

Would I care if she had?

Slamming the trunk closed, I toss her purse in the back seat and hurry to scoop up the woman I love with shaking arms to hold her close to me. For a moment I just stand there with her, waiting for my warmth to sink into her cold—waiting to feel her heartbeat next to my skin. With my brother now starting to move and the desolation of her family's farm behind me, I place her gingerly in the backseat of her rental car and her head lolls back on the seat. "Alex?" she whispers and I nearly start crying with relief that she's talking. That she knows it's me. "You came."

"Shh. Hell yes, I came. Did you think I could stay away. I'm just glad I came in time…" I place one of her slim arms into the arm of my shirt, lean her forward, drag the shirt around her back, and get her other arm in. I pull it tight over her front.

"Grady. He tried…he was going to…"

"I know. He won't do it again. Lie down," I command. "I'm going to drive you home."

She complies, closing her eyes and curling onto her side.

Just before I drive away, I yank Grady's wallet out of his back pocket and shove it in my pants next to the gun. Then, I dial 911 on Grady's phone and throw it in the dirt next to my brother who's only just coming to as a woman on the other end says, "Nine-one-one, what's your emergency?"

I make my voice low, scratchy and unidentifiable, as I utter toward the phone, "This is Grady Sinclair. I've been robbed, out at the old Wallace place...some vagrants beat me up."

I figure that's enough. The Tacoma police will know where to go. Everyone knows the old Wallace place. I know Grady will make up a good lie about what happened—how he got the bruises. I also know he won't say it was me.

We Sinclairs don't rat each other out.

We just kill each other.

Pain for pain...

21.

ALEX, PRESENT DAY.

I drive Jojo to my house—to the lake.

Our house. Our lake.

I built the whole thing for her next to our lake while picturing her reactions to it. She was behind every choice I made, from the all-glass front with self-tinting windows, to the angle of the views. She was in every damn detail, like the hand-wrought iron door knobs I ordered from a local welder because Jojo had once told me she wished the world still had a blacksmith in every town.

I chose black for the marble slabs on the floor because it was so reflective that depending on the light, the branches from the trees outside look like they're inside the house. I knew Jojo would have loved that.

The granite I picked for what Jojo and her mother had called the *heart of a house*—the kitchen—was called Black Taurus. It's a rare, dark shining stone that reminded me of Jojo's hair when it was wet while swimming in the lake. It has these deep, brown ribbons streaking through the black. Like her...it's beautiful.

The heart of this house had to remind me of the happiest moments of my life, and because I'd wanted it to have parts of the happiest times of her life as well, I painstakingly went to the Wallace farm, the burnt out Wallace farm, and secretly took out any shiplap and bead board that had been in Mrs. Wallace's kitchen. Every little piece that still looked like wood came back here. I had someone sand and repaint the parts that could be salvaged back to the original weathered white, and then I attached them together onto one big display wall.

It's a constant reminder of what I'd been a part of, and maybe a very sadistic way to torture myself daily about my guilt, but I knew that if she could have been here and if she could have sorted through the ruble herself, she would have taken each and every piece that I took. She'd have done something with it, too.

The marble tub off of my bathroom is white—a stark contrast to all of the black. I had it built for two. I placed it so it faces my huge back porch, overlooking our favorite rock and the swimming hole. The wall behind that tub is a fine inlaid mosaic work of aquamarine, blue and clear glass with sterling silver overlaid with a few genuine turquoise stones.

Not one mosaic tile is bigger than the top of a pencil eraser, and it took almost a full week to lay them out just right. I'd overseen the placement of each tile, and nearly drove the artist insane. This collective combination of blues, greens and hints of silver and clear glass was as close as I could get to matching the color of Jojo's eyes. That wall is one of my few secret pleasures, and I love being inside that tub, floating and remembering our happiest times.

Those eyes flicker open and then close again when I place her gently on the king-sized bed. "You okay?" I whisper? She doesn't answer, only scrunches her face. I can hardly believe she's here—in my home—on my bed, and hurt again. Hurt again, because of me.

Inside and out...ever wounded. All at the hands of a Sinclair.

I hit the button on my bedside that darkens the windows. The smoked-opaque color allows those inside to still look out but makes it so no one who might be lurking outside could ever see inside.

I leave the room to make a quick call to my friend who is a doctor to ask him questions about head injuries, then I persuade him to be on call for me personally should Jojo have a turn for the worse. I can sense he thinks it's me that has the injury, and he's itching to ask more questions, but that's the beauty of being a Sinclair. People are curious, yes, but they actually don't want to know too much or be too involved, so he holds quiet.

When I return to the room, despite her closed eyes, I

can tell she's awake. She's lying there, breathing like she's trying so hard to get herself together. So am I.

There is no going back now. Lines have been crossed, and re-crossed. Fuck, lines have been obliterated. I don't know who to be right now. Am I the man who pushed her away, who's supposed to hate her and who still needs her to leave town as soon as possible, or the man who loves her so much he can hardly breathe, who desperately wants her to stay?

I think of the lure: *forever...forever...forever.*

When she still doesn't talk, I go sit next to her, testing the spot on her temple that's the most bruised. I'm unable to resist smoothing back the curling edges of her hair. I shiver because the softness is so achingly familiar.

"Ouch. That hurts."

I startle and leap back. "Sorry." My hand flexes not sure what to do now. I want to touch her more. I don't want to hurt her.

"Don't be. Please. You only startled me." Her voice is thick and gravelly.

I gently move back to the bed, but I resist touching her again. "I'll ask you again. Are you...okay? Say something...let me know."

"I don't know what to say, past thanking you for saving me, which is obvious probably." She rolls on to her side to look at me, and her face is ghost-white pale, her skin broken, scratched with little bits of dried blood everywhere. "I know you well enough to know it's only going to make you worry if I tell you I'm not really okay right now. But...I'm not going to lie. I'm sort of not... okay." One tear sneaks out and rolls down her pale cheek.

Fuck.

I keep my face straight. My heart cracks wide open. I manage to point a finger at the airspace over all of her injuries. "Would you let me clean you up some?"

She nods.

I swallow, then watch her wince as she moves. "How bad does it hurt?" I ask.

"My pride, or my head? Or my heart? Or my whole body? It all aches too bad for me to own up to how much. But I'll survive." She breathes out a laugh, but it's short-lived and catching like it hurts to even do that.

Fuck. Fuck!

My throat is closing. My world is turned upside down. I do not know what to do here. Just keep loving her, I think, but damn, my defenses are too lowered. I can't love her how I do and not let her see how I feel. It's still so dangerous.

I turn my face away from her probing, questioning stare and stalk away to my adjoining bathroom. "I've got something to help. Might help some of the head pain at least." I pull out the bottle of Tylenol mixed with Codeine that I stockpile from Canada. Taking out one extra above the recommended dose, I then walk to the kitchen to fill a glass full of cold water for her. I also pour some of the good, 60-year-old scotch into a glass before I return to her side.

To her...waiting for me, in my bed...in our house. Fuck... it's a dream; it's a nightmare; it's all I ever wanted.

When I return, she lets me help prop her back against some stacked pillows and utters a small *thank you*, like she understands I need to physically be part of making her better right now.

I take a swig of the scotch and hand her the pills as well as the glass of water. "Take them. They'll help with swelling."

She pulls the drink out of my hand. "Okay." She takes the pills without even looking at them, coughing some at the strength of the scotch before handing it back.

I'm instantly, irrationally annoyed and worried, catapulted into the past. "Aren't you going to ask me what I just gave you? Christ, JoJo, I could have fed you poison just now and—and you shouldn't take those with alcohol."

"Alex." She starts up again, after drinking half of the water to pacify me. "It feels like lifetimes have passed us by." I nod as she continues. "But I think I still might know you better than anyone ever did." She settles back against the pillows and sighs. "You...don't hurt me on purpose. Not then...not now. Not you."

Her eyelids flutter closed, and I move close again to stare at her wan, exhausted face. I notice the dark circles that tell me she probably hasn't slept much since the funeral. The deep crease between her eyes and the way her nose is pinched in tells me her head is hurting more than she's letting on, and that I should have given her pills sooner.

"Back then you never knew the real me," I protest. "And considering these past few days you can't say that anymore. I *do* hurt you on purpose. It's what I am and what I am born to do and what I have done. It's what I will do more of if you stay here." The words have burned their way up my throat, and the moment they're said, I feel the thud of the lie hammering my chest.

Like she's calling me out on it, Jojo answers in a whisper, eyes still closed. "Shut up, Alex. I already have a headache."

Her familiarity, talking like we don't have walls between us at all has me wavering hard. I want to drop on my knees and pull her into my arms and tell her just how much I've missed her. I push toward my ultimate goal. "I'm serious. If you stay here in Tacoma, it will be impossible for me not to do it again. I know you found the documents—I know you now understand just how fucked up the relationship between your mom and my father truly was. You can have no reason to stay here any longer. None. I'm asking you to go. Ordering it! If you stay, you'll only find out more and be hurt worse."

My body continues to react to her. It's electric with indecision—*hold her close and keep her safe, or push her far away right now.*

She doesn't answer to what I've said. She just opens

her kaleidoscope eyes, drawing me in to her blue—her silver—her beauty, her clarity—her truths, not mine.

I also know *her* better than anyone ever did. I can read her thoughts. She never could hide her expressions.

She's saying what she's always said to me with that dead-set chin, her straight shoulders, and that penetrating stare. She's trying to reassure me that I'm not a monster. She's silently telling me that I'm not my father.

I can hardly breathe as tears sneak from her eyes. I feel frozen, watching her blink them away, and I swear I can taste the salt of them on my own tongue and feel my own tears threatening at the edges of my eyes.

Damn her for being able to strip me raw like this. She's looking at me like she still loves me.

Her small hand clamps around mine as I try to bolt, and it's ice cold. My gaze drifts down to where my hand, my heat, is already warming her skin.

"Will you stay—close? Sit here with me. At least until the pills start working? Please."

I'VE STEPPED AWAY to pour another scotch because if she gets to be in a stupor during this reunion, or whatever it is, then I deserve the same.

I also grab a small bowl of warm water and a stack of fresh soft towels before sitting next to her again and reaching for her outstretched hand to give it a squeeze to alert her that I've returned, as promised.

Right away I know this is a mistake.

I try get my hand out of hers again but her fingers have twined to latch only around my thumb—her special way of holding my hand since the first day we rode the bus together in high school. Every bit of ice I've tried to keep around my heart is instantly melted.

"Thank you," she says. "I can't stomach being alone right now."

"Yeah….sure," I manage to speak. My hand involuntarily covers the top of hers to tuck her delicate fingers into my palm.

When she squeezes back and breathes out a deep sigh like she's relaxing, I'm struck by how this simple handhold was so damn easy. Too familiar. Maybe our minds are fighting this, but our bodies obviously know this feels right.

"What if I hadn't been there?" I whisper my thoughts out loud as I start to relax enough to replay what went down with Grady.

That question is the only thing that exists in the room for several long minutes, as I'm sure she's replaying it all, too.

"Alex. You _were_ there. You were always there." She's trying to soothe me—still trying to shelter me and prove that I'm a hero instead of a villain.

I watch her other hand move up to her head. Her fingers dance across her wounded and now bruised temple, fingertips examining the small scratches on the side of her face while I gingerly take my hand out of hers and dip one of the towels into the warm water and begin to wash off the dried blood.

"I must look like hell, huh?" She pulls the covers up to her chin, shivering some as I go over the worst part of where she was clocked with the gun.

When I can't answer because she's so damn fragile to me right now, I pause and get the tumbler of scotch to my lips and take a huge swig.

She reaches over and pulls it away from me and sips it. We pass it back and forth like that, until it's gone, then she stares down at the empty tumbler, rattling the ice cubes like she needs something to do.

I realize I've never seen Jojo drink before. We were too young, and she was too good.

When she left here, she was a kid. A complete straight-edge kid who wouldn't even sip off of a beer because she didn't like the taste and because she never wanted to disappoint the memories of her mom and dad who would not have wanted her drinking underage.

I can't squelch a surge of anger.

I wanted to be the one who took her out partying on her twenty-first birthday. Me. What the fuck else have I missed?

Like she, too, feels like we were robbed, the weight of six years we will never get back crackling in the air between us, she holds up the glass and says, "Got any more of this stuff?"

"I don't think you should drink too much with the pills I gave you."

"The pain is already going away. I feel...good.

Relaxed." She smiles, looking around. I hold my breath waiting for her to notice things. "It's the world's most comfortable bed. What is this place? Is it yours?"

Her eyes are going around the room. She's a little dazed. No...she's buzzed and she has no clue where I've driven her.

"My house."

I don't say more, and instead only glance nervously at the now darkened windows. The sun has long set, so she can't see outside. I wonder if it would hurt or make her happy to know where this house sits.

"Is this your bedroom? And...thanks for giving me your shirt. I'm assuming this is yours?" Her questions are tumbling out, and suddenly she's slurring a bit. Her smile goes crooked in a cute, pain killer induced, drunken happy kind of way.

"Yes. And yes." I feel raw, trying to answer her. "And please don't thank me...for any of it."

"You always hated that." She puts her arm next to her nose and sniffs deeply into my shirt. "I can smell you on the sheets and your shirt is like you, too. All fresh...and good." Her brows shoot up. "Wait. I know this smell. It's that green striped soap bar we used to laugh about, isn't it?"

"Irish Spring. Yes." I bite back a small smile. "And it was only you laughing about my soap obsession. I still take that soap very seriously. *Manly fresh* is a constant for me."

She laughs, peals of it then, and so it doesn't bring

me to my knees, I busy myself by washing out the scotch glass back in the bathroom. I don't deserve to make jokes and laugh with her. I don't deserve to swim in good memories.

"Remember? Oh God, how we used to laugh." She giggles more.

"Yes. I remember," I say, my voice serious to push away the joy.

I have to get away from her smelling my shirt and smiling as she remembers us. Just the sight of her wearing my clothes that I should have taken the time to button better is torture. I need to get my thoughts off of how she's just right here, lying on my bed, surrounded by her glorious tousled, curling sexy hair—hair that also smells exactly how she used to smell. Damn her lavender oils and whatever she stole from the moon to make it glow and stream across my pillow like it's as alive as she is.

I return from the bathroom, clutching the crystal scotch glass like it's a fucking shield in front of me. My eyes skim over her face until I'm staring at the way her upper lip is just a little bit fuller than her lower lip, and I remember how I used to love to...

"If you're okay now," I grit out and start to step backwards. "If nothing hurts anymore then I think you should...sleep."

My breath is no longer working, and my voice is sandpaper and my body has transformed into pure wanting.

Just like before, I already know what she's going to do to me next. Instead of doing what she should, and letting me go, she says, "Alex. Maybe this it too much to ask, but could you please stay. Like *really* stay." She pats the bed. "I'd sleep so much better if you did. I can't get the images out of my head from what happened...and...I know it's too much, but...could you, until I fall asleep? Like old times?"

My defenses fall.

It's something she used to ask of me back in high school.

She'd say it when things got really bad because my father and my brother would deliberately try to hurt her —she said it after homecoming. After Grady and his teammates had torn up her dress, scared her. Scared me even worse. And of course, back then, I said yes. I held her until she fell asleep, and then I cried my fucking eyes out.

The next night, after homecoming—after I knew the deal, after my father and Grady had *brought me in* and I learned there was no way out for me—I'd held her again. I cried my eyes out again. But that second time was all for me.

Father and Grady, as the months passed by, would plan out this endless taunting and torture of Jojo. They'd time this shit to the minute. Grady would make sure I was away from her, but nearby enough to run in and rescue her. It was always last minute, like five minutes before the school bell, or he'd track me going into the bathroom and then pounce on Jojo, scaring her again, and again. Sometimes, he would create freak *accidents* where she actually did get hurt.

Then they'd let me swoop in and be the hero. They always let me pick up Jojo's pieces. I'd hold her, put her back together, and try to make her forget, try to thwart the next time. But eventually, I'd fail at that.

The memories are too much. Suddenly, I'm fourteen again, and I'm grinning about the gift of the lake. I'm fifteen asking my father for money to get the lures engraved. It's sophomore year, and I'm telling Mr. Wallace that I'll never, ever hurt his daughter—not ever —and believing it. I'm staring into Mrs. Wallace's eyes and seeing the contract my father and she made. That letter she wrote, Jojo's mom and my fucking father, how they brought me into the room to oversee the signatures. How I was tasked to get the document recorded in the city and county offices.

As much as Jojo's life was fucked, this was a whole lifetime of me being set up by my own father. Fucked over by my own mother who sat there and smiled and said nothing. Year after year of my own brother never giving me the heads up that another bullshit *accident* was about to go down, never once having my back.

Me being tricked, me being played by them all time after time—this was my destiny.

Always the end result was Jojo got hurt. That endless feeling that I needed to be better, faster—smarter than my damn Father—so I could stop it washes over me.

That pressure to try harder to beat Father at his own game ate me alive. I felt that if I could just be man enough, or tough enough, surely Jojo wouldn't get hurt anymore.

I was never fucking able to do it. I know I was just a kid back then, that what I'd wanted inside my heart was impossible. My father had backup, money and minions. *So many fucking minions!* From the police to the damn school principal who didn't intervene that first time Jojo was attacked by Grady. He was just there—watching. Watching!

Worse, any interventions or arguments on my part about what had gone down became a lesson learned the hard way. Any resistance on my part would only result in more and bigger pain for Jojo.

That Wallace girl.

That's what he always called Jojo. Never used her name.

The night Father brought me into the family plan was the day after sophomore homecoming. The night my *before* turned into a horrible, horrible *after*. How it went down, how he sent Grady in to do his dirty work, how he messed up my head permanently, is something I'll never forget. Something I try every day to shake, to undo or unmake.

But I can't do it. I am who I am, and it went down exactly as he planned it. His plan was perfection—despicably perfect.

That night, sophomore homecoming night, I grew

up. Father welcomed me into the family, and explained exactly what my new role in the household was to be.

When I fought him on it, because I did try, Father made sure I paid for it. He made sure Jojo paid for it, and made sure I could never get out of being a Sinclair ever again. He destroyed my soul.

I'm stuck here. A devil. A monster. My father's son. After what I've done, what I couldn't stop from happening, I'm a good Sinclair.

Through and through.

22.

JOJO, SOPHOMORE YEAR,
HOMECOMING.

"You look nice in that dress. Like a hot little thing..."

I jump at Grady's voice and turn, conscious of how my A-line dress sways at my knees. I sip at my punch, bad at taking complements, even from Grady, who just nearly made me ruin my dress by sneaking up behind me and whispering all awkwardly into my ear.

"Thanks," I say, pulling my lips away from the plastic cup just enough to smile politely and step away from him.

Grady nods and shoves his hands in his suit jacket pockets. "You also look nice," I say, paying back his complement, but I can't help but step away from him again. He's got on so much cologne it's sucking away the real air in the room. I want to trust him. He and I have gotten along lately. A nice change from last year when he was just a smirking jerk or bully to me most of the time.

Maybe it's because I've been telling Alex he should try to get along with his brother more—maybe they finally are getting along. I bet Grady sees how hard I'm working on their relationship, so he's trying to turn over a new leaf.

"You come here with a date?" I ask, noticing that every other girl in the gym so far seems to be linked up with another guy.

Grady shrugs. "Why commit? These dances always seem to work out for me better if I don't bring a date. Then I can be with everyone." He winks, and it makes me giggle.

"Care to dance?" He's holding his arm out like a knight in shining armor, and I make him wait a few seconds so I can scan the room for Alex first, because this is a slow dance finally, and I've been waiting to slow dance with Alex.

I don't think he will like me dancing with Grady. But it's just a friendly dance between *friends*. Besides, if I turn Grady down, he'll get all irritated like he does and might flip back to the old Grady. And maybe...just maybe...Alex will appear, and see that Grady isn't so bad, and that maybe we are *all* capable of being mature adults now that we're growing up.

"Come on." His smile deepens.

"Sure." I take Grady's arm, leaving my empty cup on the table edge as I follow him out into the middle of the dance floor. He holds his arms out in a way that forces distance between us, and I breathe out in relief, smiling at him. He's being such a gentleman, and I know it's because he wants to show Alex he respects me—and respects him.

We start to sway, and it becomes easier to hold his gaze with mine.

"You're a good dancer, Grady." I feel my cheeks redden with my awkward attempt at conversation. He quickly sets me at ease, though.

"Thanks. Our mom makes us take lessons. She makes us go to cotillion where we practice manners and shit. Junior League is her life. She expects us to go to some debutante ball when we're eighteen and pick suitable wives." He leans in, hands suddenly holding me too tight, his breath too hot and too close to my face, the cologne stifling. "Last I heard, you mom isn't in the Junior League, is she?"

"Junior League? No. I don't know what that is." I try to pull back away from him but he's holding on tight.

"Of course you don't."

I blink, filling with doubt because…is he laughing at me now? The way he's looking at me is so smug, and what he's said about there being some big *ball* planned out in the future where he and Alex would choose brides makes me feel small, stupid and really confused.

To avoid his penetrating gaze, I look down at our feet. I'm suddenly ashamed of my pearly white painted toes. Maybe mom and I shouldn't have added the glitter on each one how we did. It feels too childish all of a sudden. I'd thought at first my toes looked like diamonds, but now, under all of these lights, they're just messy.

"I'll cut in now, if that's cool." My heart skips a few beats, and my feet stumble on hearing Alex's voice. I've accidentally stepped on Grady's foot. I look up to catch him wince, but he masks it quickly and steps away from me.

"Sure thing, Bro. We were just waiting on you. I didn't want anyone else messing with your girl." Grady winks at me oddly then holds my gaze intently as he hands me over to Alex. I bury my embarrassed face in my boyfriend's neck.

"God. I missed you," I say, muffling my words into his shoulder, not resisting as Alex dance-pulls me into the center of the other couples. "What's the Junior League?"

"Nothing. Less than nothing, okay?" Alex frowns down at me when I look up. "Is that what Grady was talking to you about? He's such an asshole. Forget anything he said, okay? He likes to make drama where there should be none." He pulls me close, and I breathe in the soapy smell of him. "Let's just dance."

"And dance, and dance," I agree.

He rocks me, and it's such a relief to have his arms around me with Grady long gone that I follow his steps easily. We've been together so much. It's always so warm and intimate inside of Alex's arms when we dance. I could fall asleep in this small space where the collar of his shirt and jacket lapel end and his skin begins.

I think about kissing it lightly for several long seconds before finally opening my mouth just enough to take a small taste. And then another.

"Never dance with Grady again, okay? I don't like him touching you."

I stiffen at Alex's terse words, a little hurt that instead of swooning and leaning into my kisses, or kissing me back, or whispering stuff we are going to do later while pressing his hardness against me—which is what my kisses usually bring about—he's thinking about Grady.

Total mood killer.

"He wasn't being a creep or anything," I frown, but stop when I feel him pull away enough to look at me hard. "I'm serious. Grady, in his way—I think he was being nice for once."

"Impossible. It's not in him to be nice."

His eyes penetrate mine, and they're filled with such lonely sadness that I get sad, too. Alex often talks to me about his family being different, but it's just so hard for me to understand.

Eventually his face softens, and the side of his mouth ticks up as he pulls me in close again. "I'm sorry. You're right. I was being lame—jealousy is not a good thing."

My lips pull in, puckering against the urge to smile, but I can't hide it for long.

"You, Alex Sinclair, should never be jealous. No other

boy could compare, especially not..." I shudder, and add in a little eye roll. "Grady."

His chest quakes with a silent laugh and he presses his lips on my forehead, wrapping his arms around me tighter. He holds me like this for three songs in a row—even for the fast songs—until Grady taps him on his shoulder and whispers something in his ear.

"Okay...ummm...just stay here, Jojo. I've gotta help him with something, but I'll be right back."

Alex squeezes my arms firmly and rushes off through the crowded dance floor following Grady.

I'm left alone under the spinning disco ball and the blue and purple crepe-paper flowers the student council hung from the ceiling. Before long, I start to feel the stares of the couples looking at me lingering out here alone.

"Excuse me." I cut through the crowd, making my way back to the chairs that line the room. I look for a new cup to get another drink of punch, but can't find any, so I move to the table of treats and pick at a few of the cookie wrappers, settling on the sugar one shaped like a heart.

A few of the popular girls move around me, looking me up and down and laughing. One of them holds her fingers to her lips while the other pours what looks like vodka into the punch. I smile like I'm in on the secret, but the moment they walk away I roll my eyes at how cliche they are. I'm also glad I had some of the punch before they ruined it.

I nibble on my cookie through an entire song and a half, and I begin to worry where Alex has gone when I spot Grady weaving back toward me through the crowd.

"Jojo, you gotta come." He shouts to me. "Alex got in a fight with some guy who's been talking shit about us. He's hurt...hurt bad..."

My pulse begins to thump wildly. "Okay, where?" I'm already running after him when I ask.

He just motions with his hand and rushes through the hallway door that leads to the back of the school. My mind imagines Alex hurt, his face bruised and bloodied, red staining the crisp white of his nice shirt and the gray of his suit. I want to kill whoever ruined our night, and my hand instinctively forms a fist at my side as we bust through the doors to the maintenance area.

The stench of the dumpsters hits my nose first, but the very next thing I feel is the swift jerk on the bottom of my dress.

"It *is* some sort of freak polyester. No wonder it's so shiny. So tacky! It's not even satin...or silk." A blonde girl I recognize as one of the cheerleaders holds the long shred of my dress she just tore off of me up to the yellow light. "We should donate this to science."

"Hey! I can't believe you just tore my dress!" I hear a round of laughter and realize there's a whole crowd out here.

Half the football team at least, it looks like, and those girls who spiked the punch as well. Is that why they looked me up and down like that, to come out here and help this girl criticize my dress? I note that they don't have just a little vodka, they have a whole bottle of vodka that's so big it's got a handle fused into it making it look like a glass gallon of milk. Keeping my back to the mean girls, I turn to Grady, who's smiling at me oddly. "Where's Alex?" I demand, and scan past the laughing faces. I search for Alex lying somewhere out here on the ground.

"Grady?"

My heart begins thumping.

I spin and push at the girl who seems to be trying to grab my dress once more. My eyes roam the space around me and land on Grady again, pleading for help, hoping he will take up with this crazy girl. I wait for him to defend my honor.

He isn't Alex.

It takes a few seconds for me to realize that he's not going to. He's not going to stand up for me at all, because this girl—these girls—and the guys who are out here with them, are all moving in closer to me, as though they're all about to rip at my dress until it's gone. They'd planned to do this, and Grady's in charge.

"I can't believe you fell for that shit. Alex is fine." Grady pulls a big swig off the vodka bottle as it comes around. He holds the bottle out to me while he runs the sleeve of his coat over his mouth.

"Come on; we're just joking around. Have a drink with us. Alex wanted me to get you out here. He and I think that dance is lame. We all just want to have a little party. Be entertained, maybe by you? What do you say?"

"What?" My eyes dart around, like prey caught in the cites of a dozen rifles, but my hand reaches nervously for the bottle, because I think I should play along until I can get away from these jerks. "Why would you let that girl tear my dress?"

"Why not? Ooops!" Grady reaches out and tears my dress more, yanking another swath from the skirt, then he flings some of the vodka at me, laughing as he shouts. "She smells like a liquor store!"

I run my hand along my damp cheek and watch as the vodka soaks into my dress. My face ticks with humiliation and the threat of tears. I won't cry, though. I won't. Not here—not in front of these people.

Where is Alex?

The taunts start to come hard and fast, blurred by the drumbeat of my pulse in my ears.

Some brunette girl calls out, "What does Alex see in her? Her legs are so scrawny and scratched up. Is that a giant skinned knee under a BandAid? What are you, six years old?"

"Alex says she likes to play in the mud with him," Grady says, yanking then snapping the thin strap of my dress off one shoulder. I start to get afraid—really afraid. "Do you like to play...dirty, dirty games with my little brother? Or do you just play in the dirt."

"What? No!" He tears the other strap off. "Grady. Stop!"

Horrified, and feeling sick, I hold my bodice up with both hands, and I try to run but the crowd presses in more. Two of Grady's football friends have grabbed my shoulders and hold me fast.

"She's so trashy. Alex was supposed to be my homecoming date." The blonde girl comes to take the vodka bottle out of Grady's hands and drinks a big swig of it, coughing some, and handing it off to one of the other leering football players, before saying, "And oh my God, her shoes look like sandals a little girl would wear—and all of that glitter. Maybe Alex is a pedo."

"They aren't. They're new…we bought them today!"

She laughs through my pathetic defense, and that twinge hits my eyes again.

"Blue light special at the dollar store?" the girl adds.

I jerk my foot and try to kick out when I feel her tug at the strap along my ankle as though she's trying to break it, all while I'm trying to simultaneously squirm out of these football guys' grip. "Let me go, or I'm going to scream!"

Grady calls out, "Cover her damn mouth with your hand, idiot."

A meaty hand clamps over the lower half of my face, and I struggle against it, twisting and jerking my head violently. The force of the hand grows harder.

"You made her dress uneven when you tore it, Grady. You too, Brooke. Poor little thing." The blonde girl approaches again. "Here, let me fix you."

I feel my skirt jerk the opposite direction, and more material rips off of me.

I fight and kick as they all approach, and I hear Grady calling out, "Damn, but she's hot as fuck under this dress. I've never gotten a hard on from granny panties before, but, Jojo, every time you kick your leg high, I'm so ready to fuck you. And just when I didn't think you did anything for me at all." His laughter turns more wicked, making the guys holding me too tight also laugh nervously.

The girl—the blonde, drunk one—wrinkles her nose and looks away from me to the big trashcans and says, "It would be appropriate, trash next to trash, but I wouldn't. You could pick up a lot of bacteria from the trash...just saying."

I realize that they've torn half of my skirt away, all the way to my skin. My bodice is in tatters, and some-one's meaty hands are going after the strapless bra I borrowed from my mom. The smell of alcohol is thick. "Let's see what else she's got to offer before we decide."

I whip my head around. It's Grady. Grady's tearing at my bra! I get my mouth free, biting at the hand on my face. "No. Stop it. Stop!"

My arms shiver, and my vision grows glossy, and I swear to God I've looked up and seen our school's prin-cipal standing by the back door just looking out the square glass. I swear he's just watching what's happening to me, watching and not intervening. These people—they get away with murder. "Help me. Help!" I call out, but when I look up again his face is gone. Maybe I just imagined it.

One of the football guys starts running his hand around the front of where they've torn my dress, like he's going to grab my chest, but before he does, Grady steps up and slaps his hand away, hard.

"Dude. What the fuck? That tit is a Sinclair tit. It belongs to my family. You get to watch. That's it! Watch and learn—never, ever touch." Grady sneers at me, his own eyes hot and fixed on my chest. His whiskey breath lands on my ear, and he's panting like some sort of animal.

"You little whore. Now you're going to put out for me, just like you do for my brother."

"What the fuck, Grady!"

It's Alex. He's here.

"What the fuck!" I recognize Alex's voice; he's shouting.

I bite the hand that's over my mouth again, hard. The guy barks while stuff—trash cans, plastic food buckets, some metal milk crates, and even a big metal dolly— starts flying in every direction. Everyone scatters—some of them screaming because random objects hit them— and suddenly the principal who I thought was watching me is actually here. He's shouting along with Alex—he's on my side. "What are you young people doing out here? Drinking?"

I eye the scratches and bruises the stupid football players left on my arms as I drop to my knees to pick up the largest part of my skirt that was torn off and get it tied around my chest like a funny halter to keep my dress in place now that there are no straps.

Alex looks like a madman, as crazy as Grady did a few moments ago. He right hooks his brother hard on the chin. It's a blow that sends him to the ground.

"You don't ever fucking touch her again. What's wrong with all of you? Who tore her dress? Jojo, you tell me who tore your dress?" Alex paces around me like a lion protecting a kill. Nearly everyone has bailed, but he's desperate to sink his teeth into someone.

And that's how I feel. Killed. Dead.

Like I want to die...so I don't answer him, I only breathe in and out, and try not to bawl.

Alex kicks Grady in the leg and lunges in to hit him again, but the principal stops Alex before he lands another huge punch.

"Everyone better clear the hell out of here and get back to the dance," our principal shouts. "Alex, you get this girl home. And Jojo, I'll be calling your parents to tell them what you were up to out here. You reek of alcohol. All of you, if you don't want the same phone calls to your houses, get out."

The small crowd around us has gone silent, and then like it never happened, everyone but me and Alex has gone. Even the principal has gone.

The only one who looks back at me is the blonde girl; she's grinning at me like this was the best fun she's had in years. I glare at her until she has to look away, but once she does, I start sobbing.

"Jojo, Jesus Christ I'm so sorry!" Alex has me wrapped up in his arms, and he's shaking so hard. He's crying, and I'm crying, and we're both checking each other over to make sure we're both all right. "I'll kill Grady. Just say so, and I'll do it."

I don't answer that. Instead, I tell him how I got out here. "Grady told me you were hurt. They told me you needed my help. When I got out here I was looking for you, but they all just...like...attacked me. They laughed at me." I start sobbing again.

In seconds, I'm wrapped up in Alex's suit jacket, and he's guiding me through a gate at the back of the school. "I was looking for *you*. Grady said you were in the ladies room. Fucker said that you were sick after he lured me out in the first place for some fake friend in trouble. There were two football seniors holding me hostage in the bathroom. They said it was all just a big prank going on and that they had to keep me there for exactly ten minutes. At minute five, I slammed one of them into the tile wall, head first. The other one ran when he saw the look in my eyes, and all of the blood coming out of his friend's head."

"He...your brother tricked us. Why would Grady do this?" I work to get my tears to stop, gulping air.

"He's jealous. I told you, he's not to be trusted. My family, it's not normal." Alex gasps out, trying to get control of his own emotions. "He won't touch you again.

I promise. I'm going to tell my father tonight. I'm going to get Grady punished for this. It goes against the Sinclair code of honor. You'll see. He will suffer for this. I'm sorry, Jojo. I'm so sorry."

"It wasn't your fault, Alex." I say to him.

Because it wasn't his fault.

Never his fault.

23.

ALEX, PRESENT DAY.

My father's face, and so many of my father's words about Jojo, tumble forward, punching and slamming into my temples as I lie in my bed, holding the now sleeping girl who I will never stop trying to save.

It's not often that I attempt to recall the words and the day everything changed. That's when my own utter betrayal happened. But with Jojo's discovery of her mother's letter—the document that sealed her fate as much as my birth sealed mine—and with her tears freshly dried on her cheeks, the comparison of her family's betrayals compared to mine are just as devastating.

The only difference? Her parents were good. They betrayed Jojo to keep her safe. Betrayed her out of a deep and endless well of love for her.

My father betrayed me, and Grady, over and over again because of sheer self interest. We were never children of parents in that traditional sense. In Father's mind, we were only his possessions, chess pieces toyed with all out of boredom and hate, not because he hated us per-se, but because hate is just who and what my father was.

I was an idealistic and introverted child when Father rekindled the feud. I was a kid who read too many good books about what life and love and family should look like. Reality snuck up on me, slithered in and wound itself into each and every day without my knowledge, so when I was finally informed of my duties, I had no escape.

In retrospect, my mother should be forgiven for never standing up for us. I haven't been successful in granting her forgiveness, though, because can you both forgive and hate someone at the same time? I can't seem to find the answer to that question.

My mother always turned a blind eye to everything that went down with Father. Telling myself that she was helpless to fight it, like me and Grady, helps me get through interactions with her. She was a puppet too, doing exactly what Father told her to and trying to survive. I used to scream at her. I'd cry and beg her to do something, say shit like *be our real mother—help us somehow. Save us from him!*

I know now that my requests and my expectations were too huge. My mother...she'd been with my father since she was barely eighteen. She was too entrenched.

Once it was all over, and the pain of Jojo's parting

had lessened, I looked at her with different eyes. I figured she was pretty idealistic like me once. She probably had her own hopes and dreams. Before those big brown eyes of hers that look nearly exactly like mine went flat and dead—before she was called Wife and Mother— she must have had ideas about what her life would look like. Father must have fucked them up, too. I'm sure the things he did to her were as unspeakable and as unthinkable as what we went through.

Mother and I never reconciled, nor have we spoken a word about Jojo since. We don't get along, but we are civil. It's a business relationship, and it's difficult for me, because when I try to connect to her, or try to imagine what goes on inside her frozen and unfeeling head, I nearly go insane remembering her abandonment of her own children.

Thinking about it now with Jojo here at my side, her ribs stretching and retracting to make room for each breath, drives me deeper into memories I'll never fully bury.

I'll never forget the day I told Father I had a girlfriend named Jojo Wallace.

"You hooked her, son. Hooked her just how I knew you would once I set you loose out there up at that lake. You don't know it, but you've made me proud with this one. Motherfucking Sinclair proud, son."

I'd thought Father's admiration was because he was proud I had the prettiest girlfriend in town, not because of anything else. I'd shown him a couple of photos of

Jojo from my phone, took his praise and his happiness, and I left with it, never once suspecting.

It wasn't until sophomore year when I got the full picture. I missed the signs completely, didn't understand the cracks and the looks about Jojo that Father and Grady used to trade with each other. I didn't understand my mother's silent, watchful stares, or why at dinner they were so interested in my daily life, when before high school had started, no one had ever asked me a single thing that was going on inside my head. As long as I showed up showered and wearing the outfit the maids laid out for me to wear to dinner, not one of them had ever cared.

It all came to a head the night after the sophomore homecoming dance. I spent hours stewing in my fury after Jojo's attack. I wanted Grady to be punished for what he'd done. I wanted absolute justice for me, because I'd thought there should be some sort of *code between brothers* and that code had surely been violated. I wanted to vindicate Jojo, make things hurt for my brother—make those scales even, despite how impossible that would be after what she went through.

But I was still smaller than Grady was back then. I was intimidated by him, so I'd wanted to enlist Father's help to punish my brother. I waited until Grady was stuck at football practice. He'd been benched, and was only going to football practice because Father told him that he had to support his team. Grady had suffered a season-ending shoulder injury—one Father told us he'd gotten from falling down some stairs. I remember thinking it was probably a lie. I had this idea that Grady had either been in a fight or maybe a car accident and Father didn't want anyone to know the truth. I had been really smug about that injury, thinking it was all Grady's Karma stacking up against him. It was easy to assume the universe had noticed Grady was an asshole and finally paid him back.

I was so clueless back then. I didn't understand that Father had broken Grady's shoulder. He did it with a crowbar, as the story finally came out. That was after I told my father to go *straight to hell* when he told me he wanted me to help him hurt the Wallaces.

"Do you want me to take a fucking crowbar to your head, boy?" Father screamed in my face. "That's what I'll do to you if you fuck up this plan. Damn your ungrateful ass—always like your mother, you are, thinking you've got a voice."

Father stepped closer, shoving his nose into my face, and made his voice deadly calm. "Grady defied me once. Boy thought football was more important than family. See...Sinclair family duty and *my* plans for *my* family and *my* boys never included anyone wasting time playing fucking college ball at some second-rate school. That boy went behind my back and filled out applications. He talked to recruiters and got some sort of bullshit scholarship without telling me. He thought I'd be proud to save the family some money." Father laughed, stepping away from me. "As if our fucking family needs to save money. He humiliated me, and when is a Sinclair proud about someone going behind their back? When, Alex—you tell me…when?"

Father had flipped back to shouting, his eyes bugging out, spittle flying off of his lips. "When, Alex?"

"Never, Sir," I answered, feeling like I suddenly must be asleep, that this whole thing was a nightmare and I needed to wake up.

"I had to show him how it felt, so I went behind Grady's back too—literally. Right before I hit his goddamn throwing arm and made sure he was done with football, I was standing behind his back, quietly holding heavy metal. See?" Father's eyes lit with glee as he mimicked the motion of his swing coming down to break my brother. "You don't defy me, Alex. Understand?"

I couldn't help it. I started to feel sick.

"I've been formulating this plan since you were still in fucking diapers, boy. Since I found out there was a fucking Wallace girl up at that damn farm. Why do you think they homeschooled her? They tried to hide her from me. This plan—it's the best idea I've ever had, son, so don't insult me by calling it anything other than great. You hear me?"

I nodded because I couldn't *not* hear him. The whole planet could hear him. Everyone heard him going crazy. And everyone was terrified.

"This plan has made my fucking father and grandfather smile and sit up in their graves and applaud me, because I had a lot of crow pie to eat. I was taken in by a Wallace bitch myself, once. Oh she wasn't a Wallace by name yet, but in her heart she was. She married one right after she tricked me. She mind-fucked me and manipulated me out of my inheritance to the point my father nearly left me dead in a Goddamned ditch for falling for her. But see...on his deathbed, I swore I'd figure out a way to get our pride back. And because of my plan—and because of you and your own little Wallace whore—we Sinclairs will win this feud. I want it to be done and over. You hear me, Alex? I want this feud to be *done*. And I want the Sinclairs to be the only names left standing."

I'd been so ignorant of the depth of it all back then so I answered with so much hope. "Yes, Sir. I'd like to be done, too. Only I'd like to not do it this way, please. There must be another way? I'm sure if we just talk with Jojo's family..."

"I'll kill the girl, outright. Will that make you happy?"

"What? No, sir! You can't be serious."

He didn't answer that with words. He charged over and punched me so hard I slammed into the mahogany walls of his office. He nearly knocked me out, and I crumpled to the floor like a duck that's been shot falling straight out of the sky.

He stood over my body, one leg on either side of me. "I'm always serious, son. Now stand the fuck back up and tell me exactly what happened during homecoming."

He yanked me to my feet, and shoved me into one of his big leather wing chairs just like I was a rag-doll. "Grady tells me it was a big success. I planned that myself, down to every little detail. I even bribed that asshole principal to make sure he let it play out just right. He'd been covering the door for me and asn't to let anyone through but you. I heard the girl went home with a torn dress and smelling like vodka. Crying. Oh, crying a lot!" He chuckled, and it shook his chest. "I'll just fucking bet her parents lost their goddamned minds when they saw her. I would have loved to have been there when she told them the story."

I'd nodded. It's all I could do because my head was still full of flashes and pain from that punch. I was also so shocked, so horrified and numb, that I had no words.

"Good. Good. Well…now you know. You've been my mole all along. I couldn't tell you about the plans until now, because I was afraid you wouldn't understand. You were too young, still all stupid with your books and your fishing poles and that…crush. I saw that Wallace girl up at the lake just before your birthday. She was just like you, skinny and ugly and muddy, but she was fishing, too. That's when I decided I'd give you the lake. I knew you'd go up there; you'd fish and you'd meet her. And *fuck me* but you did. You met her the first day. All I had to do was watch and wait.

Father leaned over and punched me in the shoulder conspiratorially, then added, "And damn…but she might be more of a little whore than her mother, or maybe it's just because it's a different time. I only got to feel her mother up a couple of times—she held out on me. She made me beg. But Grady tells me that you're the one making that new Wallace girl beg for it. It drives Grady mad that I won't let him have a piece of her. But I'm proud of you son—chip off the old block with your skills, eh? You haven't fucked her yet though have you?"

"No..." was all I could say. The shock was setting in —the pain in my head all keeping me still.

"Well, you're not to fuck her. Hear me, boy? You do what you need to do to get your rocks off but you won't put your dick in her. I'll not suffer a monster grandchild. You hear me? I won't have that shame on me, nor will you. You do what you want but you don't ever fuck that poisonous Wallace girl."

Jojo shifts in my arms and moans, bringing me back to the here and now, and I think about all of the times she and I didn't have sex—all of the times I waited. And I think about when I disobeyed my father on that command.

We didn't fuck. I made love to her...twice. It was her first time, and she was beautiful. The sex was spectacular and incredible because Jojo's love for me was so real and so huge. I'd been ruined by prostitutes by then, *gifts* from my father.

Jojo gave me her everything—her heart and soul, her dreams and her hopes. And I took it all and stole it away, even though I knew it was wrong.

Then...I made her cry so hard.

24.

ALEX, SOPHOMORE YEAR.

"I love her, Father. I love her so much."

"I know you do, boy. I know you do, and I hear she loves you right back." That was Father's only response.

He leapt out of his chair and poured me my first drink of scotch. "You manned up way more than I thought you were capable of. You've taken it to a level I didn't expect."

He forced me to drink. Then he told me words I had always thought I wanted to hear: I became *a good and perfect son*. He claimed gleefully that I'd done everything even better than he could have planned, and all on my own.

All on my own.

He told me more of his plan. That my relationship with Jojo would serve to mess with her family, especially her mother—the woman Father truly wanted revenge on—until they were all dead and buried in the ground.

He claimed it was my "destiny and birthright," and again that he was "so proud" of me. I was a good Sinclair. Maybe even a great Sinclair.

After the scotch carved down my throat, warmed my body, and numbed some of the pain, my father explained more of what was to be *my part*. He told me that we each had a part. Him, me, Grady...even our mother was in on this.

All I had to do was keep doing more of the same.

"Reel her in, keep on going to her family's farm, keep doing what you've been doing but with the intent now—the conscious intent—to reel them all in to feeling comfortable with you."

He explained how, little by little, he'd orchestrate nights like tonight where we'd mess with Jojo, where we'd toy with her until her mother understood just what side I was on. We'd dangle the idea that we would break Jojo, but never really do it, all to escalate Jojo's mother's fears about the Sinclairs and what we're capable of. We were breathing life and death back into the feud, and we wouldn't stop until Jojo's mother started to break and everything hers became ours.

"Nothing hurts parents—a mother—more than when their kids are truly fucked with and in danger, right?"

That's what Father had said to my face. His eyes became unrecognizable to me.

I'll always remember how he meant it to his core. It

was completely lost on him that *I* was his kid, and he'd been fucking with me since he'd given me the lake. And Grady was his kid, and that he'd broken Grady's arm and his football dreams and made him so dark and lost. I remember understanding that nothing hurt me and Grady more than our own father had. I remember knowing that he didn't care.

Didn't care at all.

Grady arrived just as the truth settled into my chest. His shoulder still had bandages from the expensive surgery father paid for—only the best doctors from Seattle would do. I couldn't look at my brother all of a sudden. Grady just acted like everything was fine. He simply walked in and spoke. "Hello, Father. Alex."

"How was practice, boy?"

"Good."

"That new replacement quarterback going to shame the team?"

Grady didn't even flinch. He just nodded and answered like a robot. "He's getting better. Should be a good game Friday."

Even in the face of all of that, I was clinging to denial. I was in shock, but I still wasn't afraid enough. I thought to my core that I could change my father's mind, talk the man out of it all.

Ha! In retrospect, that was my biggest mistake.

I begged in front of them both. I stood and cried big fat tears down my face like a baby, and then I begged them to leave Jojo and Mr. and Ms. Wallace at peace.

Worse, I showed them all of my weaknesses. It was undeniable that my love was real. As much as my father wanted that to happen to me—to me and to Jojo —he also felt personally threatened by it. When he looked into my eyes, all he saw was his past self—a pathetic, lovestruck boy. The final straw was when I said I wanted to marry Jojo one day. I dared to stupidly suggest that our marriage, our love, could end the feud.

"End it the right way," I'd said.

My father lost his shit. That's when I got my second face punch. I don't know what my head had whacked into that time, but the resulting lump lasted more than a week.

Grady was the one who helped me up that time. With his good arm, he pulled me to my feet. His eyes were as shocked as mine that Father had done that to me, but his eyes were glinting with some odd sort of pleasure, relief that I was finally getting mine. It wasn't him being hit this time.

"Be happy. Father's first homecoming idea was that I should grab Jojo from you, fuck her and then pass her around to my friends before handing her back. But he changed his mind, said it was too dangerous, that it would be over too fast for Jojo's parents that way. He told me I could do what I wanted as long as I shamed her good, and that you delivered her all sobbing and broken on her daddy's front porch."

He spilled out the truth as if it was meant to make

me feel better. It only made the bile burn up my throat along the same path the scotch went down.

"Mission accomplished," I whispered, bitterly.

"Almost time for the bigger plan." Father smiled.

"Bigger...plan...?" I parroted, nearly blacking out from the effort it took to stand without crying.

"Yes, dumbass. Do you think I would have let puny-ass you stop me from fucking that girl tonight otherwise? She's so fucking hot. I've watched you two enough times mauling each other up at that lake. I can't get that girl's tits or the way she moans when she's coming out of my mind."

"I'll fucking kill you if you ever touch her, or spy on us or say shit like that to me again, Grady!" My eyes glared through him like fire.

Because I was still only about a hundred and thirty pounds that year and my threat to them was only air and fear, Father merely moved his hand to my throat to choke me. "Threaten someone in your family again and *you* will be the one to die. I made you. I own you. You're my sons and you both will do no harm to each other. I won't stand for it. You'll do as I ask you, no matter what that might be. I decide who lives and who dies. Do you understand? If not, everyone you care about or even have an acquaintance with will cease to exist. Do you hear me you little fuck? Stop acting like a joke."

When I nodded in agreement, he threw me halfway across the room, and he and Grady just watched me gasping and struggling for consciousness, both of them wearing twin expressions like I'd turned into some sort of a worm.

When I caught my breath and could hear sounds beyond the river of white noise pounding in between, my Father stepped his boots right up against my knees. Hard. "If you truly love that girl, like I know you do, you sappy motherfucker, you're going to listen, and then you're going to apologize to me and your brother."

I struggled to my feet to look him in the eyes, and somehow, I'd managed to swallow down my tears and nod.

"Yes, Sir." Swaying on my feet, eyes rolling some, I added, "What's your ultimate goal?" I had to know. My only hope was to figure out who these people were and how Jojo fit in between us all.

Father shrugged. "I suppose that's not entirely written yet. My goal is that her father suffers. My goal is that her mother suffers more. And I know they've been in quite a panic ever since you showed up at their farm and started sniffing around their daughter. They've been suffering for months. Now I'm bored. I want more."

"They have not panicked. They like me. I know they do." My words were so ignorant.

"Because I *wanted* them to like you, to keep liking you. And I'm willing to compromise, as long as you comply with my plan and she never knows the truth. *Pain for pain*—it can stay with adults for now. There's plenty of time to ruin her later."

I nodded, seeking some sort of refuge inside my

father's words. If he meant to 'ruin her later,' I had time to figure out a way to rescue her.

"I just found out that old bitch's cancer is back. That should mess up sweet little Jojo's heart and mind pretty good all by itself." My eyes widened with surprise, because Jojo hadn't brought that up to me, so I wondered if she even knew this news yet.

My father had been rubbing his chin, looking up to the ceiling, his face all aglow with happiness. "I can only imagine the panic that woman feels, knowing she's out of remission. Knowing she's on round two with not much of her lungs left. It's a death sentence, and I get to watch." He chuckled. "It's got to kill her that she knows she's going to die while we Sinclairs circle around her darling daughter."

He paced over to me, eyes locking on mine. "I'd like to take credit for the cancer coming back. The stress of you dating her and all, it had to play a part in this resurgence."

"How long do I have to do this?" I asked, trying to swallow down a new wave of vomit and hide the shaking in my legs.

"When Jojo's mom is dead, you can stop the game. If she approaches me first—if she's sorry and gives me back what I gave to her in good faith, well then—we'll change up the rules. I'll keep you posted, don't worry."

Grady pushed in front of me. "After Mrs. Wallace dies, can I have Jojo then? It should be my turn, right?"

He and my dad were treating this like we were all fighting over a toy!

"I can't hurt the Wallaces. I just can't." I whispered, stepping back and flinching for the blow that never came, but instead my father only laughed.

"I'm not asking you to hurt them son, I'm asking you to love them and care for them like I know you already do so unwaveringly. We're all going to go on doing exactly what we're best at, son." His smile grew and grew until it was Cheshire Cat wide. "The hurting part is all mine."

25.

ALEX, PRESENT DAY.

I lie down next to her on top of the covers to keep an appropriate distance between our bodies. I'm not even sure why I'm keeping the line there anymore. Habit maybe. It's clear that it doesn't matter how I treat her personally, the people who want to hurt her are just going to keep doing so. Grady won't stop. My mom won't let go. Happiness is not in my fortune.

Jojo reattaches her hand into mine, instantly breaking down the idea of me keeping up barriers. "What are you thinking about?" she asks quietly, scooting as close as she can scoot until I feel the warmth along her side radiate through the covers into my body.

I don't lie. I don't have it in me any more.

"I'm thinking about that homecoming dance where Grady attacked you, and how he's always thought he was going to have his way with you—get his turn. Those are the exact words he said to me while you were blacked out."

I spare a short glance to catch the disgust on her face. It's a slow melting of an expression because she isn't surprised by what I said, she's just sickened.

"I keep thinking about my father. Thinking about you." I finish in a whisper. "Your parents. *Everything.*"

Her eyes tighten at the edges. "Well...don't. Please don't." She finishes with a huge shiver, her voice just whispers, and her eyes move away from me just as I try to stare into them.

"How can I not, Jojo?"

She doesn't answer for several seconds, and I nearly pass out from holding my breath. It would be such an easy death, a peacefulness I don't deserve. When I feel her move, I expect her to turn away from me, but for some reason she moves closer, this time placing the weight of her head onto my shoulder.

It soothes. It crushes.

I don't deserve this.

Just like the puppet strings my father and my brother were consciously pulling to make me dance because they knew I'd do anything to protect Jojo from harm, she has always unconsciously been able to pull at my heart. Her tugs were always to make me be closer to her, physically and emotionally.

JoJo somehow always knew that if she felt cold, or hurt, or sad, that I couldn't resist trying to fix those things for her. It's what makes my DNA different from

Grady. When pushed to my limits, I run to save her instead of destroy her.

I can tell from the little furrows in her brow and the side of her face turning shades of reds and purples from bruising that she's obviously hurt. She's also probably still cold because the girl was always that. And because she's forced to be near me again, she has to be all kinds of sad. Her strings tug so hard, and I know I'll give in to anything.

"The last time we were together you told me you hated me. Is that still how you feel?" she asks, cracking a hole into my patched-up heart. I've played the scene over thousands of times. The hurt on her face is what I see when I close my eyes at night. It's the biggest lie I ever told.

"Do you have to ask that, Jojo? You must know it was all lies by now." My mouth goes dry with the words, and I nearly choke. Saying this out loud to her is something I've wanted to do for so long, but couldn't. I still shouldn't, but my resolve has long passed. I'm in dangerous territory, and I've lost my way back.

She picks up her head, looks me dead in the eyes, and blinks. The line of her lips turns up in that stubborn, relentless smile of hers that I'd nearly forgotten. It's so faint, but it's her tell. "I want to hear you say you don't."

I hold her precious stare for several breaths, swimming in the sea of her gaze and letting the painful past squeeze at my chest just one more time.

"I don't. I could never. And I'm—s—"

"Shh." She shoves a quick hand over my mouth. The mere brush of something of hers on my lips stuns me like a thousand volts. "It wasn't your fault."

The rest of my patched up heart crumples into dust, yet still it's beating, and I don't know how.

One of her arms floats over my waist, the other to my chest, with her hand settling in near my neck as her head finds that flat spot below my shoulder that was always hers.

I lower my arms and pull her closer so I can I nestle my chin against the top of her head, relishing how her hair remembers to twine next to my neck and tickle my chin like it's got a mind of it's own. After a few minutes, looking at her face this close becomes too torturous. This intimacy makes me want to kiss her. I mutter something about needing to get more comfortable so I can turn her so we're half spooning. To distract my hands from going where they shouldn't go, I work to tuck the blanket around us both.

When that's done, I risk letting one of my arms find it's usual resting place, all the way around her waist this time. My other arm settles along the mattress so the back of my hand can rest against her beating heart. The feel of her right here, held this close under my protection, is like a salve to an open wound I have nursed for years.

She sighs, sounding happy, and the vice I've kept on my soul releases enough to let me find a few moments of happiness too.

The slow steady beats of her heart and the sound of her breath pulling in and out feels like it's healing hundreds of deep, dark holes that make up who I've become.

The old mantras from the years she was mine resurface.

She's alive.

She's okay.

She's here with me.

I love her and she loves me.

She doesn't know all that I've done.

That last one—that's the one that kept me quiet back then, and it still keeps me quiet today. It sits heavy, and I know I'll have to tell her everything if I want this good feeling to have a fighting chance.

I wonder why Jojo is at a loss for words as much as I am, but then I think I know. Talking—coming all the way clean—will hurt us more, and this, for the moment, feels so good. She's afraid to make it end too.

If she's really the one who killed my father, then what is there to say?

I can't fault her for it, or blame her. If that's what she's done, then it's over. We're even. *Pain for pain.*

One lone tear slips down my face.

Pain for pain. Pain for pain.

One Sinclair life for one Wallace life.

"It was never supposed to be like this, JoJo," I whisper, wiping the tear away, but Jojo's stiffened at the rough and ragged sound of my breathing.

"What wasn't supposed to be like this? Us? Our past, our messed up present? Today? Which part wasn't supposed to be like this?"

"All of it," I answer truthfully.

"Tell me, Alex. Tell me your secrets and why you truly made me leave."

"Tell me yours. Tell me why you came back?" I fire back.

Our words tug and pull. We both lose.

She turns to face me completely, and her breasts press into my chest. I groan because my body and my cock have grown so taut with wanting, and I fear that she'll somehow disappear into mid-air. I can't lose her touch.

I'm almost undone when she places both hands on the sides of my face, her arching body lifting just enough to shift her gaze onto mine directly. "I will tell you. I'll tell you everything you want to know. I will give you all of my reasons—every last one that brought me back here to you. After you kiss me."

I shake my head.

"Please," she asks again, her bottom lip puffing out, inviting me. Temptation always makes me weak when it comes to this girl.

"Jojo. For all that is holy, don't ask me to do that. This time, despite what I want, my firm answer on kissing you is *no.*"

I barely believe the words as they leave my lips, but the one thing that's kept me breathing these last few years is the fact that Jojo is breathing too. I can't trade one kiss for her life, and that's what I'd be risking. I already am and already have.

"Nothing has changed, Jojo…" My words trail off because it's a lie. She knows it, too. And she calls me on it, fast.

"Everything has changed. You just don't know it yet," she says.

Everything. Nothing. Those words feel tied together somehow despite their definitions. There's something in her eyes…something behind those words she just spoke. What don't I know, Jojo? What else could there possibly be?

TO BE CONTINUED IN BOOK 2,
THE SINCLAIR HEIR…

ACKNOWLEDGMENTS

This story was born out of the truest of friendships and the biggest love of those great stories that got us into romance in the first place. We would be remiss not to pay homage to the rich backlist of epic family sagas splashed with intrigue and sensual tension woven into every page that so many of us stayed up into the wee hours reading years ago. We wanted to bring those feelings back, and we had a blast doing it. We hope you enjoyed reading this story as much as we loved creating this Wallace-Sinclair feud. And don't worry, it isn't over —The Sinclair Heir releases days after this book because we didn't want you to have to wait for the satisfying OMGs and blushing that's to come! ;-)

Thank you from the bottoms of our hearts to everyone who has ever lifted us up as authors, and who roots us on as a duo now. Our words would languish and our dreams would never get the chance to fly without you. This romance community is nothing short of awesome, and we are two lucky fish who get to swim in this amazing ocean. Tina Scott, Editing Addict, Autumn and Wordsmith Publicity, Kika MacFarlane, readers, bloggers, shouters, cheerleaders, friends—this list is endless and our love for you is just as bottomless.

Lastly, it may seem weird to thank each other...but that's just the kind of crazy kids we are. To Annie from Ginger and to Ginger from Annie—loved every minute of this.

Stay tuned, y'all...it's gonna get crazy good!

ABOUT THE AUTHOR

Eliot Scott is the love child of bestselling authors Anne Eliot and Ginger Scott. You can find them at www.AnneEliot.com and www.authorgingerscott.com.

For updates on Eliot Scott projects, be sure to follow us at www.facebook.com/AuthorEliotScott.

www.ingramcontent.com/pod-product-compliance
Lightning Source LLC
Chambersburg PA
CBHW020226260626
47156CB00002B/564